MW01119301

Confessions
of a
Corporate Slut

by
Jacqueline Gum

authorHOUSE®

AuthorHouse™
1663 Liberty Drive, Suite 200
Bloomington, IN 47403
www.authorhouse.com
Phone: 1-800-839-8640

This book is a work of fiction. People, places, events, and situations
are the product of the author's imagination. Any resemblance to actual
persons, living or dead, or historical events, is purely coincidental.

© 2007 Jacqueline Gum. All rights reserved.

No part of this book may be reproduced, stored in a retrieval system, or
transmitted by any means without the written permission of the author.

First published by AuthorHouse 12/26/2007

ISBN: 978-1-4343-4491-5 (sc)
ISBN: 978-1-4343-4492-2 (hc)

Library of Congress Control Number: 2007908673

Printed in the United States of America
Bloomington, Indiana

This book is printed on acid-free paper.

This book is for DW.
For recognizing and encouraging the passion,
I will be forever in your debt.

PROLOGUE

PROLOGUE

Over the course of my sixteen-year marriage, I'd entertained thousands, hosted hundreds of dinner parties, kissed countless asses, brokered untold deals and colluded with dozens of employees to assure the growth of my husband's company. But the day my marriage ended only my ex-husband, our attorneys and I, bore witness to the death of this corporate wife. The settlement had been negotiated out of court and our final meeting was a mere formality required by law. My maiden name restored, my severance package finalized, I was moving to Florida to begin a new life at age fifty. I had paid a high price in terms of pride and self-esteem, and my recompense was less money per year than I would have earned had I not left my own career to better my husband's.

I was sitting alone in my car in the garage under the Milwaukee County Courthouse, my head against the headrest, seemingly glued there. My arms, wrists bent backward as my fingers grazed the leather of the steering wheel, weighed a hundred pounds each. My legs felt like cement pilings driven deep into the ground. I was convinced the level of Lake Michigan had risen at least an inch from the volume of tears I had shed in the last fifteen months—tears of anger, frustration, sadness, madness, gladness, and humiliation with some triumph mixed in, too. Today my eyes were dry. My eyelids, suddenly heavy, involuntarily closed and images started rolling through my head like a bad 16 mm movie reel.

There I was serving dinner to ten company executives while convincing a desirable job candidate that he would be better appreciated and encouraged to grow at my husband's company. After dessert, he accepted the offer.

I was organizing a luncheon for potential customers and then planning a welcome party for the new employee and his wife. Secretly meeting with the executive vice-president, I was showing him a new approach to gain approval from the CEO-my husband-for a project that had previously been rejected.

I was shocked to hear my own laughter reverberate around the car, a repetitive echo bouncing from surface to surface like a ricocheted bullet. Could my life really have become such an appalling cliché? I had carefully crafted and culled my uniqueness from a very early age. Exactly when and how did "unique" sour like outdated milk and curdle into "cliché?" My laughter, changing key, took on a slightly maniacal pitch. What the fuck? How had I let this happen?

That very moment, I reluctantly began to unravel the basket of my life with John Wendall, reed by reed. I had to…before I found myself in a home for abandoned corporate wives/corporate sluts, weaving real baskets for retail. There had to be millions of us out there, walking clichés dumbfounded by the absurdity of it all, hunting like scavengers for the distinctiveness we had branded since our childhoods. We were proven frontrunners in innumerable fields who had given up working for recognition and singular achievement. Our livelihood now centered on propelling our husband's success; we had merely traded careers.

When you are a woman without children, the social expectation is that you have a career, or at least a job. Being a corporate wife doesn't qualify as a career. Most people cannot comprehend the difficulty or complexity of the task. Not exactly the same as a woman who works and supports her husband while he attends dental, medical or law school, a corporate slut actually has intimate knowledge of the business and works to better her husband's company and his image. In my case, I created an illusion. I reinvented my husband and managed his life, our lives, and his company while remaining resolutely behind him. At the height of my career, my initiatives were so cleverly couched that my husband supposed he birthed all the ideas alone.

Though I had years of experience as a business owner, an entrepreneur, a top salesperson, and a corporate manager, when I sold my company and married John Wendall I became one thing only: a corporate slut. My self-appointed title always got a laugh. "Domestic Diva" was a pretentious title I couldn't abide. It connoted a spoiled, kept woman, languishing in luxury. On the contrary, a corporate slut is a working woman, albeit an unpaid one.

I've always thought of a slut as an unpaid prostitute. Prostitution by definition is the action of selling one's talents for a base purpose. For sixteen years, I poured the best of myself, my talents, my ability, my brainpower, even my body—into creating and sustaining a successful man, a successful business, and a successful marriage. It worked for a while, but in the end, I was rewarded by being surreptitiously terminated with no notice. There was no remuneration for my services.

It was my ambitiously driven nature coupled with John's mounting demands that created a very successful manufacturing company and produced sixteen years of pyrotechnics glimpsed from a roller coaster moving forward, then backward, and ultimately reeling out of control.

CHAPTER 1

Independence and individuality are primary qualifications for a corporate slut. My particular brand of uniqueness sprang from a convoluted set of circumstances that I refer to as my childhood. Born in Pittsburgh to educated parents, my mother was a teacher and my father was president of the local school board in addition to being vice-president of sales for a company that sold limestone to glassmakers. He traveled extensively, and I remember weeks in which he wasn't home. We all missed him terribly. He was an athletic man, warm and kind-hearted who would have loved my mother to birth a football team, no matter the gender. It didn't matter if they were girls or boys or a combination of both, but enough to huddle in the back yard and play a respectable game. If only my mother had been agreeable.

Having played college football and coached high school football when he was a teacher, his gusto for the game encompassed me. Our bonding on Sunday afternoons would form my life long passion for the sport. He couldn't have known his teachings would provide me another foray into a business world where football metaphors sprinkled industry-speak like chocolate jimmies on a cupcake. Years later, when I approached a customer who was a Cincinnati Bengals fan one Monday morning, I started the conversation with, "Can you believe Chris Collingsworth caught that pass at fourth down and twenty two? How pretty was that? What a gutsy call by the coach. You have to admit, moving those chains changed the whole momentum of the game." A newfound respect covered his smiling face.

I attribute much of my fierce independence, my ability to buck the status quo, to my mother. Not that she *tried* to teach me these things, mind you. She was stellar when it came to helping with homework, but if she taught me anything about character or attitude, it was what *not* to do. I knew many kids who wanted to be just like their parents. I felt unique in my desire to be the antithesis of my mother.

She was a complicated woman. Besides herself, the person she loved most in the world was my father. She was as madly in love with him in the last years of their marriage as she was when they first met. In theory, it's wonderful to have such love, but my mother's selfishness slowly overwhelmed the purpose of parenting, decreasing the meaning of their marriage. Because my father was around so infrequently, she found herself competing with three children for his attention.

One Saturday, my dad suggested that they take us kids to the movies. He was reading the morning paper while the three of us were slurping cereal from our multi-colored metal bowls.

My mother's face fell immediately. "Sam, I'd already planned to send the kids out for an overnight tonight so *we* could go to a movie, just the two of us. I haven't seen you all week. You get to travel but I've been stuck with the kids. It's my turn now."

My dad didn't miss a beat. "Okay then, if it's your turn tonight, I'll take them to play mini-golf this morning."

We lifted our heads out of the cereal bowls in unison, eyes wide, not yet sure we could be so lucky.

"They all have chores and homework, Sam, and I have things to do here," my mother said. "I can't go with you." Her platinum hair flashed dangerously in the florescent lighting of the kitchen and her light blue eyes clouded with irritability.

"You don't have to go, Peg. I didn't ask you to go...and they have plenty of time over the weekend to do their homework." He turned to us, brown eyes twinkling, his red hair blazing atop his six-foot two-inch athletic frame. "And I'm sure they'll work double-time to get the chores done, right kids?" He clapped his hands. "Quick, get dressed so we can go."

"Sam," my mother said. "They're not going. These kids have plenty of fun all week, but I don't. I wait all week for you to come home, and when you do I expect you to make some time for me. *Alone* time."

My mother's warning tone said that there was no arguing

One could easily wonder if my mother actually wanted children. For women of the 1950's, having children was never a question; it was an expectation. To not want children would have been blasphemous and certainly never uttered out loud. The problem was not that she didn't want us. Quite simply her maternal instincts were overpowered by her tremendous need to please herself. So she handed off the parenting duties to my grandmother, who lived with us, and instead chose to work outside the home as a teacher She didn't do it for the love of learning or a fondness for children, but strictly for the money, and the freedom her own income allowed.

"I don't have to work," she'd explain when asked about her job. "It's just that I'd rather have custom-made drapes. They look better than JC Penny drapes. And if I want a new dress, I don't want to worry about spending the money." After a couple of martinis, a deeper story would emerge. "To tell you the truth," she'd say, "I'd go batshit if I didn't get out of the house. These kids are exhausting. Teaching high school

English is a hell of a lot easier than chasing three small kids around, trying to keep them entertained, happy and not whining. God I hate the whining. How many times can I take them to the zoo for God's sake?" In an era in which mothering was the career expected of women, we were the only kids in school with a working mother. Being a teacher excused her from being a room mother for any of us, explained her exhaustion if she didn't feel like taking us to a movie, and allowed her the freedom from maternity she actively sought.

She did the usual things, like feed us and buy us clothes and kiss the boo-boo when we fell, but emotionally she was as unavailable as a flat tire. It never occurred to me to ask anything of my mother, other than help with homework. I grew up relying mostly on myself, and while it was painful being force fed independence at such an early age I came to appreciate my autonomy later, in the male-dominated world of business.

I probably would've been a bitch on wheels if I hadn't been lucky enough to have the most positive maternal influence imaginable in Grandma.

She and my grandfather had divorced shortly after my parents married. It seems during the planning of my mother's wedding, my grandmother became aware that my grandfather had a mistress. Because it was a very large and elaborate society wedding, my grandmother waited until after the nuptials to divorce him. In 1948, divorce was rare. My grandfather married his mistress, moved to California, and had little presence in my life.

Grandma was a typical 1950's grandmother. Her slight figure was already stooped over by osteoporosis, and her reddish hair, done weekly by a beautician, was always in a curly coif. She smiled endlessly, her laugh a tinkle that was as contagious as the chicken pox of the era. My grandmother was an only adopted child and my mother was her only child. Having not been trained in anything other than being a wife and mother, and not being able to drive, she made her home with us in Pittsburgh, and my parents were happy to have her. She was with my mother for the birth of all three of her children and with all of us until I was nearly twelve years old. She was rarely gone except for occasional visits to a friend in Florida whom she cared for through a long illness.

Any maternal feelings I gleaned were from her. When I was sick, she comforted me. It was she who nursed me through the dozens of inner ear infections that plagued my early childhood, she who brought me milk and cookies as I watched Romper Room. She taught me unconditional love and it was in her lap that I felt the most prized. She taught me how to keep a house, and is responsible for my obsession with neatness. She imparted her philosophies daily and I digested them subconsciously.

"Roberta," she would tell me, "people are not perfect and you can't expect them to be. They have bruises, just like apples. Just because an apple has a bruise doesn't mean you throw it away. You just eat around the bruise. When you love someone, it has to be with flaws and all." So sunny was her outlook that she never told me that biting without thought into an apple slightly bruised to the eye, could reveal a worm hidden deep within.

If someone needed help, Grandma's response was automatic. She expected the same from me.

"Roberta, come help me make homemade chicken and noodles for Mrs. Dickenson. She just got home from the hospital."

"But Gram, the guys are waiting for me to play kickball."

"You can play kickball any day, Roberta, but some days you give up a little playtime to help a friend. It'll make you feel good, you'll see. Didn't Mrs. Dickenson make you cookies the last time you came home from the hospital? It's time to return her kindness, and I'll teach you how to make noodles, too. We'll have fun, I promise."

Gram was right. I helped her with the ingredients for the dough and then as she instructed, I started rolling and rolling and rolling. Before it was over my arms were shaking from the exertion and so weak from the continuous rolling and they felt like damn noodles!

"Keep going, Roberta," Gram said. "Just a little longer. The noodles need to be paper thin, just like you!"

The art of noodle-making became a game, and Mrs. Dickenson's grateful smile when we delivered her meal provided a belly full of warmth that taught me satisfaction worth sacrifice.

"Roberta wanted to help me make these for you because she remembered how much she enjoyed the cookies you made for her when she was sick. She didn't even play kickball today, just so she could lend me a hand." Gram's smile was sincere as she tossed the credit my way.

My eye didn't catch her wink, but I felt that wink kiss my cheek, like a wisp of unseen hair that tickles. That, I knew, was her gift to me. The lesson that day wasn't just about giving; it was how to deliver a gift in multiple ways.

When you fully recognize the warmth that giving provides it can become addictive. Crediting an individual for their help in achieving a goal is like paying it forward. I learned how to confer credit for the act itself believing it did not diminish the ultimate goal of endowment even slightly.

Gram taught me never to surrender if I could help it. I had no idea that the fortitude I learned at her knee would be so invaluable later in life. Perseverance was a life lesson embedded in a card game. Instead of Go Fish, she taught me to play Gin Rummy. Regardless how many times I lost, she wouldn't allow me to walk away. No quitting, no cowardly behavior, do it 'til you get it right and always know that someday, you will get it right.

"Come on Roberta, deal the cards again, sweetheart. You could win next time, you never know. You have to keep trying. You have to keep playing so someday you can beat me. Don't give up, not unless you absolutely, positively have no other choice. That goes for most things Roberta, just remember that. This time, you're going to choose to deal another hand."

For the record, I think I only beat my grandmother a very few times playing Gin Rummy. She never, not even on the day she died when we played our last game, let me give up. It was always, "Deal again, sweetheart. You might just win the next game." She at least waited until I was six years old before we started playing for pennies.

While "never give up" was a flag run up my flagpole in youth, the distinction between giving up and letting go was not clearly defined. While not backing away served me well in a business sense, I later learned that unmitigated determination in terms of human relationships can injure a human spirit. The difference between giving up and letting go remained blurry for a very long time.

*

Shortly before we moved to Minneapolis, when I was not quite twelve, she and my grandfather remarried after being divorced thirteen years. His second wife had become ill and died in California, but Granddad brought her back to Pittsburgh, her place of birth, to bury her. From the funeral home, he called and proposed to my grandmother and they eloped to Las Vegas the very next day.

Could there possibly be a more bruised apple? This man, whose likely motive was finding another caretaker, told her he still loved her.

Gram had spent thirteen years mourning his departure and the night before she eloped she explained why she'd taken him back.

"Roberta, your Granddad is a good man. He thought he was doing the right thing marrying that woman, but he never really stopped loving me. He came back for me, Roberta. He was just biding his time with her."

I was distraught at her leaving. She was my very best buddy in the world, this woman who made me feel cherished, even after I'd drawn a stop sign in red crayon on her bedroom wall. *My Gram all the way out in California?* I just knew it had to be a million miles away.

My grandparents were happily married another twenty-two years before a stroke took Granddad suddenly, but we were never allowed to mention the missing years. When anyone asked how long she had been married, Gram included those missing thirteen years without batting an eye. Honesty and integrity were her most valued virtues, but even Gram had a slight bruise, too.

*

If a child is enlightened enough to want to be different, they usually try to excel at something socially acceptable, like piano, or tap dancing, or football. Peer acceptance generally lies in being homogeneous. Individuality, particularly for a girl, isn't overly stressed. However, sometimes shit happens…life happens…accidents happen.

At age seven, I was riding my bike up a very steep hill in front of our house in Pittsburgh when I turned to say something to my girlfriend. The act of turning caused the front wheel of my bike to hit the curb, and as the bike reeled out of control I flew about ten feet and fell directly on my head. My mother told me that she heard the thump inside the house, even though it was autumn and the windows were closed. I was unconscious for approximately two minutes.

When I awoke, it was a neighbor kneeling over me with a blanket while my mother stood in the background. I was bundled into the car and driven to the doctor, who diagnosed a very severe concussion. Mother had to wake me every hour or two that night, and her annoyance was flagrant, even to me as a child. Dad was out of town and Grandma was in Florida tending to her sick friend, so the responsibility was hers alone.

When I woke after the accident, I began to stutter. I was confined to bed for three weeks and it was during that time that I began to understand the meaning of consequence.

You see, I had been turning around to say something mean. Cause and effect abruptly became crystal clear—I was being punished for intending to say something cruel to my best girlfriend. The stuttering was so severe I couldn't utter the simplest of words. I squinted, kicked, and balled up my fists, all in an effort to force words out of my mouth, but I couldn't even say my own name. My mother hated my stuttering even more than I did. It was as though my stuttering was an intentional affront to her parenting and she dealt with it with constant reprimands.

"Slow down, Roberta, don't talk so fast," became her mantra. Sometimes she'd groan aloud with frustration. "*Think* about what you want to say before you open your mouth, Roberta! Maybe the words will come out right if you just think about them. Think, Roberta, *think!*"

I was amazed. Did she really believe I wanted to talk like this? If I could slow down and get the words out, wouldn't I? I couldn't explain to her what I was feeling. I couldn't talk.

The situation worsened when I went back to school. It's hard to match the cruelty that children show one another. They have elevated teasing to an art form. They had even less patience for my stuttering than my mother, and it gave them great fodder for taunting. I didn't get through a day without being teased, often to the point of tears. My stuttering was frustrating, exhausting, and terribly embarrassing. I hated it. If I could've figure out a way not to do it, I would have.

Some months later I was playing in the street when my father called me, and I vividly remember him getting on one knee and taking my hands in his. He had the kindest brown eyes I have ever seen, even to this day. They engulfed me as he simply said, "Roberta, we are going to take you somewhere where you can learn how to talk again."

My arms reached up and around his neck and I felt the roughness of his unshaven face on my cheek as I hugged him with all the strength a tiny seven-year-old could gather. I cried, so grateful.

Children's Hospital of Pittsburgh became my home for that third grade year, where with two other students, I learned how to speak with less stuttering, and learned the method of avoiding certain words when I felt sure I would stutter. I was stupefied that I couldn't talk and astonished how hard it was to learn something I didn't remember forgetting.

But I did learn, and I did get better, and bolstered by this newfound confidence, I found a way to cope with the teasing at school and protect my feelings. Stuttering would always be an obstacle I'd have to overcome, so I chose to do so with humor. I came to regard stuttering as yet another quality that made me unique—yet another unlikely badge of honor. So the more my classmates made fun of me the more I made fun of myself. If one of them mocked me, I let loose with a string of stutters—I was really good at it, after all. Whatever they did, I topped them every time. It didn't work all of the time, but it worked most of the time. I don't know what was better, finding a new, tougher brand of confidence or making myself laugh.

It's an anomaly, I know, but my stuttering has brought a great deal of hilarity to my life. Instead of turning me inward, I twisted this malady into a platform that would launch my particular brand of humor, politely termed offbeat and self-deprecating. I still laugh the loudest when I'm making fun of myself.

*

My independence made a sudden and most unwelcome leap forward with the death of my father in 1969. I was seventeen years old and a senior in high school. My sister Sheila was a freshman at Carnegie-Mellon University in Pittsburgh, my brother Scott a sophomore at Bowling Green University, in Bowling Green, Ohio. They had both been recipients of scholarships; Sheila was a national merit scholar and Scott's athletic scholarship was for football. The family domicile was in Louisville, Kentucky.

In his sophomore year, my brother fell into a bad fraternity crowd at college, lost his scholarship, and was failing. My father drove to Bowling Green on a cold November day, pulled him out of school and brought him home so he could properly ponder his future.

One night shortly after Scott's sudden arrival home, my father woke to go to the bathroom, passed out, and fell, hitting his head on the toilet. My mother managed to rouse him and convinced him to see the doctor the next day. When he was admitted to the hospital, tests revealed a shadow on his lung, which warranted exploratory surgery. On his forty-fourth birthday, November 25, 1969, the doctors discovered lung cancer, undetected by a full physical exam performed just two months earlier.

Terminal was a word I heard from the doctors, not my mother. She never openly discussed my father's prognosis, because she refused to believe that he could ever die. Their agreement, she stated, had always been that she would depart this life first. She fully expected him to make good on that promise.

At two o'clock in the morning on December 11, 1969, my brother pulled me out of bed and dragged me to the car in my nightgown and hair curlers. I had not heard the phone ring, but Scott explained that the hospital called and requested we get there immediately. He drove to the hospital at breakneck speed. Not being told that my father had already passed, we ran down the hall to his room and pushed open the door. I'll never forget the sight of his lifeless body. I'll always regret opening that door and it took years to get that image out of my head. The rough edges of loss eventually dulled, but they never left me. My mother was in the conservatory down the hall, collapsed in disbelief. "He promised he'd let me die first…he promised me." She never considered that any of her three children might need her. She needed us.

During my father's three-week illness, mother never once left the hospital. My seventeenth birthday was spent alone in front of a TV, my brother occupied with himself and mother hospital-bound by choice.

My brother never reconciled with my father before he died. He did not see him during his illness. My sister was never told my father was ill. She believed him to be hospitalized for tests only. She never said goodbye either. I was lucky to be living at home. I got to the hospital every day.

In an instant, we became responsible for my mother. Because her philosophy of putting her husband before all others didn't take into consideration the fact that he may exit this world before her, our collective responsibility focused on meeting her needs. It was an enterprise doomed to failure because her needs were insatiable.

*

The "we" quickly became "I" as Sheila and Scott both returned to college and I was left to deal with Mother alone. Her behavior became increasingly erratic. She'd leave in the middle of the night on drives to I never knew where, leaving me at home to fret about her whereabouts and her safe return. I begged her to stay home or at least tell me where she was going or when she'd be back, but it was like talking to a mannequin. After the first dozen occurrences, I chose to stop wondering or worrying to the point of panic. It was that or be consumed wholly by my mother and her grief. I wasn't exactly sure how to cope with my own anguish and I had no idea how to deal with hers.

Some days after school, when calling her name became a mere echo of my own voice, I might find her in the basement huddled in a corner crying. Other times Mother was eager to talk, but she merely said the same things over and over: Dad would never see my upcoming high school graduation, any of our college graduations, or know his grandchildren. Soon enough the repetitious refrains of grief began bouncing off me like raindrops bounding back from the pavement in a torrential storm. She expected me to say something, offer some comfort. My failure to do so resulted in accusations of not understanding and cold heartedness. Mother believed the loss belonged to her alone. There wasn't room for anything else in her life other than grief, and certainly no room for her children. Our hurting, our loss, was not her concern.

I shopped for my prom dress with a girlfriend and used Mother's credit card. She didn't care what I bought and the only picture of me on senior prom night is the one taken in the school gymnasium. I didn't know what to do or where to put my grief. It resulted in my total lack of sympathy for her.

About four months after my father passed, Mother came into my room while I was studying. "Roberta," she said, "I have to leave for West Virginia. Grandpa isn't doing too well and your aunts and uncle don't seem to have the time to go to the farm and care for him. It's what Daddy would want me to do."

My paternal grandfather suffered from severe diabetes and as a result of complications from the disease, had his right leg amputated a few weeks before.

"And I can see Daddy every day while I'm there, too," she said, referring to his grave.

It didn't matter that I was here and Daddy was gone. To mother, her husband still trumped her kids. She left me. She took the only car we had and the dog and moved to West Virginia. She called my best friend's mother, an alcoholic unable to manage her disease, and asked her to keep an eye on me. Although I could take the bus to school, I depended on friends to take me to work and back. The only cash I had came from my job at Dairy Queen, where I earned $1.35 an hour.

Six long weeks later, she arrived home in time to attend my graduation from high school. She cried all day and throughout the entire ceremony. My graduation, like her life, became about her loss. I went out with my friends that night and got drunk and stayed drunk until the following morning. She didn't notice. The next afternoon we moved back to Cincinnati. Mother liked it better than Louisville and decided to construct her life as a widow in a city where she was acquainted with more people.

*

Around July of 1970, shortly after our move back to Cincinnati, I had a conversation with my mother that birthed my total independence from my home environment. It was the beginning of my freedom from my mother's not so high opinion of me. I decided not to attend the University of Kentucky that fall.

"Roberta, what makes you think you have a choice here?" Mother said. "You've been accepted, and you have your room assignment and even the roommate you wanted. You're going to college. End of discussion."

"Mom, I'm not going. You can't make me go. I promise I'll go to college, just not now."

I was confused and didn't know what to do, but I knew college would be a waste of time at that point in my life. I wanted to work for a year and get my bearings first. Then I'd go to school.

"Roberta, nobody ever goes back to college that says they will. This is just laziness on your part. What in the world has gotten into you? Everybody in this house goes to college and you know that. Of course, you couldn't seem to get a scholarship like Scott or Sheila. Thank heavens your dad left money for your education. It's not that you aren't smart, Roberta, you're just not smart enough. Your father would be so ashamed if you don't go at all. You just need to work hard, that's all. You'll make it. Probably not with A's, but you'll make it. You're going and that's the end of it."

My mother wore a look sometimes that was a combination of sneer and condescension. It was hateful and extremely effective in diminishing any person. When I remember her from my child's mind, it's "the look" that I remember most. Now I was face to face with my mother, "the look" filling the room.

"Mom I'm not going. There's no point in discussing it any further."

"Roberta, you are not welcome in my home if you choose not to go to college. Pack your bags and get out." The "look" liquefied, replaced instantly by a livid contortion as her arms crossed against her ample bosom. "I'm not kidding, Roberta. I don't give a damn what kind of job you get, just get the hell out of my house. And don't you dare even think about asking for my help. Don't you dare ask."

I was permitted to take only my clothes. She didn't give me a pot or a pan, or anything, including good wishes, good luck, or encouragement to start my new life.

The family of one of my close friends, from the high school years I spent in Cincinnati, owned a large real estate company. Her older brother, now in command of the business, owned rental property and rented a furnished studio apartment to me, at a reduced rate. In return, I collected rents, swept halls, and burned trash in the incinerator.

When I unfolded the couch to become the bed, it blocked the front door. There was a half-refrigerator and a two-burner range. It was shabby but clean and independence tasted good. I always wanted to work, thinking it such a grown-up endeavor. I was forever rushing towards adulthood, assuming the sufferings of childhood insecurities didn't exist in that world. No matter what my age in any given year, my father was heard telling friends, "Roberta, my youngest is going on thirty-five". I'd finally found that elusive state of adulthood at age seventeen.

My rent was two weeks' net pay. By the end of the month I was broke and had to hitchhike downtown to work. I had nothing – no TV, no radio, no car, no dishes, silverware, or glasses. Once a week I would walk to the local pizza house and carry home a large pizza. While I was waiting for my order, I would slip silverware, glasses, and a few small plates into my purse. This pizza would serve as my main sustenance for most of the week. I would ration the pieces accordingly.

Raised on high moral ground, it was difficult to justify this theft with my need, yet it didn't stop me. My mother rarely called and never offered to help financially.

I lost my virginity to my friend's thirty-year-old brother Roland, my landlord, that seventeenth year. I loved him because he brought me groceries. I thought love was what you were supposed to feel when you had sex with a man. First sex is rarely your best sex, but who knows that at the time? He was kind to me and a thoughtful lover. But in retrospect, I was overcharged, considering the cash I paid for rent in addition to all those blow jobs!

16

Finding my own way during these young years resulted in an almost total lack of fear for anything external.

"Roberta, aren't you afraid of walking home from the bar so late at night by yourself?" a coworker asked.

"Nope. If anybody lays a hand on me, I'll rip their balls off."

"Roberta, aren't you afraid hitch-hiking to work? You're getting into a car with a stranger. Anything can happen."

"Nope. If anybody lays a hand on me, I'll rip their balls off."

With an abundance of anger floating just below the surface, I was ready to rip some balls off. I couldn't wait for an opportunity.

CHAPTER 2

When I met John in 1984, my income was already in the six figures. I had earned the right to make so much money. My success in an industry populated by few females was due to a combination of hard-won fearlessness, a little luck, and punishing hard work. My career path began early and trended upward. My first full-time job was as a teller at a building and loan company, freshly graduated from high school at age seventeen. I became adept at counting money and being nice to little old ladies while assisting them in opening Christmas Club accounts. The challenge there was not the job itself, but my adaptation to an adult world and the realization that I could no longer enjoy spring break. Full-time job meant exactly that: full time.

I was dismissed from this first position after a short time because I was late for work one morning and hadn't called with an explanation.

Still unable to accept my father's death, my mother had tried to commit suicide the night before. I'd spent the night at the hospital with my sister, trying to control my rage at Mother's selfish action. I went home to change for work and accidentally fell asleep, and when I awoke I simply dressed and got on the bus. It didn't occur to me to call. I thought showing up was sufficient. While sympathetic, my employer assumed a parental role. His discharge of me, he explained, would teach me a life-long lesson in responsibility.

I walked across the street to an employment agency. I needed a job fast. The agency hired me that day as their receptionist. The idea was to train me as an employment counselor, placing female applicants with appropriate employers for a fee. It was a straight commission job, with a draw against commissions, and the goals set were unattainable. I spent most of my time there dodging the owner, who was intent on seducing me.

*

It had been a year since my father's death and my mother had remarried. She was moving to Honolulu and asked me to accompany her and her new husband whom I had never met. I was tired of the job at the employment agency and tired of managing my life. Honolulu sounded exotic and a great place to start over. I went. We stayed in a hotel in downtown Honolulu because Mother's new husband, as it turned out, had no house and no job. What he did have was a serious drinking problem. He expected my mother to buy a house with the money she inherited from my father. The first and only week I was there, he left every morning to find a job and came home every night drunk, without one.

One evening Mother and I were waiting for his return in the dining room of the hotel. He entered the lobby drunk and with another woman who was more than a friend, made apparent by their groping each other in that fervent way that says, "Please don't say goodbye just yet." My mother rushed over and pulled them apart while I stood by not knowing what to do. "Roberta, go upstairs to your room. I'll talk you later." She turned away from me and pulled him in the direction of the elevator. Wanting to avoid them, I chose the stairs. We withdrew to our respective rooms and when the shouting sounded more serious, I opened the connecting door between our rooms to find him striking my mother. Having grown up in an environment more like Leave It to Beaver, I had rarely even heard my parents argue. I suddenly felt catapulted into an episode of The Twilight Zone. I jumped on his back in an effort to halt the beating, and of course got slugged a few times myself. When he finally left in a drunken rage, Mother decided to leave Honolulu that night and return to Cincinnati. We packed, took a cab to the airport, and waited for the ticket counters to open so we could take the first flight to Ohio.

Four hours later and at approximately four o'clock in the morning, my mother turned to me and said, "I have to stay. I love him and I need to make it work."

I was so astonished I was almost speechless. I squared off in front of her, feet planted, hands firmly on my hips. "Mother," I said, "I guess you have to do whatever is right for you, but I'm going back to Cincinnati." My teeth were clenched so tightly my pulse was visible in the throbbing vein on my forehead.

Her eyes focused on a spot over my shoulder. "You can't go anywhere, Roberta, unless I say so. Do you have any money dear? Do you? Because I'm not buying you a ticket."

I turned to her, trembling with the effort to control my fury. "Mother, if I have to sell my body here for the remainder of the night, I will, until I earn enough money to pay for a ticket."

The remark startled even me as I realized I meant every word. I didn't know I possessed that power of resolve. I was leaving Honolulu and the nightmare it had become, no matter what actions I needed to take.

The look on my face told her it was true. She bought the ticket and gave me one hundred dollars. That was enough, she explained, to get me from the airport to wherever I was going and should tide me over until I got a job. She got into a cab and headed back to him, unconcerned with where or how I would live. Her only thought was putting her own life back together, and after all, I was now barely eighteen-majority age. This island was Paradise? I felt cheated.

I phoned a friend who retrieved me from the airport. She allowed me to sleep on her couch and keep my clothes in a piano bench and an abandoned toy box. I didn't have many clothes so it worked. She had two children she entrusted to my care when I wasn't working. It was part of my rent, so to speak.

I needed a job desperately. I persuaded the president of Westinghouse Security Systems to hire me as his administrative assistant. I had no skills; I could not type and my still-present stutter made me a disaster as a receptionist. I couldn't say "Westinghouse," and there is no word substitution for "Westinghouse" when you're answering the telephone. The first day my boss gave me a letter and two memos to type. He walked into his office as the telephone rang. I was struck with panic. I knew I couldn't say it. I put my hand on the receiver and before answering proceeded to wind up.

"Weh...Weh...Weh..." I picked up the phone, "*West*inghouse Security Systems." My face was red from the effort.

I can still see the look on his face as he peered out of his office in utter disbelief. He was appalled. I pretended there was nothing out of the ordinary. Seriously, the look on my face never changed. I continued to smile as though everybody who answered a telephone did it in exactly this manner.

My brain was struggling desperately to get that word out, but I was chuckling inside. Even negotiating the ordeal, I knew it was droll. This enormous effort continued all day. At five o'clock that evening I still had not completed the letter and two memos. He didn't have to tell me it was over. I thanked him for the day's pay and he hugged me when we said goodbye.

"Roberta, you've got balls," he said, laughing. "You should get into sales. You sure conned me."

*

Around this time I met Terry, who was to become my first husband. I was sitting in a bar with a date one Friday night when the drummer from the jazz trio approached my companion to say hello, then turned to me and said, "Hi my name is Terry and I think you have a fabulous overbite." I flinched at the perceived insult and promptly told him to fuck off. He explained that he meant it as a compliment but not convinced, I ignored his conversation with my cohort for the remainder of the night. Rude, I think, is the word, to describe my behavior.

Terry was short by comparison to the men I had dated. At five-foot-eight inches tall, he still managed to walk with a distinct and confident swagger, demonstrative of his leadership ability. His hair, jet black and his eyes even blacker, made him appear exotic, and the presence of a pipe, constantly in his mouth, imparted sagacity. His face bore unmistakable kindness with a touch of mirth always lurking around his mouth. Even his thick black mustache couldn't camouflage his constant amusement. I found him very attractive, in spite of what I perceived to be an insult.

Two days later, I was standing at the bus stop in the pouring rain without an umbrella. Understand that I was standing erect and not trying to cover myself. I was simply acting as if it wasn't raining. This was my way of hiding the shame I felt for not being able to afford an umbrella. I had to stand proud. A car stopped and it was Terry, mildly amused, offering me a ride downtown. He was twenty-seven and I was eighteen. We started dating and it wasn't long before he invited me to move in with him. I did. My wardrobe was so sparse I didn't need the closet he offered, but I was glad to have one that didn't resemble an abandoned toy box.

*

The newspapers detailed a grand new restaurant and bar opening in the heart of downtown. My résumé being my nerve, I approached the owner without hesitation. I was only eighteen, but I sold him on the idea of me managing his club. I had never been in the business, other than working at Dairy Queen. I wasn't old enough to serve liquor, but I was now commanding a restaurant that served lunch and hor d'oeuvres for cocktail hour, and featured live music Monday through Saturday. It never once occurred to me that I could not do this, or do it well.

I had the responsibility of keeping the daily books for the accountant, hiring and firing all personnel, scheduling personnel, managing time cards, purchasing all supplies, and opening and closing the restaurant. I also procured rental property for the bands we hired from out of town and tended to their needs. I worked Monday through Saturday from eight in the morning until five in the evening, then returned to the bar at ten o'clock and closed at two o'clock in the morning, counted the drawers and made the night deposit. I usually arrived home at three o'clock in the morning and was back at the restaurant the following morning at eight o'clock to complete the office work prior to opening at eleven o'clock for lunch.

I learned from everybody who would talk to me. That included our suppliers, the employees, the bands, Terry, and friends. It was hard and I was tired all the time. My only time off was Sundays and I didn't like to do a damn thing on Sundays. That habit has stuck with me all these years, and even today, I don't like to leave my house on Sundays. Occasionally I was so exhausted even the stairs leading to the bedroom were too formidable. Some days I just didn't quite make it up the steps, into the bed and under the sheets. Terry would arrive home to find me sound asleep draped in a contorted way, across the stairs. He asked me once if I had to choose, would it be him or the job. I couldn't answer. I didn't know. At eighteen years old I was driven.

When the owner sold the bar due to failing health, the new proprietor decided to operate the place without me. I was convinced that my knowledge was indispensable, but they made it clear that I was no longer needed. Believing this bar to be my destiny, I was devastated.

Shortly after, the salesman who sold me bar supplies offered me a job as a purchasing agent at the restaurant equipment dealer where he was employed. I took it on the spot.

Very quickly, I noticed that the people making the most money with my new company were in sales. I asked to be moved from purchasing and trained into sales. Before long, I hit the road with my fifty-pound sample case of glassware, stir sticks and beverage napkins. I was twenty one and ready to prove myself. Once again it never occurred to me that I wouldn't succeed.

*

It was late on a Monday morning when I pushed open the door to The Blue Note Bar in Newport, Kentucky. I walked towards a man standing near the beer taps, assuming him to be in charge. When he turned, I faced a heavy-set man with dark, slicked back hair, a pock-marked face, and eyes so small and murky I could barely find them on his face. He wasn't much taller than me. There were so many gold chains around his neck he couldn't have had any trouble in the snow—he just needed to wrap a few of those chains around his tires and go for it.

That thought kept a smile on my face as I peripherally glimpsed him reach behind his back and shove a small handgun under the newspaper he'd been reading. I'm sure he didn't think I noticed.

"What can I do for you little lady," he asked, without a trace of a smile.

"Sir, my name is Roberta and I represent the Roth Company, selling restaurant supplies. I was wondering if—"

"—Thanks little lady, I don't need anything today."

Nothing says "sell me something" more than the word "no." My smile only got brighter. "I'm sure you had a big weekend here and maybe you could use a few small things, like some bar napkins or maybe some sip sticks, or how about a case of double-rocks glasses? Glasses are our lead item and our prices are unbeatable."

It was like a dark cloud opened the door behind me, ran through the club, and sat right atop his face. "Look honey, I told you, I'm good. Nothing today, thanks."

I conjured the memory of him hiding a gun, pictured myself shot dead, and squeezed my eyes tight just long enough to conjure a tear. "Look, Mr.?..." I began.

"Call me Tony, honey."

"Look Tony, it's only my third week on the job and let's just say that my numbers aren't that impressive. I'm afraid if I don't do better this week I could get canned and I don't have anyone but me to pay my rent!"

"Where's your boyfriend, honey?" Tony said. "With gams like that you gotta have a sugar daddy somewheres, don't ya?"

By now Tony was smiling and I knew he was softening.

Letting the tear slip down my cheek, I looked down and said, "No, I don't. I'm too busy working to think of having a boyfriend." I reached into my purse and pulled out a cigarette. "Do you have a light, Tony?" As he held the match to the tip of my cigarette, I cupped the back of his hand, looked into his eyes, and got comfortable on a bar stool. Tony knew he had a choice-buy something or watch me cry and be subjected to my oh-so-sad story.

"Okay, little lady, whatcha got on sale in glassware?"

He gave me a thousand-dollar order that Monday and many Mondays after.

When I returned to Roth and gave my boss the order, his face turned pale. "Roberta! You got an order from Tony at The Blue Note? I'm not sure you should have gone there alone. Don't you know he's Mafia?!"

"Hey," I said my voice a little louder than I had intended, "you're the guy who gave me the damn territory to begin with, and you sure didn't mention any 'danger' then! Don't worry about it...I can handle it. You guys need to learn how to cry on demand."

My territory was the strip clubs and night clubs of Northern Kentucky and I was too naïve to understand that I was calling on the underworld bosses of the area. That naiveté led to my success. I was fearless.

My refusal to hear the word "no" netted me many sales. Like Tony, in some cases they just wanted to get me out the door and the quickest way to do that was to give me the order.

I sold only table top items like glassware, china, and cookware. Commercial kitchen equipment was in the contract division, where no women were allowed. I hung around that division though, and the guys became my friends and I learned through osmosis. I liked equipment because it was forbidden.

Terry proposed after we had been living together five years and we married with the understanding that we would buy a house first and start a family as soon as we settled in. I desperately wanted children thinking it would provide me the proper vehicle to right the wrongs of my own mother. I really believed I could hurt less if I could parent better. We bought our house after eight months of marriage and it took another four months for him to work up the courage to tell me he really didn't want a family. I was twenty-three and he was thirty-two. I wanted children and felt I could not stay and hope to convince him to change his mind. In retrospect, I should have.

Being able to walk out with relatively few entanglements was a feeling that carried over from our living together so long. I believe living together before marriage yields far less appreciation of the vows. Although my mother advised me to, I would not stop taking the pill and accidentally get pregnant. I loved Terry too much to burden him with a responsibility he did not want. There were other things, as well, but that was the crux of the matter. My inability to be less driven could have had some bearing on our split.

The day I informed my mother that we were divorcing, she calmly hung up and promptly called Terry. She offered him a place to stay. I was so flabbergasted that I laughed aloud. She had never extended such an offer to me.

*

The owner of the Roth Company introduced me to his friend Edwin, an attorney from Cleveland. I had several occasions to work with Edwin on various restaurant projects purchased for the purpose of investment. He approached me with a proposition.

He had assembled a group of investors for the purpose of obtaining the franchise for a fast food chain in Cincinnati. The parent company was headquartered in Cleveland. They were seeking a person to assist in the building of the restaurants and head up operations. What twenty something, divorced, career-driven woman can resist being head honcho? And the money was incredible—nearly double my current income. I was in. It would involve training in Cleveland for three months and having total operational control, in addition to assisting in the building of each store.

Upon completion of training in Cleveland, it was back to Cincinnati and the building of three restaurants and running the operations. Two of the stores were in strip centers and the construction was fairly easy. After the assistance of a general contractor on the first job, I was able to handle the second job on my own. There were very few subcontractors and the equipment package was set by the parent company. No discretion, no decisions. The third was the conversion of a theatre, complicated construction, in addition to running the operations of two other stores. Not feeling confident of my ability with the construction process we hired another general contractor who was kind enough to explain and patient enough to teach. My craving for almost any kind of knowledge was insatiable. I was like that pesky fly that lives in your kitchen all summer, side-stepping the swatter in pursuit of satisfaction. This man was kind enough to tolerate my persistent questions, never making me feel the fool for asking.

Although these stores were turning a profit in the first eighteen months and the investors were pleased, I wasn't satisfied. I approached the owner of a "roach coach," the mobile feeders that cruise construction sites and sell food items to the workers. I wanted him to buy one hundred sandwiches a day, at a reduced rate, so he could in turn re-sell to his customers at a profit for him. I hoped this would dramatically improve our bottom line by bringing more market awareness to our products. I finally convinced him by giving him an incredibly low price and we cut a deal, consummated by a handshake. After crunching the numbers, I determined the bottom line would be positively affected, but only if I could cut the labor costs. The only way to do that was to do the cooking myself. I was on salary, ergo no labor costs.

Monday through Friday for the next eight months or so, I arrived at the restaurant at four o'clock in the morning and prepared one hundred sandwiches for the driver to pick up at five-thirty in the morning. I usually got home between seven and eight-thirty in the evening after beginning my days at three o'clock in the morning. I still look back on this time with profound incredulity. My friends never saw me, my child (a cat named Mort) hardly knew me, and although Sundays were still an at-home day for me, they became the never-get-out-of-bed day. I have been a voracious reader all my life – I don't remember a time when I wasn't involved in a book—but I didn't read a book for two years and never had more than a Sunday off.

*

Building and managing these stores put me in touch with restaurant equipment salesmen and I began to learn restaurant equipment more thoroughly and derive a broader view of the industry as a whole. It had been three years and I had three stores up and running in the black when I was approached by the vice-president of sales for a foodservice equipment distributor based in Cleveland.

His name was Jerry. He knew of me, he said, because his sales representative in the Cincinnati market had sold me some equipment. That sales rep, upon giving his notice, mentioned to Jerry that I might be well suited for the job. The company wanted me for a sales position covering Cincinnati, Dayton, and Columbus in Ohio, and the entire states of Kentucky and Indiana. I took it. I was thrilled at the idea of an opportunity that didn't involve the hours I had been working.

Finally, I had found my chance to sell restaurant equipment. I was one of few women in the country doing so at the time. I thought the travel would be exciting. It was a straight commission job, and I was worried about that, but I had now come to realize that the acceptance of a job did not constitute an investment for the rest of my life. I had begun to understand that if this job didn't work out, I could move on. My life wouldn't be over. I gave a one month notice at the restaurant(s) and again parted with many hugs and best wishes. I never left a job without the continued friendship of my employers. Thankfully, I always formed the sorts of relationships with my employers that allowed them to allow me to grow.

*

The only thing I wasn't completely successful at was my personal life. I didn't even remember the last time I'd thought about a date, much less had one. My grandmother kept harping that I was going to be "one of those old maids with cats."

Once when she was visiting me, I had a dinner meeting with an architect concerning the downtown theatre conversion project. I was late and he called my home to see if I was on my way. There were no cell phones then. Imagine my embarrassment when I arrived at the restaurant and he told me he had spoken to my grandmother. She'd asked him if he was married. Upon discovering that he was, she inquired as to whether he had any single friends that would be suitable for her beautiful granddaughter. She even voiced her fear that I might end up being an old maid with cats. I never heard the end of that from my buddy the architect. Every time he saw me, he asked how many cats I had. "Roberta, what's the current ratio...cats to boyfriends, I mean?"

Grandma wouldn't have to worry long.

CHAPTER 3

I refer to my time selling restaurant equipment as the "testosterone years" because I worked mostly with men in a male-dominated industry. I'm convinced I grew my own set of balls during those years, and that testosterone pulsed through my bloodstream, decreasing the estrogen levels considered normal for most women. I have no proof, other than my success. Those years provided me with astounding personal and career growth. I was absorbing volumes of information daily, developing new relationships, and Jerry, my boss, was my mentor in sales as well as life.

*

We were in Cincinnati calling on a high volume customer, a gentleman interested in buying a large quantity of one of our products. I was still training and knew very little about this piece of equipment, so although Jerry introduced me as his associate, I was contributing nothing to the conversation.

Fifteen minutes into the sales presentation, the customer turned to me and said, "Honey, can you put this quarter in the meter for me?

I have the blue Lincoln parked in the next block, opposite side of the street."

I looked to Jerry, but he would not make eye contact with me and I knew he had no intention of defending my professionalism.

Off I went and returned, fuming.

After another half-hour, the customer handed me another quarter with the same request, and again, Jerry said nothing. I was seething.

Jerry closed the deal and we left with the purchase order, obviously pleased he could impress me with his sales ability. We got into his car and I calmly handed him the two quarters.

He looked at me with wide eyes that were full of question. I simply said, "Did you really think I was going to put money in that asshole's meter? Is that what you really hired me to do?"

After a very long moment of surprise, laughter echoed throughout the car as he struggled through snorts. "If we lose this sale...*snort*... because that asshole got a ticket... *snort*...you're fired!"

The deal was finalized, the order shipped and my assumption was that the asshole never did get a ticket.

*

I worked like a maniac, consumed with my need to succeed, and after a very lean first year; I began to establish the relationships needed to assure me the income and recognition I was seeking. The second year I doubled my income, and the third year I doubled it again. I was earning a reputation, thanks to Jerry's continued tutelage. I began getting job offers from manufacturers and other rep groups. If it meant leaving wherever I was at four o'clock in the morning, I was in my territory by eight o' clock. When the doors opened to the dealer, or consultant, or service agency, my spike heels could be heard clacking across the floor, keeping rhythm with the sounds of the coffee machine making its first pot of the day.

The business grew quickly and Jerry hired two additional women, Jan and Carmen, as salespeople. I was promoted to Sales Manager, with Jerry still as Vice-President of Sales. The company acquired West Virginia as part of our territory, which also included Ohio, Kentucky, and Indiana.

During the late seventies and early eighties, Gloria Steinem and Germaine Greer weren't even on my radar screen. I was too busy building my career to worry about being liberated. I thought the movement was political and partisan. I could mount a soapbox to specifically support equal pay for equal work, but did I really have to join the sisterhood? It went against my grain to become a part of a group when I had worked so hard to set myself apart. I didn't want to be among a sea of female faces blaming men for whatever position women lacked and feeling morally compelled to vote Democratic. I wouldn't have crossed the street to burn my bra – I didn't need one to begin with – unless there was a party involved.

Because of the times and my position amongst the men, I was asked constantly, "Roberta, are you a 'libber'?"

My response never varied. "When it's convenient."

*

I was left alone to set up an exhibit for the Ohio State Restaurant Show. Jerry had taken ill and couldn't be there to assist me in getting six commercial microwaves into the booth. I walked to the loading dock armed with my most devilish grin and approached a man with a flatbed cart.

"Can you help me?" I asked. "I have a little bit of a problem."

"If I can." He grinned. My legs were caught in his gaze, there was no hiding it.

"I need to get six commercial microwaves into my booth, and I can't even lift them, not to mention I don't have a cart."

The softness left his eyes. "Well, I'm sort of busy right now...the show is going to open in a few hours..."

I knew "the look." It said, "If you want to do a man's job, blah, blah, blah...."

"Would you do it for a blow job?" I said, making sure to look directly in his eyes as I let loose my loudest laugh.

Startled, wondering if I was serious, he chortled aloud. "What's the booth number? I'll have them there in a few minutes."

I used this piece of comedy more than once and it worked for me every time. Not one man ever demanded payment. This was my argument to the movement. Use what you have unless it meant giving your body to a person you would rather not.

*

I traveled with Jan and Carmen and was responsible for their training, call reports, sales, and everything business-related. My training included lectures, born from experience, about working in a man's world.

"Strap your balls on, ladies, you've chosen a career where the world will tell you that you don't belong. It's your job to prove them wrong. We belong wherever the hell we want to, we just need to be better. What's different about that anyway? If I were a man I'd want to be better.

"Don't lay down for an order unless it's a really big order. Just kidding. Personally I think it's okay to use femininity as a tool. Just know your stuff inside and out. Don't give any man an excuse to say it's because you're a woman that you couldn't close a deal. Whatever you do, never wimp out in this man's world. If you can't take hearing the word "fuck," don't work here. Nobody will try to touch you if you show them the right attitude, but if they do, rip their balls off before you even think about filing some Federal complaint. There are more penises than boobs here, so get used to it. Work with it. Suck it up. Don't cry. Don't whine. Be smarter than them and *always* sell your ass off... without selling your ass."

I took this all-female team very seriously. We competed with our male counterparts and won every time. I dubbed us the "A Team." It was a popular show at the time and as affirmation of our success, Jerry presented each of us a signet ring with the initial "A." Jan and Carmen assumed some of my territory and I was able to concentrate more on larger chain businesses, many of which were located in Columbus, where my company maintained a branch office.

*

During the day, I proved to be a formidable competitor. If there were a number of us lined up to see an important customer, I was always the first in the door, even if I had arrived last. I wasn't blind to what assets I had, and sex appeal was one of them.

I wore an ankle bracelet and it became my trademark and still is today. They were much rarer then. I made it a point to be a bit left of the popular dress-for-success fad. It was more important for me to be unique. When women's suits became popular, I wore dresses, or skirts with blouses and I earned a reputation for being fashionable.

I knew my product, knew my customers, and would like to believe that in the course of any presentation, most would forget I was a woman.

I had to be better and I was. I had the numbers to prove it. I was more driven than ever, and I developed a passion for the industry.

These were heady times. I lived to work. I drove myself and my two girls relentlessly. I wanted every award any factory or my company offered, and I wanted lots of cash for my effort. The walls of the Cleveland office became filled with sales award plaques serving as testimonials to the "A Team." Recognition was abundant, and served to push our male counterparts to achieve higher sales goals themselves. The company was ecstatic seeing growth from all angles, stating the genesis of that growth to be a woman's desire to succeed in a man's world. I was making bundles of money and I was happy. What wasn't to be happy about? I was a star. That's what they kept telling me.

*

The one thing that was missing was a relationship. On the road, I made it a point to be just one of the guys. I would see my peers, some of them competition, in hotels and bars that were popular among the sales reps. During the day, we were competitors. At night and out of town, we played. We drank, the jokes flew, the laughter was raucous - mine especially- and I could cuss better than all of them.

I would even help them pick up women. "Keith, heads-up buddy, great ass at four-o-clock."

"Thanks, Roberta, babe, but I'm still waiting for you," Keith said with a laugh.

"I would rather you live with the illusion of what it might be, Keith, than deal with the grim reality of what it actually is," I said. "Besides, you have bigger boobs than me. Come to think of it, everybody has bigger boobs than me! I could show you the tattoo on my chest, I guess. It says 'In case of rape, this side up'."

Keith almost spit his drink across the bar.

"I'm only selling this crap because I can't be a hooker. I tried, Keith, but it didn't work out for me. I not only have no chest at all – which equates to zero sex appeal for most men - the changer I had to carry got cumbersome, and I couldn't give change for a quarter to everybody!"

I ran into Alex at The Executive Inn in Evansville, Indiana on a Wednesday night. We were having a drink at the bar and chitchatting when he suddenly turned serious. "Roberta, I just don't get why you don't have a boyfriend. You're a good lookin' babe, smart, fun...Christ, you even love football! What's the story?"

"Alex, I'll tell ya," I began, "my last boyfriend, and that seems like a hundred years ago, ran off when I was trying to turn him on by talking dirty during sex. I started to stutter and the harder I tried not to, the more I stuttered. I cracked up and started laughing harder and harder, and he finally jerked on his pants and left! I guess he didn't think it was funny, or maybe he thought I was laughing at something else. I didn't actually *mean* to point. It was sort of cute though, it looked like a penis, only smaller."

I had become so much one of the guys that when one of my customers tried to arrange a date with a fellow single rep, he was told, "Take Roberta out for a date? No way. She's just one of the guys."

Dateless mostly, I was starting to wonder if I had gone too far. I had become one of the girls that are one of the guys. At cocktail parties I was the lone woman in the corner with the men, talking business and sports.

*

I started receiving phone calls from a restaurant equipment dealer in Milwaukee, Wisconsin. I'd been told by customers and dealers in my territory that the dealer had been making inquiries about me. The Binder Company, an unsurpassed foodservice equipment dealer in Milwaukee, wanted to hire me to develop a division that would specifically sell to the restaurant chain market. Having concentrated on this market for some time, my expertise with that specific market segment was widely accepted.

The dealer and I had many discussions, and after I turned down a few tenders he made me an incredible monetary offer that included reimbursement of my moving expenses.

I gave two months' notice and Jerry spent most of that time trying to change my mind. I helped train the man who took my territory and a particularly funny event occurred when I took him to meet my largest volume customer in Columbus.

We were sitting in the anteroom waiting to be called. When my customer came to escort us into his office, Bobby, my replacement, hiked up his pant leg to reveal a length of bicycle chain wrapped around his ankle. He was paying homage to my ankle bracelet. It was uproariously funny and the story made the rounds for a very long time. That joke ensured Bobby his place in line with this customer forever.

The owner of my company made me promise to return if I was not happy in Milwaukee and he guaranteed that my job would always be there for me. I was incredibly touched. It was February of 1984 that I made Milwaukee my new home. I was a vibrant, veteran career woman at age thirty-two.

I had no idea that I was about to trade everything for which I'd worked so hard, for a career as a corporate slut.

CHAPTER 4

I met John Wendall the third day of my new job in Milwaukee. It was, to be exact, February 5, 1984. Though I had developed a wealth of contacts that would enable me to successfully develop a chain division for the Binder Company, I knew not one soul in Milwaukee.

I had taken up residency a week before and John's sales rep was now calling on me. He was diligent about showing me the products for all the manufacturers he represented, and he was so grave in his delivery I had to do something to upset the funereal atmosphere. Solemnity is a condition I find profoundly boring.

"Tom, tell me about your family," I began. "How many kids do you have?"

Tom smiled broadly, exposing dimples so astoundingly deep, I thought sweat would pool there. He wore his Irish heritage like a wetsuit; it was all over him. His fair complexion highlighted the freckles scattered haplessly across a nose slightly flushed with the remembrance of a night of drinking. "Well, Roberta, I have six children. Would you like to see a picture?" You could almost hear Irish music in his smiling eyes.

"Six children, Tom? Jesus, do you ever keep that thing in your pants?"

Tom's eyes widened. "Excuse me?"

"My God! If I were your wife I would have padlocked the bedroom door and put an electrified fence around the bed."

A little flushed, he handed me the picture of his family, showing all six children to be under the age of ten.

"Holy moly Tom, has she ever owned a pair of pants without elastic in the waist? Look what you've done to that woman...six kids in ten years...another female who surely must hate sex by now."

Tom's face turned crimson red.

Probably to change the subject, Tom insisted I meet John Wendall, the owner of one of the manufacturers he represented. John was in the process of a divorce and I was single.

"You're almost as crazy as he is, Roberta," Tom said. "I think you might make a good match."

They were scheduled to lunch together that day. He telephoned John from my office and asked if he might bring me along.

We met at a well known bistro downtown. John shook my hand and placed his other hand over mine, sandwich style. "I've already heard a lot about you," he said.

"Oh? Really? I haven't lived here long enough for the bathroom graffiti to have accumulated." I was grinning.

He laughed. "No not that, at least not yet, but I did get the scoop on you from my reps in Ohio."

"Uh oh." I grimaced. "Dare I ask? Do I need to defend myself already?"

"Not bad, actually," he responded. "The extensive dossier begins with 'Single girl moving to Milwaukee, funny, smart, cute, and available.' The rest I'll tell you later...for a price, that is." His grin was sly.

"Make sure it's affordable." I winked at him. "I wouldn't want to feel cheated if the price were high and the information worthless."

After lunch, as John drove me back to my office he asked if he could call to schedule a dinner date. Being in a large group at lunch had afforded us little opportunity to speak privately.

"Well that's a ridiculous question," I said. "I've lived here for five days and my calendar is embarrassingly free."

Apparently I was irresistible because he called at three o'clock that afternoon and we arranged to meet after work at a Friday's close to my apartment.

Looking back, I can say without prejudice that at thirty-two I looked good. The perkiness of my twenties had evolved into a more mature sassiness befitting my thirties. Although petite and lean in stature, my legs were long and shapely, made more so by the five-inch stilettos that have always been in fashion for me. Short skirts, my logic directed, accented my legs and kept attention distracted from my less than ample bosom. Smooth skin not yet showing the effects of sun damage or the laugh lines caused by endless hilarity, my blond hair short, I possessed a smile that exploded into raucous laughter and deep brown eyes that occupied most of my face. I was all about attitude. My walk was confident, my wit was sharp, and because I was so damn sure I looked good, I did.

He had asked me at lunch what my drink preference was, and I had glibly answered, "A bottle of champagne with a straw." When I walked into Friday's he was at the bar holding, what else, a bottle of champagne with a straw.

His grin was roguish, his eyes somewhat small, but a warm color of brown. He had gorgeous, thick, shiny brown hair and his face displayed a boyish sense of satisfaction, pleased with his own cleverness. He was five-feet-ten-inches tall with a build and walk not unlike Donald Duck. His short neck sat atop sloped shoulders. His chest was narrow and his stomach was slightly protruded. The caboose portion of his body appeared large and muscular.

His appearance was comical, really, but it came together well with his sense of humor, as if it were God's plan to make a funny person somewhat funny-looking. His deficient shoulders later became a matter of teasing between his tailor and me. He was both charming and off-putting at the same time. He was clever and quick-witted but crude in some ways. I was equally repelled and fascinated. I'm always captivated by dichotomy. The contradiction was like a jigsaw puzzle that demanded my attention.

We drank the bottle of champagne, followed by a few cocktails, and smoked and joked. We found that we shared knowledge and a mutual love of the foodservice industry. His company, Wendall Industries, was a well-known manufacturer of equipment in the industry.

"How is it, Roberta, that knowing all these people in common we've never met? Don't you think it a bit odd? How did you get started in the business anyway?" he asked. "Me, I was born into it, and most foodservice manufacturing companies are family concerns, passed from generation to generation. Exactly how did you happen to break into such a boys' club?"

"It's a very long story, John, but I'm happy to tell it if you promise not to snore through most of it...and please hold your questions until the end!" I held up my hand, laughing. "Are you sure you want to hear all this?" I asked.

"Give me the whole story, Roberta. I want to know *everything* about you."

He took my hand in his and settled back in the barstool, and I caught him up on everything that had led me to this point. To his credit, he didn't yawn once.

Afterwards, he asked why I had experience in every aspect of the industry except manufacturing. He wondered why I never worked for a factory.

"Oh I got all kinds of offers," I said, "but they never could pay me enough money. Why would I give up a six figure income that I earn largely by commission, to work for a factory that wants to pay me $50,000.00 a year and maybe give me a car?"

John gasped. "Good God, Roberta, you make more than I do!"

"And your point is?" I laughed. "You have a problem with a woman making money?"

"No, it's not that, it's just...I guess I need to give myself a raise tomorrow. It really isn't appropriate that a woman makes more than I do."

Bottom line, as the evening concluded, both of us slightly tipsy, I thought John a bit of an asshole, but entertaining. He might prove to be a nice diversion in a place where I knew no one.

CHAPTER 5

A week later John asked me to join him for a weekend at his summer home, even though it was February and one could ice skate across the entire state of Wisconsin. Frozen Tundra, I was discovering, is apropos. He introduced me to Freshwater Falls, a resort town located in Door County, Wisconsin, where the manufacturing plant for his company was located and where his family has had a presence since the 1950's.

His house was built in 1895 from limestone mined "just up the road," as they said in the local vernacular. The two-acre estate was separated from the road by a matching limestone wall, and the fifty-foot spider pines were dressed with just enough snow to complete the Currier and Ives imagery. As we made our way down the tear drop-shaped drive, I saw the frozen waters of Freshwater Falls, which provided a winter wonderland backdrop to the house—the entire estate looked like something from a movie. The gardens lay in repose, but one could already image the splendor yet to awaken with spring.

The interior of the house was smaller than it appeared from outside – it was only one room wide, but charming and warm. It needed a facelift and fifteen minutes after unpacking my bags, I already had a vision of what it should look like. The mental exercise wasn't tied to any feeling for John. No, decorating was a pastime I loved and the house begged for some attention. I knew I could do it justice, but I hadn't imagined living there…yet.

In any event, John meant to impress me and I was properly wowed. I fell in love with the house and the area.

He was suitably pleased with himself for overwhelming me with the grandeur of it all. He built a blazing fire, poured me a glass of vodka and himself a scotch, and we settled into the down sofa, cuddling, whispering and performing the usual mating rituals….light touches to the cheek, a tender kiss on the neck, eyes filled with longing. His face betrayed an inner voice that was whispering, "I'm going to get laid tonight…finally."

After passionate kisses and desperate groping in front of the fire, he carried me up the stairs to the bedroom and undressed me slowly. But the second he got undressed, it was like a shotgun had signaled "GO" at a swim meet. John was thirty-four years old and as I was about to discover, could not possibly have been mentored with regard to sex. No kindly woman had explained to him that making love was not a substitute for aerobic exercise. As he repeatedly bounced on top of me, I was struck with the notion that I was completely out of step with this dance. He literally bounced the mattress off the bed and onto the floor that night. As he lay panting beside me, fully sated, I was curled in the fetal position next to him, convulsed in silent laughter. When I heard the standard question "Was it okay for you?" my head was bobbing so violently from the repressed laughter he thought it was genuine affirmation. Why hadn't I brought my vibrator so I could sneak into the bathroom? He probably wouldn't have noticed my absence until the sweat cleared from his eyes.

I was impressed with all that John had shown me that evening, but the climax of our evening is a memory still shaded by hilarious disappointment. It was bad sex, but at the same time it was an urgent, needy sort of lovemaking that begged for compassion. John would need some coaching, clearly. I was interested and impressed enough to want to be the coach. And as courtships go, it was far better than average. John was raised in a wealthy family and had attended private grade school, high school, and a private college. He was impressively well-mannered. After our first date, I heard from him every day, no matter where he was. He was adept at wining and dining a woman. If not escorting me to the finest restaurants in town, he was preparing very elaborate and romantic dinners at my apartment. He was an extraordinary cook. Although separated and living apart from his wife for over a year John was not yet divorced. He was rooming with a friend temporarily, so my apartment became our sanctuary.

Because I was brand new to the area, he took great pleasure in taking me everywhere. He was like a tour guide amid a fresh set of faces, delighted with the wonderment of his audience. He showed me Milwaukee in style, our chariot his spanking new black BMW. Many of his gestures were so endearing it was difficult not to be enamored. He sent flowers regularly when he became aware of how I loved them. When he learned I had a particular fondness for white roses, he sent them by the dozens. He would send telegrams when he was away from the area, traveling for business or pleasure, letting me know how much he missed me, like the one I received from Hawaii:

> *"It's beautiful here. STOP Not as beautiful as you are. STOP I wish you were here with me. STOP I miss you. STOP."*

47

I didn't even know telegrams were still available.

Usually, he would return from a business trip with a small gift. From a casual conversation, he remembered that I loved Hawaiian sweet bread and he presented me with two loaves upon his return from Honolulu. His trip to San Francisco produced a porcelain white rose he happened upon in an art gallery which, he said he couldn't resist buying because it reminded him how much he missed me. He was a gentleman, opening doors and standing when I returned to a table. His lighter was lit and waiting before I could tap a cigarette from its pack. He took my elbow when we walked and looked at me with adoring eyes. He told me I was beautiful every day. His hand, protectively placed in the small of my back as we stood side-by-side at a cocktail party, was audacious in its implication that I was his. The boldness of his assumptions caught my buried femininity by surprise. He sought my advice; he made me feel brilliant. The nurturing side of me slowly surfaced and I found myself wanting to care for him.

*

One evening while dining at our favorite hole in the wall Mexican restaurant, John was waxing on about a new product Wendall Industries was beginning to produce and market. The equipment was designed to hold food products for longer periods of time, presenting fast food operators an opportunity to improve their speed of service.

"John," I started, margarita salt crusting my lip, "do you know Don Albert, head of R&D for Burgermania, the chain in Columbus?"

"Not personally. Why, do you?"

As he lit my cigarette, I cupped his hand and said, "He's a good friend of mine. I sold him a ton of equipment when I was with the Rapp Company."

"We've been trying to get to him for months, Roberta. This cabinet is perfect for him, but our rep can't get in the door. You think you can set something up?"

"Hmmm…what's it worth to ya? Maybe another margarita?"

He grinned. "I'm not sure I can afford it."

"If I get the deal you can."

"Roberta, if you can do that, sweetheart, I promise you a rerun bouncing the old mattress on the floor again."

"Thanks, John, I'd rather have the margarita." I teased.

He was laughing so hard he had to wipe his eyes. "Oh yeah, we'll see about that."

"Let me see if I can reach him tomorrow." I was serious now, and wanting to impress him with my business savvy. "If he'll see me, I can fly to Columbus this week. But I need to know more about the product first."

"Why? I thought these guys bought from you because you have great legs," he said.

"If it were only that easy, I'd be making billions…not millions…of dollars, my friend. No, Don's a detail guy and he loves to put me through the paces…he has some perverse need to see a woman field-strip a piece of equipment."

"I think I'd like to see that myself, Roberta." John's eyes twinkled.

"There is definitely something sexy about a woman holding a screwdriver, right? Especially a woman in a short skirt and spike heels."

"Especially if it's you wearing them."

"Seriously John, I need to know the equipment before I go in there."

"Not a problem." His eyes were positively gleaming. "Come by the office tomorrow and I'll train you personally."

The look of absolute approbation can be intoxicating. He rose from his seat and moved to my side of the table, pulled me from my chair and wrapped me in a bear hug. I was drunk on his admiration, with a slight nod to the margaritas.

"You continue to amaze me, Roberta," John murmured.

"Why?" I asked.

"Because you're not only beautiful, you're intelligent, and you know equipment." His hug got tighter.

The next day, I made the contact and I was on a plane to Columbus the same week.

*

"Roberta, how great to see you!" Don Albert was hugging me before I crossed the threshold of his office. "I sure do miss you around here. I miss that laugh! You look great…how are things in Wisconsin? Do you love it?"

"Colder than a well digger's ass, Don." I laughed. "It's a bitch, that cold weather…can you imagine a wind chill factor of minus forty degrees? And people live there, go figure. Gotta love those Green Bay Packers, though. That's a bonus for sure. But listen, Don, thanks for seeing me on such short notice. I appreciate you allowing me to ship the equipment to your test kitchen ahead of time. Have your engineers worked with it yet?"

"They were kind of waiting on you, Roberta," he said, somewhat sheepishly. "They tried it some, but there are three other competitive products they're testing, too."

I put my hand on my hip, lowered my eyes, and cocked my head with a somewhat mocking smile. "Don, does this have something to do with a screwdriver? Like, me using the screwdriver for your amusement?

I wore my spike heels. That's what I love about you, Don. You're so easy. Come on, I'll show you how it works. And Don, I guarantee you there are no competitive products in terms of value, longevity, or warranty. You have my word on that."

Three hours later in the test kitchen of Burgermania the product performed as advertised, outperformed two competitors, and performed nearly equal with the third.

"Don, you've been buying from me for years. Have I ever misled you in terms of product performance? In fact, there have been things I refused to sell you, right? I talked you out them, knowing they would fail your expectations, right?"

"That's right, Roberta," he said. "I believe in *you*, but I've never purchased from this manufacturer and I don't know the dealer you're representing in Wisconsin."

"Point taken, Don, but you know me. Do you really think I'd be here laying my integrity on the line if I didn't believe this is the best deal for you? You know it's me you're buying, Don…figuratively of course."

I laughed as he lasciviously raised his eyebrows.

"You know you can't afford *me*, Don." I jabbed him. "Honestly, I'll personally guarantee it. I can arrange for you to tour the factory, we'll fly you there if it's a concern, but I tell you this manufacturer is stellar. I've seen the plant, and happen to have had several conversations with the owner."

I kept a straight face, not wanting anyone in the industry to know I was seeing John intimately.

"I'll be honest with you. Like every manufacturer of any product, sometimes a bad one gets in the field by accident. What makes this manufacturer different is that he makes it right and he does it fast. I've never seen warranty claims honored so quickly and if it's a matter of getting operations back on track, they'll air freight the equipment that day and sort the service thing out later."

I could tell he still wasn't quite convinced, so I steamrolled on. "The dealer is preeminent in the Midwest and is financially sound. I insisted on seeing a financial statement before I accepted the job. You don't think I would risk being stuck in Wisconsin working for a fly by night, do you? You know me better, Don."

"No Roberta, I *wish* I knew you better." He laughed with a wink.

Playfully batting my eyes, I continued. "He's willing to outlay the cash to stock the equipment you'll need quickly. We carry inventory so you don't have to. Returns come to us, and we'll deal with the manufacturer for you. My life is about making you happy, Don, you know that!" I belted out my signature laugh. "I promise to take back everything after ninety days if you aren't satisfied."

Without disparaging the competition, I made John's product look better based on merit, value and the guarantee of my personal service.

"I trust you, Roberta, and I'd love to give you your first big order up there in Wisconsin," Don said. "Let's work on a blanket purchase order with defined release dates that correlate with our national rollout advertising campaign." He stood and held out his hand. "Congratulations, you beat three major competitors and I'm pleased to do business with you."

Ignoring his hand, I went right for the hug. "Thanks Don, so much. That's the other advantage, right? The male rep from Barton doesn't hug you! At least don't tell me if he does! Let me buy you and your wife dinner. This particular sale means the world to me."

He politely declined the invitation, as most of my married male customers did.

Shortly after, I produced an order for one hundred and fifty Wendall Industries holding cabinets. It was a spectacular sale. The benefit for me was two-fold. The owner of the Binder Company had been handling criticism from peers regarding the amount of money it took to lure me, and was now vindicated for paying a fortune for the "broad" from Ohio. And John thought I was brilliant. Hell, everyone thought I was brilliant.

*

I was at The Binder Company a year before being approached by an independent manufacturer's rep. He had twelve superior lines of foodservice equipment and was very successful but he needed a partner. The factories, it seemed, no longer wished to be represented by a one-man band. They were looking for organizations and Dick was looking to make me a full partner so he could claim to be one. We drew up the legal papers and became B&G Inc. I was now part owner of a very successful rep firm. I thought it would be mine forever. I had fallen in love with John and I owned my own business, and I was earning a more than respectable income. Life was downright excellent.

*

A friend of John's from high school unexpectedly invited us to dinner. While dining he presented an interesting dilemma. Wayne had recently discovered that he'd fathered a child in high school with an old girlfriend. The news had rocked him. His present wife and he were not able to produce children and she was greatly disturbed by the news. She was uncertain about Wayne making contact with this woman or his child. He seemed confused by her reaction. He asked my advice, from a feminine viewpoint.

"Wayne," I said with hesitation, "I don't know you very well and I've never met your wife. I can only tell you how I might feel, were I in her position."

The Mexican Mariachi band seemed incongruous with the solemnity of the moment. Not knowing what to do with my nervous hands, I lit a cigarette. I surely didn't want to insult one of John's dearest friends, a Sagittarian predicament I've faced often; Sagittarians are famous for their always truthful but often blunt appraisals.

"This is the one thing your wife has not been able to give you. The thing you and she want most in the world . . .a child. She might feel that she has failed both you and the marriage. Now, you trot out a child, obviously delighted with the discovery and assume she will be as overjoyed as you. All of a sudden *you* have a family...not her. Your wife didn't know you in high school. It's a part of your life she never shared, and now that part of your life has come into focus. Conversations suddenly revolve around people she doesn't know, never met, and likely never will meet. I might find that a little intimidating. My guess is that she's wondering where she belongs in this scene and she's uncertain how to play it. Does she allow you room to become acquainted with your new daughter, or should she insist on being a part of it from the beginning, so that this daughter understands the two of you are a team . . . a package deal? Have you even decided that for yourself? What are your expectations of your wife? Does she know them?"

Wayne looked puzzled. "You know, Roberta, I have to admit I've been confused about this. I've been thinking more about my daughter's expectations, not my wife's. I just assumed she'd accept this. I'm not asking that this kid move in with us, for God's sake. I think I should let my daughter decide what she wants first."

"Well Wayne, you are the adult here. Kids still like direction and your daughter is most likely waiting for you to provide that direction.

She may accept your wife if she understands there isn't an alternative. You shouldn't behave as if there is. Your wife may be feeling threatened, too. You have never mentioned this woman, this old girlfriend, to her. She may think that there could be a chance you might reunite and raise this child together. Stranger things have happened, yes?"

Though I kept my eyes on Wayne, I could tell that John was watching me intently.

My eyes crinkled in a smile as I said, "Wow, Wayne, instant parenthood with a thirteen-year-old kid! If I were your wife, I would want to be included, that's all I'm saying. I think you should tell her straight up how much you love her and need her help in making this child a part of your family."

Wayne left the restaurant with a lighter heart and a new game plan. Over a "one for the road" cocktail, John said, "Roberta, I really like what you said here. It's compassionate, truthful, and it just plain makes sense. I'm glad I brought you. I wouldn't have known what to say to him. I admire the way you think. What a mind."

Who wouldn't be flattered?

*

John made me laugh. He could be so funny, and funny trumps good looks and even good sex, every day. His Rodney Dangerfield impersonation would double me over with laughter, regardless of how many times I heard it.

Although he traveled extensively, when in Milwaukee I knew his spare time was reserved for me. Although never discussing commitment, my sense was that we were headed in that direction. Because of that, I asked him to accompany me to Ohio to meet my friends and adopted family, Grant and Marie Wren and their three children.

I met Marie and Grant when I was eighteen years old and before any of us were married. My first husband was a drummer in a jazz trio with Marie's cousin. The Wrens had been a major part of my life for many years. Their unwavering support for all that is me, right or wrong, has often been akin to the life ring thrown from a boat when you are overboard. My very survival would have been questionable without it. They insisted that every man who dumped me was an asshole and would lead a miserable, barren life for lack of my presence. Even the children learned how to sneer and snicker at the mention of a lost lover. I love all of them. They know me as well as I know me. I call Grant and Marie, along with their children, my chosen family. Their adoption of me, while not legal, seemed a moral compulsion they thankfully embraced.

Grant and Marie had just had their third child, and I was honored to be Renee's godmother. Well, to be honest I had to ask- again. They turned me down in favor of blood family for both Blake and Mitch, their two older boys.

"Damn it, I don't even live there anymore," I told them. "It's not like I can teach her to smoke, cuss, and burn her bra...I'm too far away to be a bad influence. I swear I'll come back every weekend if you don't make me her god-mommy and then I *will* mentor her...I swear it!" They finally acquiesced.

Things were progressing well enough with John that I thought it was time he meet the Wrens, so I asked him to escort me to Renee's christening. John made a point of being his most charismatic self and was overly generous in both compliments and gestures. Our first evening was spent dining at an upscale suburban eating establishment, famous for its steaks. He insisted on paying the bill and was gracious when accepting the Wrens' gratitude. It wasn't often I saw John wear humble, but this night it was a three-piece suit and I found it sexy.

After the christening Mass, I helped Marie prepare food for the party, and John helped Grant ready the outside area to accommodate the many invited guests. Grant's father was quietly sitting on the deck when John approached him and asked, "Did it hurt?"

"Did what hurt?" Grant's father said.

"When you stapled on your toupee."

It was rude but hysterical. Grant had to step inside the house to hide his laughter. This was the contradiction named John. I felt part of my job was to help him realize that being amusing didn't have to include being uncouth.

At the time, I assumed his behavior was unintentional. It wasn't until much later that I realized his comments were most always deliberate and timed. But that weekend, he had been generous and made everybody laugh. He had passed this most important test. My friends told me they liked him, and it held great importance for me.

*

Despite John's occasional gaffes, I gradually became more impressed, particularly with his efforts to win my affection. When John was in town he assumed he would see me nightly. Having lived alone for many years, solitude had become, and still is, a necessary element to my sanity. I like my own company. John called every evening and if I neglected to invite him over, he pouted and behaved as though I had driven a stake through his heart. This should have been annoying but, instead, I was amused and flattered. It was wonderful, of course, to be so needed. When his constant attentions did begin to weigh on me, guilt trumped irritation. John had been a lonely child, and had become very lonely in his first marriage, his wife being "born again" and devoting all her time to the church. I felt moved that he labored so assiduously for my attention and consequently I started to take the relationship more seriously.

We had been dating for three months before attending the National Restaurant Show in Chicago in May. During the first day of the show, I was standing in the Wendall Industries Company booth when Roger, a Wendall Industries salesman who had become my friend, signaled to me and then pointed in two directions, opposite one another. I casually made way to where Roger was standing and he explained gently that he was pointing at two other women that John was dating. One lived in Pittsburgh, the other in Los Angeles. That made three of us all together. Roger said that he liked me too much to see me get hurt. Suddenly, I felt foolish.

What was I doing? Although we were not pledged to one another, no promises written or verbal, he had been duplicitous in hinting that I was The Only One. I never in my life played second to any other woman and that day I determined that given my maturity, this was not the time to begin. I gave serious thought to how I might handle the matter. That evening, John took me to the Chicago Yacht Club for dinner, a date set long before his multiplicity was revealed.

We were seated in a quiet corner at a snug table for two. The candlelight was reflected in his eyes and his calm bearing seemed to embrace the tender music and savor the moonlight as it lightly touched Lake Michigan, beams gliding across, rather than penetrating its dark waters. With purpose, I ignored the romantic ambience. I was pragmatic in my approach and came right to the point.

"John, you've been separated from your wife for over a year and I know the divorce papers were filed a long time ago, but in reality, you aren't divorced yet. There were three of us in the booth today, John, at the same time!"

John took a very deep drag from his cigarette and looked to the ceiling as he exhaled. He avoided my eyes, thinking them angry, I suppose. "Three of you Roberta? What are you talking about?"

"John," I said, "there were three women in that booth today whom you happen to be dating and screwing all at the same time. I'm not asking you to be embarrassed about it or apologize for it. I'm not angry, John. No, John...quite the contrary, in fact. Good for you!"

He finally looked at me, my laugh drawing his eyes away from what seemed to be a fascinating ceiling.

"I'm simply letting you know that while I fully understand your need to play the field, I'm uncomfortable being one of 'John's girls.' It's not my style. It's time for me to bow out and make your life a little less complicated."

With an utterly serious face, remarkable in its passivity, I continued, "John, you're a good guy. I enjoyed the time we've spent together...my heavens you've been quite the tour guide. You've been marvelous to me, and I appreciate that. But John, I find myself unwilling to compete for your affection. Let's not make this a big deal. It's just time to move on, that's all. Friends, okay?"

I fully expected him to agree. My mind's eye saw us enjoying a nice dinner, unmarred by drama or tears, the end of our relationship anticlimactic.

Suddenly, his eyes widened even as his fingers ground his cigarette out hurriedly, almost missing the ashtray. "But I think I love you Roberta...you can't leave me!" he said. "And just so you know Roberta, you have no competition...you *are* the competition."

The desperation in his voice astounded me and attracted me simultaneously. I fell in love, just like that.

At thirty-two years of age, I was ripe to feel needed in a very feminine way. Maybe not dating for such long periods made me envision my grandmother's warning, suddenly seeing myself as an old maid with cats. When was the last time someone seemed desperate over possibly losing me? Eighth grade? I couldn't clearly remember. Needing me to "be his woman" made me feel like just that…a woman. John did not see me as one of the guys. It was new, it was fun, and it was thrilling.

We agreed from that point forward to have a monogamous relationship. There was no mention of marriage, for which I was thankful. Since my divorce ten years before, I harbored no plans of remarrying. My career was my mate and that was demanding enough. Feeling needed aside, I knew I wouldn't relinquish my independent spirit so easily.

CHAPTER 6

John moved in to my place gradually. It was a night, then a weekend, then he needed a sock drawer, then an underwear drawer, and before long, I was doing his laundry. Accustomed to being alone, this proved a bit of a challenge for me.

I allowed John to live at my place with the understanding that it wouldn't be for an extended period. Although he was rehabbing a coach house he purchased near Lake Michigan, it wasn't finished. He traveled extensively, but when he was home we liked spending the majority of our time together. We were checking the progress of the work one Saturday morning and as I passed a large closet in the hallway, John reached for my arm and playfully pulled me backward. He opened the closet door and with a grin and asked, "Do you think you can get all your shoes in here Roberta, or should I have them add another closet?" I kept walking and said nothing. When I ignored the hint, he was bold in suggesting that we live together at the coach house after it was complete. I flatly refused.

Living with my first husband for five years before we married taught me the fallacy of the "Try before you buy" philosophy. *I can leave whenever I want because I'm not married* becomes of mode of thinking that never seems to diminish with the consummation of the vows. For five years before marrying him, I believed I could move on if things didn't work out with my first husband Terry. The marriage certificate didn't dispel that notion and at the first sign of real trouble in our marriage, I took off like a cat burglar caught in the act. I saw it as more break-up than divorce. After our divorce was final, I knew I had made a tragic error and attempted to reconcile. Terry was kind but firm in explaining that my capricious behavior had eternally ruptured his ability to trust me. It was one of the most painful lessons of my life. I was vehement in explaining to John that I would never live with a man again, not before I was engaged. I was determined not to repeat the same mistake.

*

A few months into the courtship, John was preparing a very elaborate dinner at my apartment. The table was set, the candles lit, and soft music invoked a romantic mood as John prepared Caesar salad and prepped the lobster. John's traveling had temporarily subsided and his every night presence was wearing on me. Elaborate dinners aside, I was so accustomed to keeping my own company, there were some nights I just wanted to be *alone.*

"Is the coach house finished yet, John?" I asked.

Without turning from his task he responded, "Maybe in a week or two."

Damn him, I thought. By now I'd realized he was putting this off on purpose. I'd be damned if I was going to do his laundry before he married me.

"What's the hold up, John?" I asked. "Haven't they installed the doorknobs yet?"

He paused half a second in whipping the salad dressing, but still didn't turn around. "Well yeah, they got the doorknobs on," he said, "but the wallpaper in the den isn't quite done."

As if having no wallpaper in the den had any bearing on his ability to sleep there. It was but another shabby excuse. Elaborate dinner or not, I found his nonchalance intolerable. I had had it.

"Dammit John, you have to get out of here! I told you I wouldn't live with another man before I marry him. You need to leave. *I* need you to leave."

My voice broke with frustration manifesting itself in tears. "Go live in your own place, John, I mean it."

He turned to me with a smirk on his face, untied his apron, and said, "Okay, Roberta, no problem."

He left the salad half tossed and the lobsters still twitching on the counter. The candles extinguished with the closing of the door behind him. I was relieved. Hungry, but relieved. I wanted my own space back, but more so I wanted him to move out so he would miss me. Miss me enough to make a commitment. A scant hour later he called from the coach house, his voice anxious.

"Roberta, I didn't mean to walk out. I should have told you right then how I feel. It's just… I don't sleep well without you anymore. It's bad enough when I'm out of town, but when I'm home I want to be with you. I want to hold you when we fall asleep. *You* are home, Roberta, being with you anywhere makes me feel like I'm finally home. Please, come to the coach house tonight, please. I miss you. I know I'm getting on your nerves at your place and maybe the change of scene will be good for us. I'll fill the hot tub and we can relax with some champagne. I need to be with you, Roberta, please."

I drove to him and spent the night. I couldn't resist this man who seemingly couldn't live without me.

Soon enough, in spite of my determination not to live with a man before he married me, the only nights John and I spent apart were when he was traveling. I even took my two kids, the cats Mort and Oscar, when I spent the night at the coach house. John began insisting I leave them there because I would only be gone a night and I "shouldn't be putting so many miles on the cats." It ensured my return. This should have been a big red flag, his neediness that so resembled my mother's. But I found myself falling more deeply in love, not understanding that his need may have been the biggest draw. I thought it romantic and endearing.

*

I gradually met John's family and friends and became more ensconced with the Wendall Industries people. It was a small group then, with only twenty-five employees in the Milwaukee offices. We were a social group and spent a great deal of time together outside the workplace. John was happy and despite being occasionally irritated with his neediness, I was happy.

It was a Thursday evening in late April and I was busy preparing my company booth for the Wisconsin State Restaurant Show to be held at the Milwaukee Convention Center. Paul, the executive vice president of Wendall Industries, was overseeing the completion of the Wendall Industries booth located in the next aisle. He waved as he approached my booth.

"Roberta, can I see you for a minute?" He was signaling for me to join him behind the curtain where we wouldn't be seen.

I slipped behind the curtain and he pulled it closed behind us. "What's up?"

"Can I just take a minute to thank you from all of us for making John human?" He was holding both my hands in earnest and smiling.

"Before he started seeing you, we went to any length to keep him out of these show booths. Now suddenly he's become a gentleman, he's stopped being sarcastic with our customers, telling inappropriate jokes, and he conducts himself professionally! At the risk of being crude, I might add that since he started sleeping with you he actually shows up at the office on time! We owe you, Roberta."

I was taken somewhat taken aback. Paul barely knew me. I thought his loyalty should lie with the man who signed his checks, yet I was flattered by the compliments.

"Well I'm not doing anything intentionally, Paul. That's the side of John I see, truly. Maybe because he knows I appreciate his better qualities, he chooses to show them more."

"Well whatever it is, keep it coming. We ought to put you on the payroll."

People commenting that John was a different person since we met and that I was the one responsible for it empowered me. Apparently the beast was less beastly because of me.

*

I was late for dinner. I was driving to Milwaukee from a trade show in Chicago to meet John and two other Wendall Industries couples for dinner at one of Milwaukee's finest restaurants. A scowl was written across my face and my aggravation was in full view as I entered the bar area. Traffic had been heavy and the additional drive time had enabled me to reflect about John's continued lack of commitment. I was thirty-two years old for God's sake, and I wanted kids. How much time was I going to waste on this guy? How many more years would I be cute? There was no way in hell I was going to ask him to marry me. What was the big hold-up?

A few days earlier we'd had a discussion about the impending lease renewal for my apartment. John's insistence that I move in with him had led to a minor skirmish. Ironically, I was cleaning the coach house at the time.

"John, why do you keep asking me when you know the answer?" I said. "The day you ask me to marry you is the day I'll move in with you. I don't care if it's a three-year courtship, but I want a ring."

He ran his hands through his hair in an exasperated way. "Roberta, for God's sake, you know how much I love you. I think we probably *will* get married, but I've only been divorced a few months. The state of Wisconsin *requires* that I'm divorced six months before remarrying."

The windows were open, and a fresh breeze cleansed the air as I looked at my surroundings. The rich wood floors of the kitchen showed evidence of my recent waxing, and the balloon shades in the adjoining dining room were of a fabric I had chosen. The closet was already home to some of my belongings. I loved it here. It was so tempting to yield my position, but experience had taught me that if I gave it up now, I would relinquish my position on every major issue forever.

"John, don't start," I said. "You know how I feel. Don't ask again, unless you have a ring. That's it."

*

Dimmed lighting and the tinkling of live harp music made the elegant restaurant somehow sentimental. Two other Wendall Industries couples and John and I were seated in a banquette, rich tapestry upholstery offsetting the stark white cloth on a table crowded with crystal and simple gold banded china. I was struck by the richly romantic atmosphere, subdued and understated, yet elegant.

As we were seated, John asked the sommelier to serve a bottle of Perrier Le Fleur champagne, superior by anyone's standards. The sommelier served it with a flourish, and he backed away from the table with a wink to John. With raised glass tipped in my direction, John began a toast. "To Roberta, the most beautiful woman in the world... my heart, my love." Slightly embarrassed, I smiled behind my glass and took a long drink.

John lowered his glass and took my hand. He appeared slightly amused, but his eyes were full of love. "Roberta," he said, "I love you." There were "ahhh's" from the two couples at our table, as well as a few surrounding tables. "I would be honored to have you as my wife. Will you marry me, Roberta?"

I gasped in total surprise. Bombarded by stares, and with tears of elation streaming down my face, I said yes.

It seemed the entire restaurant broke into applause. The sommelier returned with a fresh bottle of champagne and began pouring once again.

It's odd, but I don't remember the couples who shared my engagement dinner. My attention was focused solely on John and the ring he chose. It was his mother's. It was a five-carat square-cut emerald, surrounded by three carats of baguette diamonds. I was stunned, in a very beautiful way. More important than the magnificence of the ring was the significance of the gesture. He had never offered this ring to his first wife. It was a special ring for a special love, reserved especially for me.

We agreed to a long engagement – neither one of us was in a hurry. I loved playing house with John because it wasn't twenty-four/seven. Our combined travel schedules and individual businesses kept us apart often enough to satisfy my need for solitude. I didn't cook often because of my demanding career schedule. On weekends, however, I would prepare meals and we loved having couples over for dinner. We'd roll up the rugs and dance for hours, laughing at the Disco Ducks we were not. Trivial Pursuit became a passion and Mystery Parties were my favorite, where we all stayed in character and costume and solved a murder. Some evenings alone, we cuddled on the couch, watching television and alternately rubbing each other's backs. If I had been on my feet for nine hours straight in my very high heels, John would rub my feet for hours without complaint. The next morning they were never swollen or painful, and I called him my healer. The sex still wasn't great, but it had gotten better, and mutual satisfaction was at least sometimes achieved. In time, I was confident it could only improve. John still sent flowers every week, and I would send him a romantic Hallmark card every Monday, saying how much I loved him. I always found a way to hide a few cards in his suitcase before he left for a trip. He delighted in finding them. He called me at least four times a day to say hello, tell me he missed me, or ask me my opinion on any business matter. On the rare occasion that we weren't separated by our respective career travels, we were together everywhere. If he was working on a motorcycle in the garage, I sat in the garage on a lawn chair reading my book. He said he felt better when I was in the room with him. He just wanted me near. If we were attending a black tie event, he took me shopping and chose my dress. I had no objection. He had remarkable taste and the dresses cost thousands of dollars. I never was asked to wear something I didn't love.

*

It was a typical below zero day in Milwaukee and just after five-thirty in the evening when John was suddenly standing in my office doorway.

"Hi sweetie." I rose to kiss him. "What are you doing here?"

"I came to walk you to your car." He was smiling his *I've got a secret* smile.

"My car is right out front, John."

"You know it's ten below zero, Roberta, and I thought you might be more comfortable walking to your car in this." He stepped just outside the door and returned with a full-length mahogany mink coat. "May I?" He held the coat for me to slip into.

My hands flew to my mouth and tears sprang to my eyes. "Oh my God, John, it's absolutely gorgeous! Is it mine, really?"

He pointed to the inside lining. "See, it already has your initials embroidered."

"Oh John!" My arms flew around his neck, my lips reaching for his. "Thank you *so* much! I don't know what to say." I was spinning and spinning, the warmth of the fur circling my legs.

"How am I gonna get my lady to stay in Wisconsin without a mink coat?"

John laughed, but his eyes were deadly serious when he pulled me tighter and whispered, "I don't ever want you to leave me, Roberta, not ever. Promise you'll never leave me."

"Oh John, honey, I won't," I said. "Don't be afraid...I'm not going anywhere."

*

We had lived together for three months and had not even discussed a wedding date. I took John to the airport one Saturday and when he opened the car door, he turned to me and said, "Roberta, I want to get married in September. Get started planning."

With that bomb, he closed the door and walked into the airport. My mouth was still open; September was only three months away.

Just a month later, John was diagnosed with melanoma. He abhorred the thought of pieces of him being cut away slowly and wanted to forget the surgery, but I was able to reassure him, and I never left his side. I walked him into surgery and when he opened his eyes, mine were the first eyes he saw. I was at the hospital all day, every day, playing cards with him, or Scrabble, watching TV or just watching him sleep. I crawled in bed with him if he wanted to be held. He needed me and I was there. I loved him.

Just after John was released from the hospital and a short time before our wedding, I was presented with a prenuptial agreement. I believed John as he kept insisting that it wasn't his idea.

"My lawyers insist that we sign this before we marry," he said. "They've given me no say in the matter. It isn't a big deal. You are very well protected in this document. My attorney Michael has become so fond of you, I think he intentionally slanted it your direction!" He continued laughing as he said, "I think you'd be better off divorcing me the day after we get married."

"You are so sweet John," I said. "Don't worry about it. I understand and it's really nothing, right? Something you put in a drawer and never look at again? I'm not marrying you for your money, John. I don't need you to support me financially and I never will."

"That's right, Roberta," he cooed as he took me in his arms and kissed me long and lovingly. "It's because of the lawyers, nothing more. If it was up to me, I'd rip the damn thing into a million pieces. I could care less...I know how much you love me and I know you aren't marrying me for my money. I love you, Roberta. Thank you for understanding."

I had no objections, really. I had never known anyone who had signed such an agreement so I was unable to consult with friends about the matter, but I did seek legal counsel—recommended by John's legal counsel—before signing the document. I didn't know anyone in town not associated with John.

In reality, I paid little heed when I should have. This document was the ultimate reason I later received such a paltry severance package. At the time, I made more money than John and it never occurred to me that I would leave my career. It didn't occur to anyone who knew me either. My career was who I was. It defined me. I also had enormous appreciation for John's career and assumed that appreciation was reciprocal.

Little did I know that it wouldn't be long before I found myself on a street marked "ONE WAY."

*

A mere eighteen months from the day we met, John and I married. The wedding was simple, with one hundred and fifty friends, family and industry people sharing our happiness. Our eyes met with shared mirth when we said, "in sickness and in health." We already knew that part

It was a morning wedding, followed by a brunch at a beautiful restaurant on a striking fall day in 1985. After, the party adjourned to the coach house where it continued past midnight, with music, dancing, and lots of laughter. The following day we left on a cruise of the Baja Peninsula. We were very much in love.

CHAPTER 7

In the early eighties, women in their thirties railed against needing a man for almost anything. I recall seeing a t-shirt emblazoned with the motto, "Women need men like fish need bicycles." I publicly supported the position while still declining to join the movement.

Public discourses aside, hormones rear up like wild Mustangs and before you're aware that estrogen has flushed the testosterone away, a private longing begins. It's the centuries old longing to be a wife and a mother. It's the desire to feel a head resting on your bosom, man or child, whose only comfort can be found in your petting. It becomes a double whammy when fear of never being wanted again, losing your looks, and being an old maid with cats unites with the longing like conjoined twins. The impact was powerful.

*

John's parents founded Wendall Industries the year he was born. His father invented a product pertaining to the sanitization of dishes in a commercial application that brought them fame and success. His mother marketed and sold the product in an era when most women didn't work at all and surely never fast-tracked a career path. She was the only woman in the foodservice industry at the time and spent her children's formative years working trade shows and lobbying the state's boards of health to enact laws that would ensure that their product was mandated for use.

I'm not sure John ever knew, but stories had circulated for years about how Lily, his mother, had slept with whomever she needed to in order to achieve her goals. She had no role models, no peer group, and no one to tell her what not to do. She was flamboyant and wore it well. That particular trait mutated when passed to her youngest son and flamboyancy hung on him like a forgotten parachute flung haplessly over a tree. He just never got it quite right.

John and his older brother James were mostly raised by housekeepers. On a whim, Lily would take them out of school in the middle of winter, drive with them to Florida and enroll them in a school where they knew no one. Then she would leave to travel the southern states, housekeeper ensconced in Florida. To me, it seemed unbearably sad.

Although my childhood was far from perfect, I couldn't imagine never going to the drive-in with my parents, or to the museum or planetarium or botanical gardens.

Lily committed suicide when John was a sophomore in college, and his brother James had long before left home for California. The morning of her death, John received a call from his father Gabe while in class. He simply said, "John, come home, your mother is dead." James' return for the funeral ended a three-year absence from seeing or speaking to his father. "Dysfunctional" in this family was bold, underlined, and italicized.

The insurance company ruled it accidental death, and Gabe was awarded a large life insurance settlement. He used the money to build a factory in Door County, Wisconsin, to honor Lily because she so loved the area. When I met John, his father had passed two months earlier, so I never had the opportunity to properly thank Gabe for his failed and never-patented invention, John.

Our backgrounds were not so similar. After losing my father at age seventeen, my brother, sister, and I struck out into the world without the aid or sympathy of our remaining parent. But, no matter how out of sync my family was or became, it did not compare to the total lack of normalcy that was the framework of John's life. I enjoyed and endured much in my coming of age years and managed to exit the tunnel smart, successful, happy, and always laughing. My successes were mine and were hard-won. I was proud of my accomplishments and liked who I had become; I was unique, by design. At thirty-five, John was still stumbling with his identity. His father told him he was an asshole and a fuck-up so frequently, he was confused about its accuracy. I felt horribly for him.

His past was privileged but riddled with parental neglect and his need to be loved was overwhelming and all encompassing. Fixing his insecurities appealed to the woman in me. It appealed to the mother I had never become. Much of my strength was born from bad parenting but John's reaction was opposite. The consequence of his parental neglect resulted in sometimes bizarre behavior, his insecurities as visible as a full moon on a clear night. My emotional response was that I could right the wrongs of his parents by parenting John myself.

CHAPTER 8

After we were married, our primary focus was having children. I was thirty-three and John, thirty-five. During John's recent thirteen-year marriage, he had not been able to sire children and testing determined that his sperm were not mobile. Ironically, the problem was his but the treatment—G.I.F.T., or gamete intra-fallopian tube transfer—belonged to me. His contribution was to masturbate into a jar and complain mightily about it.

G.I.F.T. was arduous, painful, and invasive. Fertility drugs are administered daily via injection to promote the production of eggs and ultrasounds are conducted daily to assure the manufacture. Blood is drawn daily to monitor hormones.

At the time of surgery, performed by the use of laparoscope, eggs are retrieved and evaluated. A sperm sample is collected prior to the procedure, prepared, and brought to the operating room. The best eggs (usually two or three) and sperm are mixed together and transferred into the fallopian tube(s) with a small catheter. It requires general anesthesia.

The fertilized egg (embryo) travels down the fallopian tube for four or five days and then enters the uterine cavity for implantation. In theory this journey down the fallopian tube helps with development of the embryo and improves the chances of implantation. A pregnancy test is given two weeks post laparoscopy.

It was demanding. I couldn't leave home, couldn't travel my territory and I was constantly asking my partner or factory personnel to cover my ass. I produced so many eggs that I looked pregnant and it actually hurt to walk. I felt miserable most of the time and it was the only time in my life I have ever been overweight. When we weren't in the process leading up to and including the surgery, I was traveling and playing catch-up.

John and I once had a three-week period where the only place we saw each other was in the airport. He traveled, I traveled, and the fact that he owned a foodservice manufacturing company and I represented not only his factory but eleven others made life one colossal conflict. At national trade shows, I had sales meetings to attend, other factory booths to work, and he wanted me with him to entertain his customers. His booth was the only one he felt I should work.

*

It was a particularly busy National Restaurant Association show the year of 1985. The aisle traffic was almost impossible to navigate and the combination of laughter, sales spiels, and restaurant equipment demonstrations produced a cacophonous din. John's voice rose above the fray as I started to exit his company booth.

"Roberta, I need you to spend a little more time here," he said. "The man who wants to represent Wendall Industries in the Pacific Rim is coming in a half-hour and I want you to meet him before I decide if he should have the territory."

My eyes widened. "John, I have eleven other manufacturers who are expecting me to spend time selling *their* products in *their* booths. Can

I meet this guy another time? What about later this evening after my Baulsen sales meeting?"

John took my arm and turned me slightly, so we would not be facing the hordes of customers making their way through his exhibit. "What Baulsen sales meeting?" His face was a mixture of anxiousness and annoyance. "We have a dinner meeting tonight with my export agents from New York. You said you could make it."

"I did?"

Was I losing my mind? Did I obligate time to John that was already allotted to one of my own events?

"John, I can't skip this sales meeting for Baulsen. I'm receiving an award for the most improved territory." My voice wasn't as strong as I would have liked. A painfully organized person, I was confused by the thought of my double booking. I had successfully avoided such calamities my entire career. In addition, I felt it my burden to meet both obligations and satisfy everybody involved.

"John," I said with a slight tremor in my voice, "let me get to my next booth. I have an appointment there with a customer. I'll come back before the show closes and we'll figure it out, okay?"

"But what about the man who wants the Pacific Rim territory?" he countered, still holding my arm firmly.

My brow furrowed in thought. "Ask him if he can meet us in the lobby bar of the hotel around ten o'clock tonight. How would that be?"

"Ten o'clock, Roberta?! Isn't that a little late?"

My voice took an edge as I said, "Too late for what, John? How badly does he want the territory? Nobody wishes there were more hours in a day than me, but I can't pull any more hours out of my ass than you can! Let me go, John, I'll be back later."

I strode from the booth, harried and annoyed, feeling his eyes boring a hole in my back. I couldn't help thinking if my skirt wasn't so straight, and my heels weren't so high, my stride could lengthen and I could get away faster. I didn't dare turn around for fear of engaging in more conversation that could make me even later for my next appointment.

*

In the end, I was present to receive my award but skipped the subsequent Baulsen dinner to dine with John and his New York export agents. The gentleman vying for the Pacific Rim territory appeared pleased for the meeting, regardless of the late hour and when John was certain of my approval, became our new representative.

He didn't mention my sales award, nor express any desire to see me receive it. He forgot to congratulate me, consumed by his many corporate concerns.

*

I was overwhelmed with responsibility, not to mention a surfeit of hormones causing emotional reactions that were wholly unfamiliar to me. After every G.I.F.T. procedure, negative results made me feel as though I had miscarried. I never felt so emotionally unstable. John was sympathetic some of the time, but mostly, it wasn't about him, so it didn't deserve his consideration. He let me know he had grown weary of the process and of me not being myself.

During all of this, we purchased a massive house on Lake Michigan in late 1985, demolished the greater part of the interior, and were rehabbing it.

This house was a grand, five thousand square-foot three-story English Tudor with an authentic red English tile roof. It sat high on a bluff overlooking Lake Michigan in a staid and upscale suburb north of Milwaukee.

Decorating was my domain and I was scrupulous in keeping with the style of the house. I made it thoroughly English, with plenty of chintz, Queen Anne pieces mixed with Chippendale, and a spattering of antiques and Chinese accents. Every upper class English home housed Chinese pieces as proof they were wealthy enough to travel and purchase items abroad.

The jewel tones of the furniture were balanced by muted stripes of neutral wallpaper and silk drapery adorned with heavy fringe. Just off the oversized mahogany-paneled foyer was a mahogany-paneled library with a limestone fireplace. The burgundy leather couch became my coziest winter spot to read and the antique game table was ideal for playing cards.

The many cocktail parties we hosted gave our living room life. It was exceptionally large and a roaring fire in the traditional fireplace nicely offset the beautiful music played by various hired pianists on an antique Steinway grand piano that John's mother gave him as a child. We kept the instrument in good tune. Our guests could drift into the sunroom, which was adjacent to the living room and separated by original leaded glass panel doors, to a traditional hand-painted antique Chinese desk. I labored to achieve elegant yet understated surroundings.

The kitchen and lake room area was where we lived daily and I made sure it was casual but still English with oversized and sturdy dark brown wicker furniture with striped ticking upholstery.

Upstairs, we converted the master bedroom into a master bedroom suite by converting a smaller bedroom into my office and enlarging the bath. John would complain about hauling wood upstairs to burn in the conventional fireplace at the foot of our four-poster mahogany bed, but once the fire was lit, the work was forgotten, overtaken by the ambiance that a fire can convey. A little champagne heightened the romance of special moments in front of that roaring fire.

The third floor was a ballroom complete with hardwood floors and also housed a large cedar closet. Every room upstairs and down had spectacular views of Lake Michigan. Some days foreboding, some days sparkling, the lake assumed a mood that made me curious to study it, every day. From our rear deck that ran the length of the house, you felt as though you could swan dive right into the water.

I loved that house when it was completed. It was formal, but warm and welcoming. I was proud of the result of my efforts. At the time, however, it was a considerable endeavor, in addition to working and trying to achieve pregnancy.

Life was frantic, every minute, every day. After the third G.I.F.T. procedure, we started discussing me selling my half of the rep firm. I was all for it. Burnt to a crisp, I was exhausted from working, and I wanted to raise my own children. No nanny or housekeeper for us, I wanted to be "super mom."

*

My head was cradled in my left hand, as my right hand twirled spaghetti around and around on my fork. It was barely dark as we finished our supper in the kitchen. The back door was open, allowing the very first breezes of spring entrée into our home slightly stale from heated winter air.

"Roberta!" John's voice startled me. "What is it…where are you… you seem a million miles from here."

"Oh, I'm just struggling with the idea of selling my half of the rep firm." I answered.

"I thought this was settled. I don't understand what the struggle is. We want kids…you want kids. You refuse to have a nanny. We can't do that with you working."

"But, my independence," I started "I've been working since I was fourteen. I've always had my own money." The sentence was incomplete, just like my thoughts.

"So, you don't trust me, Roberta." It was a statement, not a question

"It's not that John, it's just hard to depend on somebody other than myself."

"So, you don't trust me Roberta." The statement now seemed more an accusation. "Like, I'm not going to take care of you?"

My eyes were brimming with tears of apprehension as I asked, "Will you, John? Can I trust you to take care of me?"

Rising from his chair, he strode around the table and pulled my held gently into his stomach. Stroking my hair he said, "Oh baby. You know I'll always take care of you. I promise. I love taking care of you. Money won't be an issue. I'll just deposit what you need in your account every month so you won't have to ask me. Trust me Roberta. Let's make a baby Roberta."

I was struggling with what was the biggest decision of my life so far. Internal battles are tricky in terms of identifying the enemy. In any battle, there has to be a winner and a loser. When you're fighting with yourself, do you lose when you win? And how do you measure that loss! I'd been walking down a path alone for so many years. Maybe I didn't want to walk alone anymore. It was time to let someone join me. I married this man. It was time for me to trust him.

I sold the firm.

CHAPTER 9

We exited the attorney's office, entered the elevator and I dissolved into tears. For the thirty-five floor descent, I cried while my husband looked mildly amused. Through my tears, I saw a look of triumph in his eyes. We had just completed the sale of my company and I was now officially his wife, and only his wife.

On that day, a corporate slut was born. Although the decision appeared to be a joint one, I was suddenly overwhelmed with the realization I had been conned. My God, this was a sham! *He* wanted this. Had I just sold myself into slavery? I never thought it possible, but I had just traded my career for love. After months of back and forth rhetoric, the agonizing decision had been made and I gave myself no choice but to move ahead.

However, I was scared and I don't scare very easily. Never, since I left home at the age of seventeen, had I depended on anyone else to care for me. I had full trust in myself and knew that only I could do the best job of caring for me, only me. Now I had put my welfare into the hands of another. But as with any job move, I told myself that if it didn't work out, I could move on to the next job. My professional reputation had grown so that I knew there was always another job waiting, should I desire it. Hell, I got calls every week. This was just another job move, and again, the employer had found me. I was never looking, but I always was found. With those thoughts, I managed to swallow my fear.

Sadly, I never was able to achieve pregnancy, but I never returned to my old career either. I had a new career.

My job description for the next sixteen years was to aid and better John's vocation, and to play a major role in the growth of his company. I mastered it. A great many of these tasks were accomplished from behind the curtains and there were a few in which I was able to take a bow. To the goal-oriented woman I had become, it didn't matter that he would garner most of the credit.

Being a woman selling foodservice equipment, I had been distinctive in my field. As a result, I had received positive attention, many awards, as well as accolades to confirm my success. I took that for granted.

With this new career, I thought I didn't need recognition or praise. I thought knowing my own achievements would suffice, because it was the end result that was vital. It wasn't until later I realized that praise is mostly what drove me to success all those years before becoming a corporate slut. Living without it eventually eroded my confidence and made me vulnerable to his abuse.

Always an overachiever, my new corporate slut job became yet another challenge, another accomplishment to be made, and I needed to be the very best corporate wife/slut ever. I needed this for me. I approached it with the dynamism that had become my trademark. The jobs leading to this point had been various, related, and mostly male dominated. I was good, really good. In any transaction, I almost always had the biggest cock at the table. I didn't lose many deals and had earned the respect of my peers and my competitors alike. Many fine things were said about me, along with murmurs of, "Don't fuck with

Roberta" and "Roberta doesn't take shit from anybody." I could bring these talents to my new role. Of course I could.

My work was cut out for me. I'd never been much of a cook because I was single and uninterested. Now I bought dozens of cookbooks and became an accomplished cook. I didn't stop there. I bought books on napkin folding and flower arranging and got busy learning the finer points of my new career. I asked John to stop sending his weekly flowers and started buying and arranging flowers for the house myself. Folding the napkins took almost as long as setting the table until I got the hang of it. I became a wife extraordinaire, and John was appreciative.

His first requests for business advice came disguised as an innocent statement or a silent question asked by means of an eyebrow raised or a tilt of his head. Never one to hold back my opinion, he was always assured of my response.

I was clearing dishes from the table one evening when John said, "Jesus, the sales department was all over my ass today…they want to realign the sales territories."

When I glanced over, his eyebrow was raised in question as he looked over the top of the motorcycle magazine he was perusing. I was in, like a bug trapped unsuspectingly by a spider web unseen. After hearing his version of both sides, I issued a twenty minute opinion in favor of the sales department. The following day, the territories changed and John was lauded for his flexibility.

A key qualification for a corporate slut is knowledge of her husband's business and his industry, and it helps a great deal if you're a whole lot smarter than he is.

It was in this way that John trained me to be a corporate slut and I in turn taught him how to treat me. People react to the person they see. John saw the tough, hard as nails broad I presented and he expected strong and unemotional responses to every situation life presented.

I'm not sure if it was the act of leaving my career, learning how to cook, or nurturing a child-like adult male, but I was slowly becoming more a woman than a broad. I thought he saw that very thing.

*

When John hosted a luncheon at his company for twelve dieticians whose business he was seeking, I prepared the meal, transported it to the company, and served it to his business guests. I thought myself the perfect corporate slut because I was aiding and abetting. The wife had prepared the meal; the corporate slut would help consummate the sale.

As I began serving the luncheon, without provocation John launched into a litany of stories about my spending habits, about which he always publicly railed. It was largely untrue and I was embarrassed, but rather than deny his baseless accusations and show him to be a fool, a corporate slut no-no, I made a joke.

I turned to his business guests and said, "You know John asked me the other day, 'Roberta, if I didn't have money would you still love me?' And I replied, 'Sure John, I'll always love you.....I'd miss you, but I'll always love you.'" It got a huge laugh and diffused the embarrassment instantly. At least I had shown his guests I could hold my own. Later and privately, one of the dieticians commented, "Thank God you don't take shit from anybody, Roberta. He met his match in you."

*

I always wanted a real family – a family kind of family. Mine was buried with my father. I craved the kind of family in which everyone genuinely liked each other, wanted to be together and planned activities for the sole purpose of sharing with one another. I met them. They were John's extended family – his step-family – the family I always wanted and I made them mine. I fell madly in love with them. All of them.

John's stepmother Emily became one of my closest allies. She had married John's father Gabe a year after Lily's death and they were happily married for thirteen years before Gabe died. She was a proud and gracious woman with an abundance of social grace. Attractive and diminutive, she carried herself with dignity. Her build was small and she was always stylish, relishing current fashion. I could have easily, without embarrassment, worn her clothes. Her blond hair was styled in a manner typical of her age, and her eyes remained a startling blue, even as she grew older. I remember her eyes the most. Alive with intellect, they always carried a laugh even as her mouth was reluctant to follow. The sound emitted was more tinkle than guffaw. She enjoyed her life without apology. Emily was much loved among friends and a matriarch in the true sense of the word. She split her time between northern Wisconsin and Florida. She lived next door to us in Wisconsin and we were with her frequently in Florida, particularly at Christmas. I came to love Emily as the mother I had always wished for.

June was John's niece by marriage, though closer to us in age. She was helping me clear the dinner dishes after enjoying a jovial family meal at Emily's house. "Roberta, what have you done with John? Where is he?" She was giggling in a whisper.

"I have no idea what you mean, June." I purposely kept my eyes averted to avoid laughing.

"Since he's met you, he's a changed man, Roberta. He's so nice and fun and he even played with the kids tonight. He was *never* like this. I love it. So does Emily, by the way. She's so happy to see him become an active member of the family. Family is everything to her."

"I wish I could take the credit June, but John is just being himself, honestly. He loves all of you. It's just tougher for him to show it. I think he was a late bloomer and I gather his father was tough on him. Maybe with his father gone, he'll have more confidence in himself. Wait and see." My sincerity was honestly delivered.

"Whatever…we just want you to know we love you and we hope you're around for a very long time," June said. "I mean forever. No matter what you say, the whole family thinks you've changed him and we appreciate it! As long as he behaves like this, he's welcome anytime."

As was I. John's stepsiblings' children are still an important part of my life. I am godmother to one and have a namesake in another. I adore them all and am thankful that they came into my life. They have elected to stay there, no matter what John wishes.

*

It was the Wendall Industries Christmas party of 1987 and John and I had been married two years. It was a formal affair that year. The party was held in an elegant hotel ballroom. The Wendall Industries wives were happy for an occasion to dress formally, and their husbands, in black tie, were all handsome. I think Attila the Hun would be attractive in a tuxedo.

I arranged for the tree in the ballroom to be decorated with ostrich feathers, white baby's breath, and red and silver ornaments in deference to the company logo colors. Smaller tables of eight were made more intimate by a décor of red linens with crisp white napkins, enhanced by centerpieces of white and red roses set in clear vases filled with raw cranberries. Mood lighting augmented the enchanting effect.

After the last dessert plate of chocolate mousse was cleared, John rose and approached the podium to give his speech.

"Ladies and gentleman, respected members of the board, not so respected members of the board..." He paused to let the laughter subside. "...it's been another great year at Wendall Industries and both Roberta, my lovely bride, and I would like to thank all the people responsible."

I was shocked by what he said next.

"I would like to say a special thanks to my lovely wife, who has taught me the true meaning of family. Not only have I been blessed with an extended family by way of my father's second wife and her children and grandchildren, I have been especially blessed with my Wendall Industries family. I want you to know how very important all of you have become to us, and how much your presence has enriched our lives. You're my family and I thank you for my place in it. Roberta, come up here with me."

Amidst a standing ovation, I made my way through the crowd, people touching my arm or grabbing my hand at every juncture, and joined my husband at the podium.

"Ladies and gentleman, family, may I present the First Lady of Wendall Industries, my wife, Roberta." As the applause grew louder my tears finally spilled over. I had never felt so proud of John, or felt more like I belonged. I finally had a family – a large and caring family and I loved him for giving me that dream.

CHAPTER 10

John was a true Gemini in that there was always two of him – the good John and the very bad John. The good John was charming, bright, and very funny. He could, when he wanted, display exceptional social skills and be a generous host. The John I loved was kind and munificent. He made me laugh every day, told me he loved me every day, told me I was beautiful every day, and brought me gifts large and small. He thanked me every time I cooked a meal, even if it was Sloppy Joes, and he wrapped around me every night in bed, spooning me with a tenderness that insisted I forgive him everything. He loved me so much I felt compelled to love him back. To do otherwise would have been cruel.

But the bad John could be crude, cruel, and malicious. I specifically remember an instance in 1984, the year I met John. We were at a wedding in Miami Beach at a very upscale resort. We weren't even married yet and John had surprised our host, the groom, by bringing me. I was unaware until much later that John thought this was funny. The groom did not, and the bride was decidedly unhappy. It was a weekend of mostly formal affairs where headcount and names were important.

The wedding was on Sunday afternoon, but John had already consumed enough scotch to shed any sense of propriety he may have otherwise felt. We were sitting at a table with a mixture of the groom's older relatives, aunts, and cousins, when a cousin approached. She was an attractive woman from New York, an attorney bound for a judgeship, and politely asked if there was anywhere for her to sit. John promptly stood and announced, "As long as I have a face, you'll have a place to sit." Following the collective gasp, all eyes were on me. Bad, bad John. Hello pooper-scooper.

"Oh my God, what brand of scotch has a voice like that?" I laughed. I looked directly at the cousin. "Let me apologize for John's crude behavior. He's educated enough to have found better words to tell you that he obviously finds you very attractive. It's evident that the scotch has affected his better judgment, and by the way, should I be jealous or what? I think he likes you! At this point I would tell you that you're welcome to take John, but when he sobers up, I think I'll want him back. You may have to fight me for him." Her eyes revealed that, lewd language aside, she was actually flattered.

This John made an occasional appearance, but he showed up less and less, and everyone assured me that I was responsible for the positive changes. John became my mission and I was convinced that this was God's plan for me. My life's work became the tasks of building his self-esteem and convincing him that he was bound for greatness.

Women who believe they can fix men are either arrogant or have an abundant want to nurture. Glancing in the rear view mirror, I now see that I possessed both of those ominous qualities. In the vernacular of the period, I had my shit together. Success in my career had yielded a confidence not only in my abilities, but a belief that I had great acuity regarding life in general. I saw in John a decency that I believed I could help him realize and in doing so, I deemed his happiness would be assured.

His lack of confidence was the root of his bad behavior, but I was certain his character was of good quality. My protectiveness was quite often like that of a mother protecting her young. A disparaging remark from a relative or employee elicited not only a rebuke from me, but an explanation as to how his lack of love growing up warranted extra understanding. In short, I asked people to look deeper and see the man I loved. The man I loved, I assured them, was a superior person. Could I love anything else? This conviction enabled me to sell John to the world just as I had sold many products in the past. The fact that this product walked and talked was insignificant.

In one hand, I held a megaphone and I sang John's praises. "Ladies and Gentleman, allow me to present one smart man who has been victimized by lack of good parenting. His occasionally dubious behavior is but a shield to hide his lack of confidence. I beg you forgive these minor insecurities and look to his clever and inventive mind. A little eccentric, I'll grant you, but isn't that the case with so many of our brilliant minds?"

I called him a visionary and within a few years, most of the industry did too. Had I earned commissions on this particular sale, I would have made millions and ensured my financial security for a lifetime.

In the other hand, I held one giant pooper-scooper to clean up all the shit he left behind. I was mending fences, and soothing hurt feelings, and explaining bizarre and sometimes anomalous behavior.

He once told an upper level employee that because he didn't invite us to his home often enough, he may not be promoted. Over a martini laden lunch, I assured this competent and valued employee that a promotion was still within his grasp and that he had misunderstood the remark. It was my job to convince him that John meant no such thing. I did my job.

I became a one-woman PR firm, with one, sometimes hugely insubordinate, client.

John's behavior when he was younger was often so moronic he had lost a great deal of credibility within the industry. His supercilious airs coupled with his sarcastic commentary served to disparage the people he deemed unworthy of his attention. His humor was quite often just enough off to be offensive, and some of the demands he made were outrageous.

When employees/friends were visiting in Florida, he made them again wash the car he asked them to wash earlier because it wasn't clean enough. It was midnight when he initiated the order and he stood watch over them until they completed the task to his satisfaction.

Initially, I was able to keep the good John in the forefront for very long periods of time, and the bad, mean-spirited John only made intermittent appearances.

It took me many years to grasp John's motive. I did come to understand much later that everything John did was with purpose. Most acts of kindness were designed to reap benefit, whether it was loyalty or favor.

*

Not only did I cook almost every night, but we began entertaining regularly. John loved people around him and to party was our modus operandi. He over drank regularly, but it didn't become uncontrollable until much later. Let me be clear. This was fun for me too. For the most part, our life together at that time was harmonious. My self-deprecating humor complimented his sometimes debasing style. My confidence as his wife was still such that I could field the slurs he cast my way with aplomb.

"Last night Roberta and I met after work for a few drinks" John started explaining to our dinner guests. "You know how that goes. We were just tipsy enough that by the time we got home, we couldn't wait to jump into the sack. I reached for her blouse and said 'Roberta, let me help you with those buttons'. The problem was..."

"I was already naked," I finished the joke. "I inherited my Mom's great laugh, but unfortunately I inherited my Dad's chest. God can be cruel sometimes."

We played off each other beautifully and gained somewhat of a reputation as the couple of the industry, to the extent that our names had become one. We were known as RobertaandJohn. Being the cuter of the two, it was I who got top billing!

We were in collusion when it came to company issues and the majority of our conversations reflected that. He actively sought my opinion and we discussed and strategized. Implementation was his job so the credit was attributed to him and my ego did not suffer from it. Together we found ways to increase opportunity and achieve growth. It just didn't include parallel personal growth.

I felt I had the best of both worlds because I had the advantage of never leaving the industry, which I loved. I saw the same people I had always seen and was in a position to maintain those relationships.

Working one booth instead of twelve at trade shows was heaven. John expected me to be in the booth, and I gladly complied. I brought in contacts from my days with the chains and knew his products because I had sold them. I worked. No complaints - I loved to work. In the evenings, after the show, we hosted the hospitality suite before dining with international customers, or sometimes going out with the sales people. I was an asset, decidedly. Much to my surprise, I found great joy in caring for a man and a home, or in our case, five homes. I loved him. It was satisfying for me to have him enjoy a dinner I cooked, or look at me with great pride when I pulled off another fabulous party. It was new and fun and yes, there were many fulfilling times. I thought John loved me as his wife and was proud of me as a business asset. The wife and business asset walked hand-in-hand at this point in time. I wanted to be invaluable to him as both. We may not have been happy every day, but we were happy most days.

John never hired a sales employee until he or she had been invited to our home for dinner and I was able to give him my assessment. He wanted me everywhere with him, including after-work drinks with the guys. My youth as a tomboy, my career spent mostly with men, and my ribald humor combined to make me one of those girls who was one of the guys. I was often the only wife included in business functions and it was never questioned. He sought my advice, most often took it, and the idea became his. To me, if the result was positive I need not care where the praise was directed. While flattered for a good long while at these attentions and his insistence that I be at his side always, I found that my alone time, always a must for me, was becoming less frequent. Should I insist on reading my book upstairs instead of with him in the garage, he became resentful and hurt, like a child who still wants you to toss the ball when your arm is about to dislocate from your shoulder socket. Enough, already! In the interest of parity, I tried to balance both.

*

About a year after I sold my share of my rep firm, the secretary of the company took maternity leave and I volunteered to work in the office for those six weeks, free of charge. I thought it would be fun to speak with my old customers, do quotes, run the service calls, and generally be my old professional self for a while. I was itching to get a custom fabrication drawing and work up the quote for custom stainless dish tables, or anything that was intellectually challenging. A small part of me understood that I was beginning to feel consumed by John and his demands. Much of what I did demanded my energy, but not always my brainpower. I enjoy intellectual challenges and I thought it would be a nice break.

John didn't like this six-week endeavor, but instead of verbalizing that, his demands just kept piling on. Suddenly he had customers he wanted me to go to lunch with, trips that required my attendance, and questions asking if I had washed that one shirt (out of hundreds, literally) that he absolutely, no question, had to wear that day. He intentionally made my fun experience stressful and was deeply chagrined that I would not cave in to most of his demands. It became quite clear that I could do absolutely anything I wanted with my life, as long as his life didn't change in the slightest.

It's not easy to imagine a tough, self-governing woman heeling to such a force. But because my approach to not working was working, heel is exactly what I did. It was a different title and the pay structure was not traditional, but it was a job, a career, and I was as obedient as I had been in all my other positions. That is to say, I picked my battles. In my other jobs, I had picked them wisely. Somehow, with this job, I got a bit off track.

CHAPTER 11

CHAPTER 11

My father died a week after my seventeenth birthday and two weeks before Christmas. Since then, the holidays have been rough for me. Christmas is about family, and Daddy was always the best part of mine.

The memory that shouts loudest is of my brother, my sister, and me sitting on the top step of our house in Pittsburgh. We were eight, six, and five respectively. It was still dark and we were forbidden to go downstairs until my dad went before us and lit the tree. We were excited and giggling as he finally descended the stairs, wrapped in his grey plaid bathrobe. When we saw the glow of the lights, we tumbled over each other, laughing all the way down the steps to open our presents.

My gift that year was a stand-up grocery store, with cardboard cans of vegetables, cardboard boxes of cereal, plastic fruits and a real grocery cart. Well, it was real to me. I loved it. How ironic that later in my life I came to hate grocery shopping. That Christmas morning, I loved my grocery store and everything that went with it. It remains one of the happiest memories of my childhood. I still recall the pajamas each of us wore and I still remember the feel of my dad's grey plaid bathrobe as I hugged him with every bit of strength in my little body. If I try hard enough, I can even feel the stubble of his red beard on my face. We had many happy family Christmases, but when I hear the word Christmas, this particular memory comes alive and it makes me sad.

My father has been gone from my life longer than he was in it and I remember him every single day with a smile, but at Christmas, the memory of his beard on my face is heartrending. I can't say why. Since my father's death, I can count the number of times my family has come together for Christmas on one hand. Without him, my mother found no value in celebrating.

John's Christmas memories from childhood were so negative he never spoke to me of them.

*

It was Christmastime and John and I were in Florida with Emily. I don't recall the year, exactly, but John had retrieved the tree from her garage storage area at Emily's request. He then quickly extricated himself from having to help decorate with a feeble excuse about needing to pick up cigarettes. As the car backed out of the drive, I expressed aggravation that he was such a grouch around the holidays. Emily turned to me, sadness on her face, and she began an abysmal story.

"Roberta, you have to better understand John and his youth. There was at least one occasion that Gabe told me about, maybe more for all I know, where he and Lily left the kids with the nanny at Christmas while they came here to Palm Beach without them."

I was shouting in my own head, *Are you serious?* But I didn't interrupt Emily.

"It's horrible, I know. I think Gabe told me because he felt guilty all those years and was looking to me for some sort of forgiveness." She lifted her head and those bright blue eyes held mine, even as her normally serene hands began nervously rubbing together. "Roberta, I couldn't give it to him. I told my brand new husband it was one of the most appalling forms of child abuse I could imagine."

She reached for my hand then, and we held hands in silence for a moment before she laid her other hand upon my cheek and said, "Roberta, be patient with John around the holidays. The memory of it has to be horribly painful. You need to find a way to start your own tradition, together, and make it filled with joy. Make it about the two of you first, before you try to make it about John's family."

It was that day I determined to change the holidays for both of us. I wanted to create our own memories of Christmas, hoping they would obliterate our collective past sadness. I went about this with serious intent, convinced I could make Christmas a better time.

The first year in our house on Lake Drive, it took me a full week to decorate the English Tudor. If I remember, I had a tree in most every room, and the stairway was wrapped with evergreen boughs and ribbons. The landing was home to a full Dickens Village. The library was traditional English, with evergreen and fruit swags, dozens of candles and dishes brimming with ribbon candy and chocolates. There was a decoration on every shelf. Stockings hung on the living room mantle for the four of us – John, me, Porsche and Harley, the latest cats that were my "kids." The grand piano bore a massive Christmas centerpiece and tiny sparkling white lights winked merrily everywhere. The tree in our master bedroom was decorated in the Victorian style, and there were four more stockings displayed over that fireplace, too.

Every room yelled Christmas and huge wreaths on the front double doors welcomed our guests. I bought every holiday album I could find, from classical to rock, and the house was alive with Christmas music every night when John arrived home. I bought a set of Christmas china and invited people for holiday dinners. I thought achieving joy at

Christmas could help him understand that the most pleasure he could ever derive would come from giving, holiday or not

It didn't work out. It seemed nothing could alleviate his sadness, and every year, the approach of the holidays was like watching a storm cloud gather over Lake Michigan marching forward. Our house was surrounded in a sad yet semi-hostile aura.

As the years went by, the decorations became fewer, but John didn't notice, and we never did establish a happy Christmas tradition that we could share together. We were in Florida with Emily every year she was alive, but John would never join me in my crusade to make Christmas merry. Christmas most certainly was not a victory. *This*, I thought, *may be one thing I can never change.*

CHAPTER 12

I secured my first job at Dairy Queen when I was fourteen years old for the expressed purpose of not taking an allowance from my father. My independence, I explained to him, was crucial to me.

Now as a corporate slut, I was getting an allowance to be used for groceries, dry cleaning, housecleaning, my clothing, hair, manicures, and gifts. The amount of gifts required was astounding and this expenditure broke me every month. Wendall Industries now employed approximately one hundred fifty people and we received invitations for every wedding, and birth announcements for every child. We began a gift exchange with John's step-siblings and their children. Tack onto that, all the Wendall Industries family members in Milwaukee with whom we exchanged birthday and Christmas gifts, and John also had eleven god-children. No matter what I spent for whom, John said it was too much. If, in a moment of frustration, I insisted he buy a gift, he spent at least three times what he'd allow me to spend. Then he made sure the recipient knew it was he who purchased the gift, with a bit of a nudge in my direction indicating that I would not have spent as much. Long forgotten was his promise that I would never have to ask him for money. I don't think there was ever a month I didn't have to ask for extra money and justify it with a complete written accounting. I was thoroughly diminished by the process yet I could not seem to find a way to avert the ensuing scene. I felt defenseless in this regard, because I produced no income. I knew I had it good, relatively speaking, and I recognized that not every job was perfect and nobody loved his or her job every day. I had found a way to live with the imperfections of every job and I would find a way to live with this. I determined to suck it up and give him the accounting; hoping that after a time, his trust would grow and we could drop this embarrassing monthly event

*

Memory is a funny thing. I can't remember what I had for lunch yesterday, but I remember every last detail of one particular evening. We had only lived in our house on Lake Drive for a short time. It had been a somewhat hectic day for me, but I still managed to prepare one of John's favorite meals – meat loaf, mashed potatoes with gravy and fresh green beans. I had just finished loading the dishwasher and cleaning the kitchen and was standing by the desk.

"John," I said while leafing through my mail, "I had my eyes checked today. I cannot believe how much they changed! No wonder I've been getting headaches. I had to order two new pair of prescription glasses, regular and sunglasses, and new contacts. Geeze, it was six-hundred-fifty dollars altogether and I have to wait ten days."

"How did you pay for them, Roberta?"

"I put them on the credit card you gave me," I truthfully responded, not thinking twice.

I was opening mail and didn't see him. He came at me from my blind side and slammed me into an adjacent hall closet door hard enough to leave me momentarily breathless. He was an inch from my face as he screamed, "Don't you *ever* use my card again unless you ask for my permission! I don't give a damn if you have to phone first, but don't you *ever* do that again!"

It took a moment for me to catch my breath. I was at first stunned and then blinded by anger. I pushed him away and headed up the stairs to my office, taking two steps at a time. I retrieved the card from my purse, cut it into pieces, bounded back down the steps, and threw the pieces in his face.

"If you ever lay a hand on me again, I'll be out the door before you can turn your back, John. Don't you *ever* touch me like that again or I will be gone! Get it? *Gone!*" Tears, hot as lava, flowed freely down my face.

John slept in the guest room that night, knowing better than to object to the locked bedroom door. The verbal bullshit I could take, but I would never tolerate physical abuse.

His sincere apology in the morning earned my forgiveness, but he never gave me another credit card, and I never asked for one, either.

This was the very first and decidedly last purchase I ever charged to his account. We always maintained separate accounts for everything. Never in our sixteen years did we even have a joint checking account. Money was always a major issue between us. He was the only one allowed to spend it.

*

I had worked the booth at the show in London for the better part of the morning. With John's permission, I left to enjoy some free time with Lola. She was the better half of an industry couple we'd become close to. Lola and Trevor owned a non-competitive manufacturing company in Chicago, and lived only an hour from us. We became quite the foursome and traveled the world together. I relished any time with Lola, my pretend sister, the sister I always wanted, and we were off for lunch and shopping. I found a suit that seemed made for me and I was so proud of my purchase.

Upon John's return to the hotel, I modeled it for him. "It's beautiful," he said as he took off his suit coat and loosened his tie. "How much?"

I did a little sexy dance step in front of him. "Five hundred dollars." In 1988 five hundred dollars for a woman's suit was plenty pricey.

"*What?*" He planted himself in front of me, leaning forward. His voice lowered in fury. "Where the hell are you going to wear that thing? What makes it worth five hundred dollars and what makes you think you deserve a five-hundred-dollar suit?"

My happy feet stopped suddenly. I was frustrated and bitter at John's double standard. In a cold voice, as cold as the wintry, damp London day in January, I said, "Well, John, I'll probably wear my suit the same place you wear your thousand-dollar suits, like trade shows, where I *work*, exactly like you, and earn the right to buy a five-hundred-dollar suit so I can show the world how successful Wendall Industries is." I took a step towards him, put my hand on my hip, and stood my ground. "Does that make my motivation somehow different from yours?"

He glared at me but said nothing.

"And so you know, John, the suit is not returnable."

"Well," John snapped back, taking a step closer. "I guess you'll have to keep it then, won't you. You bought it knowing you couldn't return it and didn't give a damn how much of my money you were spending. That's just typical, Roberta, of your self-centered, irresponsible behavior when it comes to shopping. You're just like your mother – you just love flushing money down the toilet, your only concern being yourself." He put his own hand on his hip, mocking my gesture.

I tried not to change my expression, but the remark about my mother hurt. John always managed to throw in a clincher designed to deflate me. I shouted back, "Jesus John, give it a rest! Is this five-hundred-dollar expense going to prevent us from eating next week?" Then suddenly deciding I had to make light of the situation quickly or risk ruining the rest of the trip, I waited a brief moment before saying, "Hey John, can you see them?"

"See what?" he replied.

"A pack of wolves. I think they're headed for the back door."

For a moment he looked at me like I was crazy but then he laughed. It was over. My joke had gotten us over the hump. The remainder of the trip was great and even had some elements of romance. It was London, after all. Ironically, that suit became his favorite. Whenever I wore it, he complimented me sincerely and with a smile. He probably was remembering the wolf joke!

Of course, it's never about the money, it's about the power. And he, who has the money, has the power. I didn't know how much money John had. It wasn't a concern to me. No bills, other than mine, came to our home and the only financial data I saw was the tax return every year. Without exception, every year I was stunned and angry that he was so stingy with me when "our" income was more than healthy.

*

I was at the Wendall Industries office one day when John was out of town. As I rounded the corner, I nearly bumped head-on into Michael, the corporate attorney, personal attorney, and close advisor to John. He was a revered member of the three-man team I jokingly referred to as the posse. His controller Raymond, his corporate attorney Michael, and his Executive Vice-President, Paul, made up John's posse. Never a major decision was made, business or personal, without input from the posse.

And on occasion each one of them turned to me for counsel. It was our own little version of ring around the rosy. John had no idea there was such a game swirling around him. Had he known, the fury unleashed would have reduced all of us to a smoldering pile of ash.

Michael and I laughed as he grabbed my elbow to prevent me from staggering into the wall. Since our first meeting, Michael and I had been friendly. His head turned first to the left and then the right before he pulled me into a satellite employee kitchen. He pushed his glasses back to a comfortable position on his slender nose. He lowered his voice so that I could barely hear him over the usual general office noises.

"Roberta, you cannot believe how upset John got with me yesterday!" He was clearly a little proud of himself. The corners of his smallish mouth turned slightly upward and his stance became relaxed, confident that no one was listening. "He was whining about your spending again... I can't believe him...and I simply said, 'John, I can't believe how lucky you are...you should stop complaining. I think that in terms of what you have, Roberta is incredibly frugal. I wish my wife spent as little as Roberta does.' Would you believe he told me to mind my own damn business?"

"Seriously?" I asked with concern. I didn't want Michael to have any trouble because of me. I liked him.

"Well, I thought he was joking at first, but when I saw his face... well, Roberta, in all these years, I think it was the most angry he's ever been with me! He was infuriated!" Michael, though slightly smiling, seemed just a little twitchy.

"Are you upset that he's angry?" I asked. As a rule, people went to inconceivable lengths not to upset John.

"Nah, not really. Not over that. It isn't exactly a Board of Directors issue. I was just surprised, that's all. I *do* think you're frugal!"

I thanked him for his support, pleased that he acknowledged my common sense approach to spending. I felt, however, that Michael was trying to garner my favor, in exchange for falling temporarily out of John's good graces. The conversation, though private, held significance later.

CHAPTER 13

The year of the Gulf War, John conveyed the dismal prediction that this could be the first year in company history Wendall Industries may not make a profit. The economy was poor and sales were down. Always the team player, I started cutting coupons for the grocery store, bought head lettuce instead of Bibb, and did not purchase one thing for myself for about eight months. I was truly concerned with John's very fragile ego. To record a down year on his watch may affect his legacy.

Eight months later, John came rolling in the driveway with his brand new one-hundred-and-twenty-thousand dollar Porsche. Shortly after, he came home with a Harley Davidson box. I opened it to find a beautiful pair of motorcycle boots, and I complimented them by saying, "These are great and you really did need new boots."

"Thanks," John said. "Wait until you see the bike I bought to match." We had no debt, no mortgages, and no loans. John paid cash for everything. I was aghast but what could I say after he emphatically stated that it was his money to spend as he chose.

I began to grasp the concept that his control of the money provided his biggest leverage over me. I knew I couldn't change that.

It isn't that he didn't buy me things. I had beaded formal gowns costing thousands of dollars, jewelry, fur coats, and anything tangible that made him look great. He used to parade me around at parties saying "Show him what I bought you."

*

Lola and I were sitting in the lobby of the Peninsula Hotel in Hong Kong, waiting for the personal shopper we had hired for the day. I was thinking about gray pearls. Lola's long, lean frame was draped languorously over a loveseat, as we sipped our coffee in silence. She was keeping her head down, soft blond hair hiding most of her face, chin dipped low, and studiously examining some imagined thread on her sleeve. She was thinking I couldn't see her smile. I stared intently at her, knowing she could feel my gaze, and finally, she jerked her head upward and looked directly at me. The laughter burst from her followed closely by a wide grin.

"Please don't ask me Roberta, I promised John I wouldn't tell you. I'll take care of you, I promise." While agreeing to allow me to purchase the pearls, John had told only Lola how much she could spend on my behalf. I was to play no part in that decision. With a glance at the revolving door, her elegant and bejeweled left hand reached for her Chanel handbag, as she affably extended her right hand to greet our hired shopper for the day

We were driven by limousine to a reputable wholesaler in Hong Kong and when I told her what I was seeking, she asked how big and how much. I pointed to Lola and said, "I don't know, you'll have to ask her."

The wholesaler looked at Lola first, then me, and said, "Oh...are you two gay?"

We laughed uproariously. I got my pearls, thanks to Lola, but she never to this day revealed the amount John had allowed her. The pearls are sensational. I still have them but I never told anybody the great sadness I felt that moment at the wholesalers.

I was beginning to feel powerless; somewhat like the prey of a python, being strangled and digested a little at a time. The wife part of me was being swallowed slowly. I could almost see my stiletto heels protruding from the belly of the beast. Laughing at the visualization even as I tossed it aside, I assured myself that I was still me, wasn't I?

It wasn't until after we had been married many years and things were getting ugly, that John began telling me on a regular basis how ungrateful I was. I genuinely tried, but somehow I could never thank him enough and it got tiresome after a time. I began exploding back, "How dare you blame me for being spoiled," I said on one occasion, "*You're the one who spoiled me.*" It's a poor defense, I know, but I was implacably firm in defending my logic, my voice never wavering as I indignantly waved my arms in the air for effect.

CHAPTER 14

It was rare that John and I dined away from home while in town. One particular evening we chose a casual German restaurant not far from our home. It was just after the Christmas party of 1987 and a freezing cold winter night. The heat of the blazing fire and the smell of German cooking warmed our moods as well as our bodies. Volatile marriages are similar to bi-polar disease, with distinct highs and lows. During our highs we enjoyed relative peace, with the good John decidedly in the forefront. We were at just such a juncture this particular evening.

I began a small speech I had been rehearsing in my brain for some time. "You know how you're always referring to the employees at Wendall Industries as your family?"

John lit a cigarette for both of us and handed me one before he responded. "Yeah, they are."

"Well, if it's one thing I've learned from not working, John, it's that wives are rarely included in that mix, when they make a lot of sacrifices to make sure their husbands succeed. Look at me, for example."

He looked up, relaxed and interested with a bit of question on his face. "Go ahead," he said.

"I hate it when you're gone for long periods of time and the trade shows are always over weekends, which dramatically affects the amount of free time we have together. I get it. I even travel with you a lot of the time because I can help. I know the business, but I've heard a few wives complain a little. Imagine having to come home from a business trip to hear a whiny woman complaining about a lack of attention! It can't be nice for the guys."

His head cocked a little to the side, but his eyes were intently studying my face. "Go ahead."

"My philosophy is that happy wives make for happy male employees. What if we brought them into the fold? If the wives love the company too it would assure that their husbands would work doubly hard. I could do a little behind-the-scenes work, like starting a theatre group for all the wives. I've been attending Repertory Theatre since I moved here, so why couldn't I invite all of them to join me? It could be a Wendall Industries Wives Club sort of thing."

His face lit up. He reached across the table to squeeze my hand and said, "Do it, Roberta. It sounds great. You're right, these guys are away a lot, and the last thing I want is a good salesman leaving us because his wife is unhappy with the hours he spends at Wendall Industries."

I began a very stringent campaign designed to make the company employees and their wives a family with everyone treated accordingly. We entertained Wendall Industries personnel extensively and later on I hosted an "orphan's dinner" once a week for all the employees who were single and had no family in town. These were casual, in the kitchen, meatloaf kind of suppers, but the bonding was unmistakable and a lot of business was accomplished. Many a marketing idea, new product name, and sales strategy were formulated over dinner at our kitchen table in Milwaukee or at our summer home in Freshwater Falls.

Our closest ties were to the men in the sales department, and the wives became my pals. When somebody new was hired, I immediately took charge of the wife, provided there was one. We always hosted a very large welcome party so that they might become acquainted on a social, more casual level with the Wendall Industries family and it was my pleasure to show the new wife around town and help her with any services needed. If a new employee was single, he or she became one of my orphans and was at the house for dinner once a week, and weekends too if he or she seemed lonely.

Nobody was going to be unhappy at Wendall Industries if I could help it. It was bad for business. I was the first one to take food when someone was ill, send cards for all occasions, celebrate every birthday with a party, and I did it willfully and sincerely. I loved them all. We partied together, we cried with each other and John's employees became our closest friends.

John and I became quite insular, socializing very little with anyone outside the company. I thought this industrial version of Camelot a good thing-a happy place where harmony and camaraderie were plentiful. I may have become Queen of the castle, but I didn't realize that one day I would be standing outside the wall I had designed and help build.

CHAPTER 15

In 1988, about three years after we were married, I was in Freshwater Falls preparing for weekend houseguests as always when John called sobbing. Real men didn't cry in 1988 and John was no exception. Hearing him blubber and hiccup, thoroughly strangulated by tears, was alarming. Roger, the current president of Wendall Industries, was supposed to be mentoring John, preparing him to assume the role within the year. While calling on a large chain together, John apparently told a crude joke in the presence of a very prudish female purchasing agent. She had exited the meeting in disgust, leaving Roger red faced with anger and embarrassment as John stood by utterly bewildered. *What's her problem*, he was always apt to think. After informing John that he felt him unsuitable to manage Wendall Industries, Roger suggested that John become chairman of the board, and Paul, the executive vice-president, be promoted to President. He was distraught and uncomprehending, feeling as if he had been fired, yet thinking the Chairmanship might not be all bad.

He made the two and one-half hour drive so that we might speak in person. As he sat at the kitchen table, eyes rimmed in red from crying, I explained to him that I would support any decision he made.

If he chose to be Chairman, they would remove him from day to day operations; he would collect the money and essentially retire. He'd lose the opportunity to put his stamp on the company that his parents founded. That was fine with me, I explained. We could sail, travel, and we were young enough to thoroughly enjoy a privileged life. There was plenty of money. However, I told him that we could fight it. He was the sole stockholder, Wendall Industries was privately held, and should he want an opportunity to operate the company, I would not only support him, but help him in every way I could.

I suggested we contact his stepbrother, who was chairman of the psychology department at a prestigious university. He might help us enlist the aid of an industrial psychologist to assess the situation.

This strategy had been used earlier in John's life when he was convicted of a felony for dealing drugs in college. Stepbrother Ben came to the rescue when Gabe wanted to write John out of his will, his company, and his life. After an industrial psychologist, recommended by stepbrother Ben, ascertained John capable, Gabe was convinced, with the help of Emily, that John could fulfill his legacy.

John, without much thinking, tearfully admitted he wanted to operate Wendall Industries. I took the lead, not realizing that I was fulfilling his expectation, and became head lobbyist for the "John Wendall for President Campaign." It was a full time job. I talked to every employee before the shrink ever set foot on the property, without John's knowledge, of course, but we discussed my meetings in a roundabout way every evening.

Over cocktails after work with the sales department I made my case, stating decisively that John had a right to try this – he was born to it and it was his legacy. He started at Wendall Industries as a child, working at the factory and earning his position. Upon graduation from college, he maintained a sales territory prior to being vice president of sales, and was one of the only executives ever known who could strip any of his products and reassemble them in the field. My belief was that he would take Wendall Industries in a new direction. He also had plans to sell the company to the employees at some point, giving them a unique opportunity for an equity portion of a very profitable concern. And he thought of them and treated them all as family.

The chief financial officer agreed to lunch with me, and the customer service department listened attentively while I chatted amiably in their area with them over coffee and donuts on a snowy Milwaukee morning.

Deliberately choosing a time when John would be out of town, I made the short drive to Wendall Industries. My purpose was to confront Paul about his motives. I asked politely if I could have a word with him. We moved quickly into the test kitchen, adjacent to the service department, and I closed the door behind us. The thud of the door closing must have sounded ominous, because he turned to me, eyes full of question and concern. There was a small stainless steel table and a few folding chairs in the center of a cold grey cement floor. The surrounding equipment some tested and some not, looked like orphans waiting to be adopted. For a fleeting moment I thought the new toaster, mouth wide open, was watching my performance.

I asked Paul to sit, but I remained standing, wanting to maintain a position of power. I was angry. Protective of John, always, I felt like a mama bear protecting her young. Sitting at the table, Paul looked smaller than his five-foot-four frame. He chose not to face me, but rather concentrate on the table folding his hands, one over the other, fisted.

"I understand you want to be president of Wendall Industries, Paul." My tone was intentionally sharp. "I'm not sure where I heard such a goofy rumor, but it's a joke, right, Paul? You couldn't possibly be serious."

I could see beads of sweat forming on his brow as he looked up at me, his hands springing apart and starting to gesticulate wildly. "Roberta," he said, "honest to God, Roger came and asked me. He made it sound as if this is what John wanted. I've been here since college, almost thirty years now..."

In one step, my hand was grasping his arm. "Bullshit, Paul. Do you think because you carried Lily's hatboxes way back when, you have a right to rob John's legacy? You do get it Paul, don't you? If Lily and Gabe had wanted you at the helm, they would have asked you, not Roger, to be president those many years ago. That didn't happen, did it?"

I intentionally entered his personal space, trying my best to intimidate. "I have a feeling they didn't find you worthy, in spite of all that ass-kissing."

I was leaning over him now, both hands flat on the table before him. "John trusts you with major decisions regarding this company, has delegated more authority to you than anyone in this company, and here you sit, ready for the big coup, the big overthrow, the biggest betrayal of all, before he even gets his shot. This is something he was born to, and you're ready to take it all away from him without a glance backward, aren't you? You think it's a secret, Paul, your need for power? You can take the man out of the military, but you can't take the military out of the man, right?" I was making reference to his rank of colonel in the Air Force Reserve.

Paul stood so quickly he overturned his chair. His gray hair might have stood on end had it not already been so closely cropped to his head. His face decidedly pale, lips slightly trembling, he tried to take my hand. I stepped backwards and swatted his hand away from me.

"Roberta, please," he said, "I think I got caught in the middle here. Roger told me *everybody* wanted this, the board of directors, John, everybody. Honestly! If John wants to be president, you are absolutely right, he deserves it."

He was becoming short of breath. "I'll tell Roger right now I want nothing to do with this. I'll tell him I refuse to be president. Roberta, please, you have to believe me, I would never hurt John. I've known him since he was a baby...I love the guy."

"Save the crap, Paul." My whole persona was now a virtual thunderstorm, lightning included, I pointed my manicured finger in his direction. "*If* John asks me, and you know he will, I will advise him with a clear conscience to fire you. This will go his way, I can assure you. He *will* be president of Wendall Industries, and nobody should have to live with a right hand man so willing to betray him. You know that I know the truth, Paul. That's *exactly* what you intended."

His shoes squeaked on the cold grey cement as he turned and ran out the door, but not before I saw the look of panic on his face. He looked even shorter than when he was cowering in his chair a few minutes earlier.

He made a beeline for Roger and told him he no longer had any desire to be president. That pretty much nailed it. In addition, the reports came back positive that the majority of the employees would prefer working for John than Paul.

Hail to the Chief, we had a new president. John was so proud—of himself! I never received an acknowledgement or a thank you. Hell, I was the architect of the plan, and I helped save his sorry ass. Yet John sincerely believed that the right thing happened, with only divine intervention. Oh yes, you bet I was divine.

My awareness of John's inability to give back was now becoming clearer to me. Giving, to John, was a material perception, not a spiritual one. For emotional support, John was always on the taking end. That was fine for a very long time when I had ample supply. As the years went by, his inability to support me made me weaker and the erosion of my confidence was slow but very steady. It took years for me to notice its absence.

As for the rest of the story, Paul's fate was not as I predicted. It was a rare occasion that John did not heed my counsel yet he allowed Paul to remain in his position of executive vice-president. Paul had intimate knowledge of the company, and because John was aware that Paul was still painfully uneasy, he felt it more beneficial to exploit Paul's guilt than to punish him by discharging him. Paul remains at Wendall Industries today, lips permanently affixed to John's backside.

CHAPTER 16

In May of 1990, we were five years into the marriage and John was to turn forty. It took a year to plan his surprise party, which was held in Chicago at the annual National Restaurant Show a week before his birthday. It was a perfect venue, because all of our industry friends attended this show every year. He was shocked yet truly elated as two hundred and fifty people shouted surprise when he entered the ballroom, thinking he was attending a banquet honoring an industry consultant. This was the sort of grandiose event he relished.

I had arranged a dinner coupled with a roast in a beautiful ballroom of The Four Seasons Hotel in Chicago. The dais was adorned with John's childhood pictures. Positioned on each place setting was a four-page mini-biography of John's life, told in a comical manner. The linens were black on black, signifying the mourning of his passing youth and, though difficult to find, I managed for the flower arrangements to be black, white, and red roses. I had chosen six people to roast him and at the conclusion, I was to give a speech.

My stuttering wasn't a secret, but it wasn't public knowledge either. It's not the sort of thing one speaks about with pride at cocktail parties. I wrote my speech and practiced relentlessly. I made my way to the podium and delivered a fabulous and funny missive, without a single stutter.

At the end, having had that last scotch too many, John rose to give his rebuttal. I expected to hear, "I want to thank my lovely wife..." Instead, he leaned into the microphone and said, "I am so proud of Roberta for giving that speech. It's unbelievable that she didn't stutter once. Can you believe that? Roberta honey that was amazing."

The silence was vociferous. Not even a titter of laughter, just gasps-audible gasps. Most of these people had no idea I stuttered. I was crushed. It was one of the most embarrassing moments of my life. The only one in the room who did not understand my embarrassment was John.

The next morning when he was relatively sober, I still could not make him comprehend my unease. Finally, like an exasperated mother, I left him with, "OK...just don't mention my stuttering publicly again."

Please dear Jesus, I prayed, *make sure he doesn't do that again.* Silent prayer was becoming a part of my daily life.

*

It was late September, early October of 1990 that I began to feel overwhelmingly exhausted. I had been working non-stop on a charity function to benefit mentally challenged young adults. The project was to build and equip a commercial kitchen at a local technical school in order to train these young adults to work in restaurants. I loved this project. A fellow rep pulled me in and somehow I came to be in charge.

We were able to get all the equipment donated, but needed additional funds to build the kitchen, and we were having a very large dinner dance fundraiser in mid-October. I was closely involved in every major aspect of the project and the fundraiser, too. I only mention this because today, if you visit John's company website, he states this as one of his proudest achievements! Ok, so he called some of his factory buddies for me and got some equipment donated, but that was the extent of his involvement.

At any rate, I attributed my fatigue to the work and all of my other daily life stuff, which was significant. I have always had a high energy level, but around three o'clock every day, I had to lie down. I couldn't even remove myself from the chaise lounge in the lake room to cook dinner. I finally decided to see the doctor.

The doctor took a chest x-ray and the following day called to tell me he had found a suspicious spot and scheduled a CT scan for the following morning. I was a smoker and probably smoked one and a half packs of cigarettes a day at that point in time. The next morning after the CT scan was completed and I was leaving the scanner room, the technician said, "Roberta, call your doctor this afternoon."

"OK, sure. Why? Did you see something?" I asked.

"Just call your doctor."

I didn't have to, he called me. There was definitely something there, very small, but enough that he wanted me to see a thoracic surgeon. In spite of the fact that I smoked, he thought it unlikely to be cancer, but they needed to determine exactly what it was.

The following day John accompanied me to the thoracic surgeon. I was slightly nervous. My father died of lung cancer at age forty-four and he never smoked. I was only thirty-eight, but had been smoking since age fourteen. The surgeon explained that it was highly unlikely to be cancer, due to my age and excellent general health, but he needed a biopsy to rule it out. This spot was in a very unfortunate location, extremely difficult to get to and would require the big cut. No laparoscopes for this procedure in 1990. The cut would start under my right breast, wrap around my right side, and go half way up my back – the same incision my father had.

I explained to the surgeon that we were scheduled to leave for London, Paris, and Amsterdam right after the charity function and he said, "Sure, go ahead and go. I'm sure it's nothing and it can wait a month."

I was already out the door when John grabbed my arm and in a moment of clarity told the surgeon "No way – Europe will be there another thousand years, but we need to take care of this."

The surgeon explained the biopsy would be conducted in the operating room and, if cancerous, would result in removing the upper third of my right lung. Ok, now I was scared, but John was more afraid, so I hid my fear. I tucked it in that place in my mind that one chooses not to visit, just like the back hall closet where all the old sporting things were. My surgery was scheduled for October 31, 1990.

The weeks preceding my surgery were sprinkled with moments of my reassuring John. He was worried. I asked friends to come sit with him during the four-hour surgery. It was the only time I asked him not to travel. I was to be admitted for a minimum of ten days and I would be in intensive care for a day or two after surgery, and I wanted him with me. I needed him.

Nobody fully prepared me for what was to come. After the surgery, I opened my eyes in intensive care to the worst pain I have ever, to this day, experienced. I have an extremely high tolerance for pain, but this was so acute that I preferred not to breathe. It seemed easier to die than to take a breath. No one explained that a rib would be removed. And since the results were positive for small cell cancer, the upper third of my right lung was also removed. My breathing was so labored and painful that an anesthesiologist was rushed to ICU to insert a catheter into my spinal cord to deliver morphine directly to the site. It was touchy because the drug actually slows breathing and they were trying to increase my breathing to enable more oxygen intake.

When I wanted John to hold my hand, a friend told me he was in the gift shop crying. In the haze of the drug I remember thinking, *Get your shit together, Roberta. You can probably handle this, but he can't.*

Forty-eight hours later, I was moved to a private room on the oncology floor. It was early evening when John marched in with four couples; they brought take-out Chinese food and bottles of Saki. For John, any occasion was an occasion for a party. They began filling the sink in the bathroom with hot water to warm the Saki, and then promptly forgot that they left the water running. The sink overflowed and water began flowing under the door. There was laughter and utter chaos and I could hardly bear it. The pain was still overwhelming and my only focus was just trying to breathe. It was rare I couldn't rise to the occasion and do the expected thing. In this case I was expected to entertain, make a joke of my experience and invoke my quirky brand a humor to make them all more comfortable. I was drugged and miserable and was much relieved when the nurse made everyone leave. *I let them down,* I thought. *I can't be funny tonight; I don't feel like being funny.*

I couldn't fathom John's inability to be there for me. My weakness seemed to elicit disparagement rather than sympathy, and it contributed to my agony immensely. The third day after surgery John phoned my room to tell me he was leaving town to attend to some business. It was only a day trip, he explained. He had chartered a plane and would be back in the evening.

I hung up the phone with tears just streaming. I felt horrible. *This could have waited,* I thought. As the day progressed, I continued to feel worse. My surgeon had left for vacation right after my surgery and his colleague came to check on me. When I explained that I felt worse than the day before, he looked at me and said, "Didn't anybody tell you this would hurt? Hell, this is worse pain than open-heart surgery. Why isn't anybody here with you? Don't you have any friends?"

I literally had hundreds of cards from friends, family, acquaintances, and industry people, and so many flowers they took some from the room because they feared the plants were taking too much oxygen. But he was right. I was utterly alone this dreadful day. I couldn't reply. I was weak and I couldn't breathe. When he left, I started to cry. My surgeon was a wonderful man; his colleague was not. I closed my eyes thinking how nice it would be to see Daddy again, and Grandma, and even Teddy, the family dog we had for seventeen years. I was ready to go and prayed God to take me. I'd had enough pain. My tolerance had crumbled.

I was lying perfectly still, in abject misery and praying to die, when a friend of John's walked in a short while later. "Roberta," he told me, his voice riddled with alarm, "you look horrible."

He went running to the nurses' station. My internist, the doctor I credit for saving my life by getting that first X-ray, happened to be at the desk. He is a Pakistani and not given to excitement, but when I haltingly explained the excruciating pain and he observed my labored breathing, he began barking orders. He called for a STAT portable chest x-ray, which revealed a collapsed right lung and a partially collapsed left lung.

They started cutting and inserting chest tubes right there and shoved another IV in my neck. The veins in my arms, not good to begin with, couldn't tolerate another needle. I already had one ruptured vein. The anesthesiologist was suddenly there putting another catheter in my spinal cord to alleviate the pain. I was close to death.

It was an epiphany. I closed my eyes and told myself that if I was able to overcome this, I wanted to be a better person, a better friend, give more, open my heart more, and be a better wife, a better daughter, a better sister. I would listen more and talk less; I would get smarter, more evolved, reach toward self-realization with more vigor. I knew I could give more and be more if I got closer to understanding who I was.

Dr. Rah explained that I needed a blood transfusion because I had lost more blood than anticipated during the surgery. This was during the time when the blood supply had become tainted with HIV and hepatitis C. I was confused, in a drugged haze and so sick I couldn't make a decision about my own well-being. John was not answering his cell phone. In spite of the fact that Dr. Rah said it would greatly aid in my recovery, I said no. There wasn't time to get a donor, as the screening process for blood was too long. I wasn't sure if I had done the right thing, and John was nowhere to be found to help me figure it out.

John didn't call all day and it was late evening before I finally reached him on his cell phone. He was having dinner with Michael, who had made the trip with him. When I told him I almost died, he told me not to exaggerate. He seemed mystified and angry that I was upset. His anger at me the evening of the day I almost died was a crushing blow. I had always been there for him and just assumed he could reciprocate when I needed him so urgently.

The next day John became a bit sheepish, but never apologetic, when Dr. Rah explained there had been no overstatement. He brought me a pot of my beloved Blue Mountain Jamaican coffee from home. Weakened and needy, anything was something. It was a small gesture, but I cherished it.

I stayed fourteen days instead of ten because of this major set back. The oncologist came with good news. The spot on my lung was smaller than the tip of a baby's fingernail, and because they had removed so much lung tissue surrounding the area, there was no need for follow-up treatment. I would not have to endure chemotherapy or radiation, just blood work and chest x-rays every six months for the next five years.

He explained the recovery would be six months to a year and I would have to work hard to regain muscle strength and breathing strength due to the huge incision and the excision of the upper lobe of the lung. In addition, because I had refused the blood transfusion, I would be feeling weak and tired for quite a while. There must have been an angel on my shoulder, even though there was no knight in shining armor to protect me.

Self-reliance was my mantle. I lived it, preached it, and wore it proudly in full public view. I'd been on my own for so long I knew no other way. This first chink in my shield turned into a huge dent with the realization that there was no knight for me. There would be no guardian, no rescuer from horrific unexpected life-stuff. I had reversed the roles, and I feared it too late to put them in the proper order. To be his protector, I thought, was why John married me.

*

I was home in mid-November and though John had been present when the doctor explained how lengthy my recovery might be, he pushed me from the moment I got out of the car in a nagging *I want my life back to normal* kind of way. He wouldn't quit smoking in my presence. When I asked, he told me to get used to it. I started smoking again a year later and the only one who didn't care was John. It was ok with him.

Friends brought food, flowers, and love. Marie and Grant came to visit from Cincinnati, and I was grateful to them not only for their love, but for taking care of John. When he kept insisting I go out with them, they took him away so I could get some rest. They occupied his time, made him drinks, and laughed at his jokes so I wouldn't have to. When they left, he attempted to make me feel guilty because he had to host my friends all alone, without my help. I just rolled over in bed. What could I possibly say?

*

Thanksgiving had become a tradition we shared with four other couples. It started the year we were married and the intent was for people to come together for the holiday because they had no other family in town. It was my favorite holiday because we spent it with our closest friends, had no family feuds, and we always had an incredible amount of fun.

We were not the host house that year and I didn't feel able to go, yet John nagged me until I did. I was weak and still in a great deal of pain. Already thin, I lost an additional fifteen pounds and my blood counts were still very low. The pallor I carried was alarming and my eyes were sunken and dull. I barely ate dinner and begged to go home soon after. Our friends looked at me sympathetically, but everyone was afraid to suggest to John that he take me home. Nobody liked to make him angry and he was irate and drunk. His wrath could be withering. It was an inauspicious start to the Holiday season and on the silent drive home, I offered another silent prayer. *Get me through December with my mind unharmed and this broken down piece of crap outer garment of a body intact.*

*

We hosted an annual black tie New Year's Eve party in our home for about fifty people that John never suggested we might skip this year. I had great difficulty dealing with the caterer, the entertainer, and the details but he insisted I fulfill my role, do my job, and be me. He had not exactly bargained for my weaker side and I could see in his eyes that it was barely tolerable for him. It never occurred to him that I didn't like it much either.

Our party started at ten in the evening and we served a midnight buffet. When John and I were entertaining, we were rarely together. He was host and I was hostess, most often on opposite sides of the room. That year, as the piano player struck the first chords to Auld Lang Syne, I had an unexpected and emotional reaction. All eyes turned to me, many of them teary, knowing I almost didn't make it this year. John forgot about me. As people surrounded me with ginger hugs and tears, I began sobbing because I couldn't find him. I was the last person he kissed that New Year's Eve. John was drunk and I don't think he ever wanted to remember how close I came to dying. I slowly made my way upstairs shortly after and collapsed in bed while the party roared on until four o'clock in the morning.

My confidence started to display hairline fractures; I was certain he couldn't love me if I didn't get myself back together and become his corporate slut again.

*

Shortly after the New Year of 1991, I was finally able to start exercising. I began working with a trainer to build the muscle in my right shoulder and work on expanding my right lung. Lungs don't regenerate, but they can expand to their original size. After some time, I was up to walking four miles a day. I wanted to be me again too. I needed to get back to my job.

We began entertaining again and I booked houseguests for every weekend of the summer at our summer home from Memorial Day through Labor Day. It was our usual schedule. I was busy planning menus and activities. I kept a diary of our guests and menus and made every effort to not duplicate meals for the same people from year to year. It was a job. Because there were not a lot of choices in Freshwater Falls, I purchased most of the food in Milwaukee and transported it. I personally did all the shopping and cooking and that was no small task.

It took almost a full year for me to be pain free and rid myself of the exhaustion. I couldn't wear a bra as even that small pressure was agonizing. Not that I needed one, mind you. I worked through the exhaustion because it was easier. I tried to ignore an annoying sense that I was giving up too much of myself for this corporate slut job.

I began volunteering at a center to teach adults to read. Reading has brought such joy to my life that when I read about the alarming amount of illiteracy among adults, I wanted to help. I loved it. I had to give it up after six months because the corporate slut was needed.

I was back to working trade shows, traveling, drinking after work with the guys, and entertaining. I made time for everybody who wanted my attention. John's closest colleagues had always turned to me for advice and Paul and Michael often told me I should be sitting behind that big desk instead of John.

I became more involved with John's extended family, particularly the great nieces and nephews. And my brother's son, who had always been in my heart, became a focus of my attention. He starting visiting Freshwater Falls for two weeks in the summer and it solidified our bonding, which still grows in strength today. I think of him as if he was mine and I would give my life for him. Still.

When I got back to speed, our lives resumed normalcy, or what we deemed normalcy. It was travel, party, entertain, work hard, and play harder. We were happy because the business was expanding rapidly and the corporate slut was working harder than ever.

My improving health permitted the return of fervent hugs and renewed my belief that John needed me and loved me. I forgave his lack of attention during my illness, choosing to believe his fear of losing me the culprit. Human frailty is a condition I understand, appreciate, and embrace. My own flaws are often as glaring as the sun reflected off a mirror and I hope to be forgiven quite regularly. His kisses renewed their intensity and the wife helped John bounce the mattress to the floor now and again, laughing, as expected, on the ride down. I found restored comfort with his arms wrapped around me as we drifted into sleep. We were all focused on John, just as he demanded and desired.

*

A few years later I endured another unexpected body betrayal when two discs herniated in my lower spine. Confined to bed for six weeks, I was largely caught up in blaming my mother for inheriting her bad back and wondering if I could sue her for substandard workmanship. When I tired of that exercise, I transferred my annoyance to John and his feeble attempts to care for me.

He rose in the morning, served me some breakfast, and put enough food and water on a tray to get me through the day. In the evening, he would generally bring home some kind of fast food for dinner. John had been a gourmet cook before we married and prepared elaborate and romantic dinners for me while we were dating. But since walking down the aisle, I couldn't remember one meal he had cooked other than breakfast. God forbid he would come home for lunch or prepare a real dinner for me. Dating to marriage is the optimum example of bait and switch, I have learned.

I literally willed myself better in record time. Great customer notwithstanding, I couldn't take another night of Kentucky Fried

Chicken. Again, he was impatient for his life to be back to normal. I prayed so fervently for a knight in shining armor that I was convinced he may appear magically in the form of John. Of course, everyone knows that prayer is futile if the goal is selfish. John never learned how to be sympathetic to a weaker Roberta. Again, I was overwhelmed with that sense of *Get back to work, Roberta. You hold no value if you're not well and can't work.*

This last illness drove John and the wife side of me apart. His snoring had become unbearable and we began sleeping in different rooms. I missed the feel of him in the bed and his arms around me falling asleep and the intimacy that brings. Once in a while, we still had sex, but he would go to his room after and that was even a greater loss of intimacy. His desire for me as his wife had begun to wane.

Surprisingly, without that, we became more of a team in the company and work sense. It is remarkable to me that in a time of great stress in our personal life - no affection, no sex, no sharing of personal feelings, no intimacy - the business side of our relationship continued to grow and thrive.

*

I arrived home from my night with the Wendall Industries wives at the theatre. As I pulled into the garage, I noticed the lights in the lake room glaring. John was always asleep when I returned home late, but as I walked up the stairs from the basement and before the door was fully open, he said, "Where the hell have you been?"

"Out for a drink, honey, after the theatre. Why, is something wrong?"

"Why were you out for a drink? Do you always go out for a drink after the theatre? Seeing what's available, Roberta, or what?"

This wasn't typical behavior for John. He was never jealous, knowing that my work with men made most of my friends' men. He had no reason to distrust me.

"Honey, what's wrong?" I said. "You know better. Talk to me… what's really the matter?"

He slumped into his recliner and lowered his head. "Oh Roberta, I really want to start an international division. We've been talking about it for months."

Surprised, I said, "I thought that was a done deal, John."

"There's a board meeting tomorrow and I think they're going to vote against me. They think it's too soon to go global. What should I do?"

The corporate slut kicked into high gear.

"Okay, let's figure this out. Is cash outlay the problem? Do you have to borrow to purchase overseas warehousing? What is the timing to be fully operational? Will inflating the sale price to cover shipping and warehousing keep us competitive in that market? What's the profit margin? What's the ROI? What's the cost of training, how much personnel…let me see the paperwork."

After a few hours of dissecting all the information, I leaned back in my chair and said, "The reality, John, is that you are the sole stockholder. Your Board of Directors is internal. They are all employed by you, even your attorney. You trust that your board gives you the best advice they can, but looking at it objectively, are they idea-based, long term thinkers or afraid of what may affect their profit sharing bonus at the end of the year? That's the thing about internal boards, John…no new blood…no new ideas. If you're asking what I think, I believe your instincts are good with this venue and you are ahead of the game.

"It may be a few years of minimal red ink that could turn into many years of huge profits. If it fails, you're young. You'll earn the money back. If you're concerned that the employees may lose by way of bonus, set up a different corporation that doesn't affect them. You can take the loss and the profit, and should you want to share when the profits warrant, you can merge the companies. I say go for it. When you pursue your passion, the money somehow seems to follow, right?"

He went for it. It's doubtful that he approached his board the next day beginning with "Roberta told me….." However, he did call me around ten o'clock that morning to tell me he put the wrong pants on with the suit coat he had chosen. His tie wasn't right either, he said. Could I bring his pants and a tie over? He definitely needed me. Everybody could see that!

*

John interviewed a young dynamic woman to head the international division, and of course brought her home for dinner and to spend the night. Dana and I were to become the closest of friends

We began traveling worldwide extensively and quite often with Lola and Trevor. Lola remains among my closest female friends – like a sister, really. And we bonded over two similar males who made so many demands of us that we didn't need to speak of it freely. We just knew how and when to support each other.

For the most part John and I had wonderful times on these trips, even if the romance was sporadic. We still held hands, teased each other, and jointly marveled at our new experiences in unfamiliar countries around the world. When we traveled to London on the Concorde, we were like children riding a roller coaster together for the first time. We both had wide eyes, and that thrilling childlike sense of wonderment as our speed reached Mach 1. I can still hear the two of us giggling, trying desperately to look sophisticated, as though we belonged there. Being irreverent at times was a hobby we still shared. There were still moments of great fun.

CHAPTER 17

I started working at the company for real pay. The Information Systems (IS) Department, at John's behest, hired me as a consultant to develop and publish a web page. I had asked for a raise in my allowance but instead of paying me in after tax dollars, the posse thought it more practical to have Wendall Industries hand me a paycheck. I had to do something tangible—they couldn't exactly pay me to be John's unofficial, never publicly acknowledged common sense. Silently propping my husband or helping to reverse his poor decisions was not a written job description. It may have been a difficult sell to the IRS, or John for that matter. I was to be at Wendall Industries some of the time, but work from home most of the time and still fulfill my corporate wife duties, of course.

A year before, I had begged John for a computer and he had enlisted the help of his new Information Systems Department head, Josh, in pursuit of that goal. Josh patiently taught me the basics and endured my panicked phone calls, but computer technology for anyone is largely self-taught through experimentation. I had only been at it a year and, while far from expert; I had advanced a little beyond novice. My first day at work, I was introduced to Mark, the new IS whiz kid who was to help me learn the process. He handed me some software and told me to install it at my work computer and the laptop I used at home. It was Microsoft Front Page® and proved complicated software for a beginner website developer.

Mark rarely took my calls or answered my questions in enough detail or depth. He left me hanging out there on my own, swinging from a limb of ignorance with nary a textbook or teacher in sight. He spoke computer lingo intentionally, I think, to screw with me. The terms "html" and "tags" may have been familiar to him, but I had no idea what he was referring to. Always able to solve the mysteries of new ventures on my own with relative ease, I strove to do so again. Frustrated after a month, I finally asked Mark to lunch to confront him with the "what's up" question.

I chose a Thai restaurant near the office, aware that it was his favorite lunch spot. I was nervous about this meeting. I admired Mark. He was a wiz kid, technology wise, and I was thoroughly intimidated by his knowledge. We settled in a booth, and Mark looked everywhere but in my eyes. I was struck with the notion that he wasn't looking at me because he didn't like me. The kid thought I was a doofas. Far from stupid, I was just dealing with brand new territory.

"Mark," I said, "I'm a little confused as to why you haven't returned so many of my calls."

Mark's voice always surprised me. It was a very deep baritone and difficult to reconcile with his slight stature, balding head, pale complexion and blue eyes that swam behind very thick glasses.

"Roberta," he said, "I have tons of other work to do, although you might not realize that. Josh has me writing code to upgrade our billing procedures, and the sales department needs me to write a program so the independent reps can track their own orders and tons of stuff. Just because you're the boss's wife doesn't mean this web page is the most important project I have.

But then his eyes widened behind his glasses, as if he couldn't believe what he'd just said. "Not that I'd want to piss you off, of course. I can't imagine what you'd tell John about me or the whole department, for that matter." Suddenly it dawned on me that Mark thought I was a spy, out to gather information on his new department. In his mind, being in charge of the boss' wife had all the makings of a total nightmare. Yet he barely knew me.

I was relieved. My loud bawdy laugh began before I could stop it and, in a moment, Mark was laughing with me, unable to resist the moment of levity.

"Mark, is *that* the issue?" I said. "Me being John's wife? You think I'm going to discuss this stuff with him over dinner?" I laughed again. "You think I'm nuts, Mark? You think I don't know what I can't talk to him about? Listen if I report to you, my allegiance is to *you*. I have one person to satisfy, Mark, and that is you. Fire me if I don't do a good job. You can, honestly. I'll walk out without an argument and make sure you get no hassle from John."

His look was wary, but he allowed me to continue.

"I'm a quick study, Mark and, if you give me a shot at this, I won't let you down. I'll make you look good, Josh look good, and John will give IS all the support you need, based on performance. Mark, what I hear in the department or from you stays with me. Trust me on this. I'm on your side."

I didn't earn all of his trust that day, but Mark began to work more closely with me, gradually teaching me more. Finally, I was able to convince him that I was just Roberta, just one of the guys once again, doing a job like anybody there. I would actually be more advocate than critic, as they all came to realize. IS eventually had the largest budget of any department in the company.

Over time, Mark became my mentor and one of my closest friends. We lunched on average of three times a week and I came to love his wife and daughter. Together we were able to launch a website within six months and it even received some far-flung award when I showcased it at the next trade show. The objective of the website was to begin the process of going completely interactive within a few years and cutting mailing costs by half by making the sales reps' reports and specification sheets available online. I was to be a part of that and I was also responsible for updating the web page daily. It was a work in progress and it required my constant attention. It was a challenge and I loved it. Under Mark's direction, I excelled.

My next project was to launch a contact management program for the sales department; enabling them to synchronize customer information and schedule meetings with each other from anywhere they had access to a computer. This was difficult and required an exorbitant amount of my time, but I loved it. Nobody is more resistant to change or learning technology than sales people. I used to be one, so I understood. My success in this particular enterprise was largely due to my experience in both sales and my new area, IS. I proved myself to be an effective liaison.

Nothing suffered for it, either – I was still cooking, still entertaining, and still traveling. My luggage included a laptop computer now, enabling me to maintain my Wendall Industries work from most places we traveled. I just had longer days. I still sent two hundred and fifty Christmas cards every year, decorated the house for all occasions, had birthday parties for everybody, orphan dinners weekly, ran all the errands, handled the social schedule, fielded occasional calls from John's posse, was consulted regarding business trips, and managed an occasional blow job for John when required. That's what our love life had become. I didn't even think about sex much anymore. We were at the apex of his career. Who had time for sex? Multi-tasking was my life and I did it without thinking, but I couldn't determine a way to have sex, cook dinner, and conduct business simultaneously. If the desire were strong enough maybe I could have. I was that good.

CHAPTER 18

Because most of John's communications with me were routed through his personal assistant, Sally, she and I were practically best friends. When calling me from the office I would pick up the phone to Sally saying, "I have John for you. Hold for a moment, please." The corporate slut was treated just like any other business associate.

No matter how many times I told him it bothered me, it never changed. The corporate slut appreciated the respect; the wife was hurt by the cold indignity. Why couldn't he just pick up the phone and call me himself?

The respected corporate slut loved being around the office. I knew most of these men as long or in some cases longer than John. I was becoming the "go to" person to "get to" John, and I bought the entire concept without realizing the long-term impact. Anybody at Wendall Industries who wanted to sway John's opinion would approach me first, particularly if John was in a mood, which was becoming more frequent.

A typical moody day might find John in his office complaining loudly over a streak on his window the cleaner missed the night before. If one happened to intrude during this crisis of major proportion, a perfectly plausible inquiry might be met with a scornful, "It may take me a while to come up with an answer to a question that stupid. I'll get back to you." The derision painted so clearly on his face could reduce even his most competent manager to a cowering, incomprehensible idiot, stumbling over his words as he stumbled over his feet trying to escape.

These men took me to lunch, pulled me behind closed doors, and picked my brain searching for the approach that would net them their desired result. I was rarely wrong when predicting John's reaction or suggesting the right way to approach him. Being so often consulted made me feel important, and feeling important boosted my confidence. I may have been a corporate slut, but I was a confident one, striding into every new day gleefully keeping the secrets of John's employees, and with absolute certainty of my brilliance.

Yet any praise that came my way was terribly annoying for John. Knowing that I abhor public discord, he began openly demeaning me. He knew I wouldn't fight back and risk everybody's discomfort. I quickly learned to lob any praise I received his way. Whatever initiative had drawn attention to me, I gave him credit. "No, it wasn't my idea...." became a frequent refrain. It was easier than taking the insults John threw at me when I took a bow.

Despite my efforts, I still sometimes endured public degradation. One night we were driving home from a party with another Wendall Industries couple. It was late, and John was driving dangerously fast on an icy road. When I asked him to slow down, he turned all the way around in his seat to scream, "Shut up you fucking bitch!" I still remember the sour taste of that horrific humiliation. I actually cried from the shame of it. These attacks were always personal – directed at the wife, not the corporate slut. John rarely questioned my business acumen—in fact he relied on it—just my worth as a woman. Like a cat toying with a mouse he would bat at me, scratch me, pick me up, and shake the hell out of me without ever slaying me.

*

My closest friends, the Wrens from Cincinnati, were in Freshwater Falls with their family for their annual vacation.

It had been a grueling day. Blake and Mitch, the two oldest Wren children, had a small accident on the Wave Runners. Thankfully, neither child was hurt, but John was unhappy with the damage caused to his brand new, never-been-ridden toys. Every time a child would approach him with a request—innocuous trifles such as "Can I have a soda, please?" or "Can I use the fishing poles?" —he'd snap at them. I was busy trying to run interference, make sure the kids got what they wanted, keep John calm, and make Marie and Grant feel comfortable and welcome in spite of John's behavior. Scooping poop, in other words.

Consequently, I became the object of John's wrath. That was okay with me. Better me than the kids. I was used to it. I would have preferred he insult me privately, but that wasn't John's way. What would be the fun of that? "Roberta," John snapped, "When in the hell are we going to eat? What happened, Miss I'm-So-Organized? Did you lose your stupid menu planner?"

John turned to Grant for commiseration. "Can you believe she's so dumb she can't get a meal on the table without having to write everything down?" Instead of answering John, Grant looked to me, eyes questioning, expecting a retort worthy of the 'I don't take shit from anybody' Roberta.

Instead, I just ignored John. That particular day, I didn't want to exacerbate his pissy mood.

*

"Get that away from me," he said. It was just after dinner and I was serving dessert "I'm sick to death of that chocolate covered, chocolate chip cheesecake! Do you have to serve it every damn weekend? It's not that special, for God's sake...really, it's not. People won't tell you because they don't want to hurt your feelings, but you should hang this one up, Roberta."

The poor Wrens stared at their plates. We were all relieved when John pushed back from the table and went out for a walk.

Grant waited until everybody else was in bed. I was on the screened porch, both cats on my lap, legs propped on the ottoman, chain-smoking in an effort to relax. Grant folded his six-foot-three-inch frame into the sofa. Leaning forward, both elbows on his knees, he tried to make eye contact in the dark.

"Roberta," he said, "what the hell is wrong with you? How could you allow anybody to speak to you that way? What happened to the Roberta who never took shit from anybody? Where is the 'don't fuck with Roberta' Roberta? I don't like the way he treats you, I don't like it at all."

"He didn't mean it the way it sounded," I said. "Things are so busy at work because the company under his leadership is growing so quickly, and we've been on the road so much and there's lots of pressure, lots of guests, lots of entertaining. John and I don't have enough time alone and that's my fault for not scheduling it. I'm the one who does the scheduling, Grant."

Faintly aware that I was trying to convince both of us, the words continued tumbling from my mouth in between nervous puffs on my cigarette. Grant listened to all the nonsense, kissed me goodnight, and went to bed. I knew he didn't buy it. My exhaustion preempted any deliberation in relation to his words. Deep down I knew he was right, but I couldn't even begin to deal with it then. I'd have to figure it out later, I told myself.

CHAPTER 19

We were into our seventh year of marriage. The beginning of October 1992 John and I received an invitation from close friends for a "hat-o-ween" party for Halloween. Everyone was assigned a hat and had to choose an appropriate costume to accompany it. The invitation indicated that three couples were hosting the party and due to the size, the venue was The Italian Community Center downtown. The theme was clever. I saw the invitation posted on every refrigerator in every home we visited for a month.

The hat assigned to me was a straw hat with a price tag attached. John's was a top hat, which enabled him to wear a tuxedo. I dressed as Minnie Pearl of course, and didn't wash my hair so I could get the effect of her frumpy hair. I wore no makeup and looked perfectly ridiculous when I walked into the ballroom with two hundred people dressed in black tie shouting, "Howdeeee!" and "Surprise!" It was two months before my birthday, but this was my surprise fortieth birthday party. Everyone was dressed to the nines but I looked awful - like Minnie Pearl with dirty hair.

I was humiliated and in tears, and turned and ran out the door, intending to go home and change. Paul was the one to stop me, explaining that Lola had an outfit for me, complete with the appropriate undergarments and shampoo and makeup. It was too little too late—I'd already been thoroughly embarrassed.

In spite of the fact that many people told him I would be humiliated, John went ahead and executed his plan. Again, he made me look foolish, but how could I possibly complain when he had done all this for me? As often happened in those days, I felt foolish for feeling foolish. It wouldn't be right to call him an asshole, I told myself. Not after all this.

This line of thinking becomes a trap. I was the recipient of a grandiose and magnanimous gesture yet made to appear foolish, in this case, by the manner of my dress being discordant with the propriety of the event. What fashionable hostess extraordinaire would be caught dead without makeup and perfect hair unless the playing field was level and all her compatriots looked the same? If there is an escape from that trap, the door is so well hidden you cease to believe it exists.

Moreover, "all this" was elaborate and sophisticated. John paid for the facility to upgrade its sound system. He had a set constructed to replicate the "This Is Your Life" stage of TV fame. As I took my place on the stage, he, playing the role of John Edwards, introduced my mother, who he'd flown in from Hawaii. Next, my best friend from high school who I had not seen since we graduated in Louisville, Kentucky, glided out from behind the curtain. When my ex-husband walked out from behind the curtain, the room went silent. Terry and I laughed and held hands, as we had remained friends. His speech about me was the kindest of all.

Each table was set with forty magnificent pink roses – pink being my favorite color – and the ice carvings were of elephants with their trunks held high, another favorite of mine. There were gigantic blown-up pictures of me everywhere. There was the requisite naked baby picture hanging from the ceiling, and the high school prom photo. I was overwhelmed with everything.

All my friends from Ohio came to celebrate with me, as well as industry friends from all over the country. John read wonderful and flattering speeches from many people in my past and after the initial awkwardness it was a night of non-stop laughter and remembrances.

At the end, John led me onstage, pulled me to him, and said into the microphone, "I love you, Roberta. Happy Birthday." This was the John that made my heart swell. I was convinced that he really did love me. After all, he'd just said so in front of a few hundred people.

After dinner and the program, several hundred pink balloons were released from the ceiling and my favorite band in Milwaukee played until the wee hours. John arranged for shuttle buses to take people back and forth to the hotel where everyone was staying. The following morning there was a beautiful brunch at the hotel. It remains one of the most talked about parties ever.

Just when you're not sure where all the love went, it sneaks around the corner and pinches you. I fell in love with John all over again that weekend. It's what kept me coming back, kept me working hard, those moments when I believed he loved his wife. Love doesn't die suddenly; it chips away in small pieces like paint on a windowsill. Every once in a while, the windowsill gets a fresh coat of paint and it takes a while for the chipping to start again.

After these grand gestures, there were months of tranquility in our lives. I was so grateful for his effort to please me, convinced it was over the top love, I lavished him with praise, affection, favorite dinners, and-yes, his very favorite blow jobs. Life became as good as we knew it to be and we were as happy as we thought we should be.

Except when I wasn't. The tranquility would inevitably end and my times of happiness grew ever shorter. I had long wanted to say that

I was forty and fabulous. It's what I should have been, having danced through my twenties being perky and skated through my thirties being sassy. To be perfectly truthful, I was forty and fucked up. Maybe not fucked up entirely, but I was caught between sporadically being aware of my unhappiness, denial of that unhappiness, and backsliding into not being quite sure if I was unhappy. The situation was too daunting, too complex, and too painful to hold my complete attention. A random peek was all I would allow myself.

CHAPTER 20

John always wanted to purchase the property south of us in Freshwater Falls because securing it would restore the estate to its original size. The owner was an elderly man suffering from Alzheimer's disease, just recently diagnosed. John began talking with him about buying the land and a log cabin structure situated on the property. It was a situation requiring tact and delicacy.

We happened upon this gentleman in the grocery store in Freshwater Falls one Friday evening. His Alzheimer's was progressing, and when John and I approached to say hello and make nice, he seemed not to recognize us. John shook his hand and said, "It's me, John Wendall."

The gentlemen, stooped over with the burdens of old age, peered through his glasses and said, "John Wendall? I know him. Everybody thinks he's an asshole, but I like him."

I had to walk into the next aisle so I could laugh freely. How refreshing to hear it aloud from a person John couldn't denigrate on the spot. John needed him, or rather his property, and wouldn't risk losing it by insulting him. After regaining my composure, I rejoined them. John wasn't laughing.

We owned, or rather John owned, our old Freshwater Falls house, built in 1895. In addition he owned the house next door that his father and Emily had built. He had purchased it from Emily when his father died and she paid him a dollar a year in rent. The additional property, if we were able to procure it from the elderly, senile man, would give us a few thousand feet on the water and a compound to fit John's ego. Negotiations involved not only the man but his family and after several attempts and more time than anticipated, John's offer was finally accepted.

The log cabin was deemed uninhabitable and had to be demolished, and there ensued much discussion about which type of house to build. John originally intended to build a small A-frame structure to house company people from Milwaukee who traveled to Freshwater Falls regularly on business. At the time they stayed at our house. I had grown weary of a bunch of Wendall Industries employees or Wendall Industries customers staying in my house all week. By the time I arrived, I would have to rearrange and set up just to get ready to prepare for weekend guests. I could barely find things, and I was exhausted from attending to so many people's needs. I wanted to build our dream home, our retirement home, and finally have a house in which it was convenient to entertain. It only made sense, entertaining comprising a large part of our life. We could continue to have Wendall Industries employees stay at the old house.

I won that battle. The posse backed my position after many consultations and John finally acquiesced to building a party house. I couldn't lose with the posse behind me! I once jokingly asked John if I should call Raymond, the vice-president of finance, to ask permission to buy panty hose. I left the room before he could respond, afraid of the answer.

My office in Milwaukee was located adjacent to the master bedroom. One evening John was changing after work when I walked in and discovered a document in the middle of my desk. He spoke to me from the dressing room. "Michael wants you to sign that so I can get it back to him tomorrow."

I read it to discover that this document waived any rights I may have to the new house we were just beginning to build. I was stunned and once again crushed. It hurt to the bone.

I joined John in the dressing room. "You really don't think I'm going to sign this, do you?"

John concentrated on loosening his tie. "I don't know what it is exactly, Michael just asked me to have you sign it."

I explained the intent of the document, half hoping John had not read the agreement, would join my outrage and together we could would rip it up without delay. When he calmly continued undressing I flew into rage.

"I will never sign this paper, John! *Never*. If you go ahead with the house, I won't contribute to the decorating or building process and I will never live there." I was hysterical. "How could you possibly *not* want to share this with me? There is no 'I' in team, right? You *always* call us a team, John, always. This house is supposed to be a team effort."

Too late, he threw his hands in the air, feigning surprise. "Roberta, I didn't even read the thing, and it's been a bitch of day, so I'm not going to read it now. Before you get yourself worked up into frenzy, relax. I'll have Michael call and explain everything tomorrow."

"John, that's bullshit," I said.

"Roberta, what part of 'a bitch of day' didn't you understand? I'm tired, damn it. You know I wouldn't do anything to hurt you. Leave it alone. We'll resolve it tomorrow."

This type of conversation was his typical defense. He could never discuss any personal issue directly with me if it seemed it might result in confrontation. I had won too many confrontations. If there was a serious problem, he dealt with me through intermediaries like Michael or Raymond, and less frequently, Paul. Passive-aggressive behavior was perfected by John Wendall.

Michael came to the house the following day and confirmed the document to be a waiver of my rights to the new house. Anger couldn't begin to describe my mood.

"Here's the deal, Michael," I said. "The house is titled in both of our names, or John can deposit one million dollars in an account for me alone. It's half the estimated value of the completed house, correct? Two choices, Michael. He has two choices. If he elects to do neither, and I guess he can, he can build, decorate, and live in that nine thousand-square foot monstrosity by himself. I'll contribute nothing. I won't run the job, I won't decorate, and I'll certainly never live there. He can enjoy it alone."

Michael, to his credit, looked distraught, running his hand over his smooth, bald head. Keeping his head buried in a sheaf of papers assured that he couldn't make eye contact with me and I took this gesture to mean he was embarrassed.

"Roberta," Michael said, "I think John is afraid if he gives you a million dollars, you'll cut and run."

I turned and looked out over Lake Michigan, pondering. *Would you, Roberta? Would you take the money and jump a train out of town? How the hell did you get here anyway? You are dependent, girl, really dependent. When did you let this happen?* Yet, so intimidating was the thought of leaving, I discarded it like an insult from a person of no merit. It entered and exited my brain almost simultaneously.

In spite of my pleading, John would not discuss the issue with me. His lone comment was, "The lawyers are doing this to protect me and

I can't control that. Michael is a trustee of my estate. You'll have to change his mind, not mine."

Michael would call from time to time, but I held firm. My demands were unchanged and I wouldn't entertain further discussion.

"Please relay to your client that it isn't about the money, it's about our marriage," I said. "You know, Michael, the team. It's his word, not mine. It's what he calls us, you know." I made no effort to hide my biting sarcasm, but my stomach was in knots for all those months.

Hurt as I was, our lives were not remarkably changed in terms of work or entertaining. I still oversaw the website, I still organized and executed dinner parties, I still scooped poop when the need arose.

Six months later, I opened an envelope addressed to me that contained the title to our new house in both of our names. I called John immediately to tell him how much I loved him and to thank him. I cried, believing this to mean our marriage was the union he had always stated it was, privately and publicly.

*

This new project would be all consuming. We found the plans in a book, oddly enough, and it was a home that had been built in Florida. It was precisely what we wanted, with a master on the first floor and most rooms facing the water. We added an enormous screened porch facing the water and had three en suite guest rooms upstairs.

In addition, the library housed a Murphy bed and a full bath. Because John and I slept apart, the library became my bedroom. He insisted on keeping the master for himself. I had the master in Milwaukee, he stated, so this one was for him. What kind of perverse logic is that? I didn't tell my girlfriends about that disagreement. I don't know if I was more embarrassed by the fact we slept apart, or that I'd lost the fight.

Wanting the outside to appear old like our 1895 house, we opted for the same limestone structure with a slate roof. The appearance of an old house that was part of the original estate was imperative to John. It had to be grand. In addition, we made some rooms larger, moved a few walls, and added the all-important bar. This nine-thousand square-foot house was the conception and birth of a compound, made up of three houses and five acres of land that was later named "WendallWorld." The logo for WendallWorld became ubiquitous, adorning a large flag raised above our house, a plaque at the entry, and T-shirts that read "I'm going to WendallWorld" on the back. There were collared golf shirts with the logo embroidered on the pocket. The plush terry robes I placed in the guest rooms were embroidered with the logo, in a color that matched the guestroom.

We began this project in 1993 and it was an expedition, this house. It consumed most of my time and there were many days I traveled back and forth from Milwaukee to Freshwater Falls in the same day, a two hundred and fifty mile round trip, because John didn't like to be by himself. Unlike our Milwaukee house, he wanted approval rights on everything from wallpaper to draperies to chotskies. The new rule became, if he didn't like it, we didn't get it.

This resulted in countless trips to Chicago, home of The Design Mart, to return any sample he found unsuitable and to obtain others. He refused to accompany me, as he was too busy with the business. Emily was stunned by his boorish behavior.

She asked him one evening what was wrong with him. "Roberta has outstanding taste," she said. "Your father let me do anything I wanted in decorating the house. Let her do what she wants!" He paid no heed.

After the umpteenth drapery sample he declined and six trips to Chicago, I finally turned to him, shoved my favorite fabric in front of his face and said, "See this? Do you like it? No? Well you're going to learn to love it because this is what we're getting."

For a time, it silenced him. He hadn't been nearly as involved in the Milwaukee house on Lake Drive. I was so thoroughly accustomed to knowing what John thought, that this necessity to be immersed in the details of the interior design was a mystery to me. I didn't appreciate his sudden need to aid in the choosing of wallpaper and fabric. It would be five years before I fully understood his meddling.

*

Northern Wisconsin is beautiful and I fell in love with the area and our properties in particular. It was filled with towering birch trees, remarkable for their white trunks, and the hardwood trees, maple, oak, and sycamore. The waters of Lake Michigan more closely resemble an ocean, with blue water translucent in its cleanliness. Even the Bay side of the peninsula, where we were located, has clear, cold, water, but the Bay waters are milder than Lake Michigan. The pine trees surrounding our homes had been there hundreds of years and created a stately disposition to the entire estate property. It screamed *Tradition* emphasized by the limestone houses standing solid in the background.

The soil was perfect for my favorite flowers like iris, Queen Anne's lace, lily of the valley and hydrangea. Old-fashioned flowers suit me. I found comfort seeing the same flowers from my childhood home in Pittsburgh bloom in my garden in Freshwater Falls. It felt as though the flowers and I had traversed the years together. The flowers, unlike me, remained unscathed and unaffected by time, but seeing them blossom every spring conjured memories of feeling brand new as my bike came out of the garage for the first time since winter. Ahhh...freedom to grow and seek new soil.

Gardening became a passion for me, a quiet hobby that yielded so much satisfaction. It became an escape, a place to either put my thoughts together or toss them wholly asunder. My garden provided peace for me in an increasingly chaotic WendallWorld.

Every morning I awoke in Freshwater Falls, I found my faith. It was brilliantly presented in the rolling green turf and the riot of color scattered about the gardens. Weeds were surprisingly absent, as if afraid to poke their heads through the specially blended, bright green, perfectly manicured grass to ruin God's postcard. Viewing this miracle of nature evoked a prayer of thanks every day.

*

I believed that I had never lost my freedom, never lost my independence, never lost any part of what made me, me. I was still Roberta in my mind – self-determining, independent, and tough-minded. Not until I was very far out of the circumstance did I look back and understand how lost I already was. I was far too dense at that point to be afraid of the forest, because I had become so familiar with the trees. We have all heard the term total denial, and I owned it. I still firmly believed I was in control, when I had practically wrapped control in a gift box and given it to John.

CHAPTER 21

Shortly after the construction of the house began, John hired a famous architect from Fort Lauderdale to design and build his dream restaurant in Freshwater Falls. Knowing his desire to build a restaurant, the city approached him and asked him to be part of a downtown revitalization project. Restaurant consultants told him he couldn't make it here. And if conditions were perfect, never true in any restaurant operation, he might break even and this wasn't likely. I had operations experience and I, among many others, told him it was foolish.

John insisted on moving forward, ignoring all advice to the contrary, and I told him not to talk to me about anything concerning JR's On the Bay. JR's stood for John and Roberta, and was my idea. I may not have wanted any part of it, but I wanted my name on it, damn it. Opening this restaurant was the only endeavor in our marriage in which I did not support my husband. For the first time since we'd met, I was not the confidante I grew accustomed to being. Instead of being hurt, I was surprised to feel relieved. This was freedom, truly, with no demands made of me or my time pertaining to this particular project.

It was a five hundred-seat restaurant in a town of nine thousand people that swelled to a few million in season. The season in northern

Wisconsin is approximately six weeks. It was upscale in a rustic environment, with an American menu of steak, chops, and JR's signature ribs. The motif was nautical, with rough hewn timber interior beams and an aluminum roof. The centerpiece of the bar area was a large stone fireplace, making it cozy in the winter. It was directly on the water at the foot of the old bridge with an adjoining marina that we did not own or operate, and the new maritime museum was across the street. This restaurant was another monument to John's ever-expanding ego. It had become an ego that left little room for me, corporate slut or otherwise.

*

It's impossible to explain to even your most intimate of friends that your life is transitioning in a negative way when you're covered with jewels, jetting to places like Europe and Hong Kong, living in beautiful homes, and driving expensive cars. The task is made more difficult when you can't find the answers because you're not sure what the questions should be. *Shouldn't I be happy? We have all this stuff. Most people would be thrilled with all this stuff. I'm grateful, but am I happy? I don't really care about this stuff. Should I care about it?*

I found myself trying to find a way to measure happiness and determine how much happiness it would take for me to stay in the marriage. If I was cooking, I thought of it in measures. Did the cup have to be half-full of happiness for me to stay or would a quarter-full be sufficient? Was it time to leave if the happiness factor got to an eighth-full? Knowing that all relationships have ups and downs, how long should I give the cup to refill before deciding?

If I was working a spreadsheet, my thought process would go more to the percentage side. Did I need to be fifty percent happy, or would twenty-five percent do? Trying to measure my happiness became so confounding for me that I eventually abandoned the idea without ever finding an answer. Shit, it was just easier to be happy; happiness is a choice, after all.

*

It began as a tug, a slight head pain, or some sensation that wasn't identifiable. All of a sudden, tedium overtook me. I began bumping into boredom far too often to disregard the notion. In the midst of what I thought to be an intellectual conversation, I'd be hit with the realization that this person wasn't stimulating. Then I'd wonder when and how I'd *ever* found this person interesting. I realized I felt intellectually starved.

Then there was a kernel of an idea formulating that our friends may not have been our friends if they weren't paid to do so. They were employees. They put up with John's abuse because they wanted to keep their jobs. How did they really feel about me? I was the nice one. Of course they loved me, didn't they?

Many times I felt like an employee myself, albeit employee of the month, every month. In other words, I got the good parking space.

I earned my title. We had customers of the company in Door County for the weekend and after giving them the grand tour of their accommodations, my home, I overheard the wife remark to her husband, "I can't believe she doesn't have bottled water in the rooms."

Bitch, I thought, wearing my winning smile. "May I get you a cocktail, shrimp, cheese? I can bring it to your suite if you'd like to freshen a bit before dinner." Roberta - employee of the month.

"Jesus, John. I can't believe the balls! Brass balls! Do they think I *work* here? I mean, I do work here, but for Christ's sake, I don't *WORK* here!" I exploded. One of the rep firms was scheduled to bring all of their families for a long weekend, twenty people in total. They were to occupy all three houses. It was two days prior to their arrival and I had just received a fax listing the groceries they would be requiring.

"Roberta, it's not a big deal," John said. "Just run to the grocery again and leave it alone." The tone of his voice indicated he was trying to calm me. It was the same voice I was accustomed to hearing on PMS mornings, when my first words were apt to be "leave me the hell alone" or "don't you dare look at me like that."

"I don't think it's rude," he continued. "I think they're trying to help you by letting you know what they want. It's better than having a houseful of food they won't eat, right? You make everything a big deal, Roberta. It's not a big deal, just do it."

My tires screeched out of the drive as I headed to the grocery, my most dreaded chore, for the third time that week.

In addition, after these folks arrived, when their children objected to whatever I prepared for breakfast, lunch, or dinner, I quietly made another meal or two meals, whatever they wanted. Their parents voiced no objection nor came to my defense in any way. I was starting to hate this job more often than love it.

I have always dealt with stress by losing weight. I have never been able to eat when I am upset. My head and my gut are like identical twins, joined together in thought and behavior, like it or not. When the head isn't together, the gut bears the brunt. This behavior has been with me since childhood. When the stress is alleviated, the weight returns. With everything going on, it was no wonder I began losing weight.

"Look at her! You can almost see through her."

John was drinking coffee with the housekeeper while I straightened the pillows on the sofa. He was using her as his sounding board.

"I think she's anorexic, for God's sake," he went on. "What kind of a woman becomes anorexic with a lifestyle like this? What in the world does she have to be upset about?"

Finally he turned to me. "Are you anorexic, Roberta? Are you?"

My laughter was immediate and strident. "By the time the food gets to the table I have no desire to eat it. I go to the grocery store, place the food from the shelf to the cart, out of the cart onto the belt, off the belt into the bags, and back to the cart. From the cart, it traverses to the trunk of the car, from the trunk of the car to the kitchen counter, from the kitchen counter to the kitchen cabinets, back out of the cabinets to the pot, the stove, the oven, where it makes its way to the plates. At this point, I am sick to death of this food. I've had way too much contact with this food and want no further relationship with this stinkin' food!"

My delivery made even John laugh. It sounded believable, but the real truth was I had lost my appetite for more than just food.

CHAPTER 22

CHAPTER 22

My menstrual periods were barely an event for me, ever. Even as a teen I had experienced no difficulty. Suddenly, I was burdened by unbearably painful and very heavy monthly episodes that soon occurred every ten days.

I refer to 1994 as The Year of my Hysterical Hysterectomy for a few reasons. The first was my outright panic-stricken demand to be spayed. Second was John's lack of care for me. The latter would eventually provide a platform for my private comedy routine, performed for girlfriends only, entitled "Compassionate John."

*

"How come when we spayed the cat, she didn't lay on the couch for a week? What's the difference…cat…wife. An ovary is an ovary, right? The cat was jumping on my lap the next day. What's with you Roberta? Come jump on my lap. Here Roberta, here Roberta, come on girl". I would stride across the floor, protruding my butt, my shoulders sloping, as my friends roared with laughter.

My gynecologist/fertility doctor felt I should try one more G.I.F.T. procedure in an effort to achieve pregnancy. I was forty-two years old. The thought of being sixty years old and seeing my child graduate from high school was unappealing and I was beginning to think that God did not want John Wendall to procreate. Should the world have to handle another John Wendall? Should I?

Although Dr. Chang denied that all the infertility treatments had an effect, I still believe they created this problem. I finally told him, if he wouldn't perform the hysterectomy I would find a doctor who would. We had become good friends, Dr. Chang and I. Being his first G.I.F.T. patient I saw him almost daily for five years. We had developed a relationship of sorts, one of great mutual trust. Any woman who has been through infertility treatment establishes a vast self-awareness of her body and how it feels. I knew with certainty that my body felt sick with these monthly symptoms and Dr. Chang finally trusted those instincts. He agreed to do the complete hysterectomy using a laparoscope. A pioneer in this field, I had no trouble entrusting myself to his care.

Our next battle was about my being admitted to the hospital. I can't attribute the word "hate" to many things, but being admitted to a hospital is almost number one. I make no secret of it. Generally speaking, most hospitals won't take me after witnessing the hissy fit that ensues at the mere suggestion of my being an overnight guest. I wanted to return home the same day of the surgery, but Dr. Chang insisted I stay at least one night. We ended the argument by his agreeing that if I felt well enough, I could go home. He was certain I wouldn't. John and I were leaving for Italy three weeks after my surgery, so I was determined to heal quickly. Nobody can begin the healing process in a hospital bed. It is impossible to rest in a hospital.

Ok, hysterectomy scheduled, I now had to figure out how to tend to John's needs during another down time that was certain to cause him disquiet. I'd been sick before and knew better what to expect, or in John's case, what not to expect. I had to make it as easy for him as possible.

I prepared day by day menus and cooked three weeks worth of meals and put them in the freezer, with written instructions stating exactly how and when to cook them. I ordered the Christmas cards earlier than normal, had a few dinner parties prior to the surgery because I wouldn't be entertaining during my recovery or do all those corporate slut things that matter.

We arrived at the hospital at six o'clock in the morning; I was admitted and taken to a room. As I was donning the surgical gown, I suddenly became aware of a searing pain, though not of a bodily sort. This ache seemed to be centered in my soul. This was it, the very end – there would be no children, not even by accident. I knew this, of course, but once I put on that gown the finality of it sliced through me like a knife through sponge cake and my pain exploded forth in tears.

John threw his hands in the air. "What the fuck is it now?"

His exasperation, his monumental self-absorption, had an immediate calming effect. I no longer wanted to share any feeling, any emotion, any of my essence with the fool standing in my room. I recalled my last G.I.F.T. procedure. I was on the surgical table and they were just starting to administer the anesthesia. Dr. Chang was holding my hand and suddenly I grasped it tightly and said, "Please, if this sperm sample is no good, *please* run to the lobby and grab any man and get some good sperm. I mean anybody but you, because we know it can't be you." Dr. Chang is, of course, Chinese. I went under to sounds of laughter reverberating from the surgical room walls.

Now, I wished Dr. Chang had done that very thing. It was the same doctor, same operating room that morning, but when Dr. Chang took my hand that day, he leaned over and said, "Roberta, you need to be sure about this because we both know it marks the end of our efforts. No babies. Not ever. Are you sure? How's your head with that?"

I nodded in the affirmative, but I felt a tear slip. I was mourning the loss of a child I never was able to conceive or birth. A smaller portion of that sadness came from knowing my doctor was more in touch with what I was feeling than my husband. I was grateful that at least somebody was.

Unbelievably, I went home three hours post surgery. From the recovery room, they had taken me to my regular hospital room and laid out the rules. Eat this Jell-O, go to the bathroom and walk around the unit floor once and you can go. I still hold the record – the only patient of the hospital or Dr. Chang to undergo a complete hysterectomy and go home the same day. I was in the hospital at six o'clock in the morning and home in my bed at two-thirty in the afternoon. My mindset was that this procedure was no different from the four G.I.F.T procedures of the past. I wanted nothing more than my own bed and quiet. Frankly, since the lung surgery, everything else was just a walk in the park.

We arrived home to a backhoe and bobcats in the yard. John was staying home under the pretense he needed to care for me, but he had scheduled the new drain tiles to be installed in the yard that day so he could keep an eye on the work. Of course, he neglected to tell me of his plans. The majority of the yard had to be excavated and I need not tell you the noise that entailed. I wasn't shocked, I wasn't angry, I was resigned. John helped me to bed and headed outdoors.

"Roberta, I'm standing in the hospital room where you are supposed to be! I can't believe you went home. I only said you could because I was sure you wouldn't *want* to! It's insane, you being home so soon." Dr. Chang's clipped delivery conveyed his anger with me for leaving. I could barely hold the phone to my ear and I was still a little woozy.

"I thought we had this discussion in your office," I said weakly. "You said I could come home if I was up to it, so here I am."

"Roberta, you need to understand that this is very different from the G.I.F.T procedures. The incisions are the same, but you have stitches inside, holding your bladder in place and a few other things, too, and if you aren't careful, serious complications could arise. No stairs, Roberta, do you hear me? I can't believe you! I have never had any patient leave the hospital the same day of a complete hysterectomy. You're going to give me a heart attack, I swear!"

I had never heard him so irritated.

"No stairs, I promise, Dr. Chang. Don't have a heart attack – I'm fine, really. John is here taking care of me." I solemnly swore I would behave.

*

The fax machine was ringing non-stop, the phone was ringing uncontrollably and the doorbell wouldn't quit. I must have had twenty flower deliveries.

I crawled to the window, raised it, and shouted, "John, please come in here a minute. I need to talk to you."

He walked into the bedroom, his expression wary.

"Honey, please, I need to get some rest," I said. "Dr. Chang just called and he's worried that I came home so quickly. The fax is going nuts – better check it, the office may need something, and the doorbell is ringing non-stop. If you just take care of things for a few days, I'll get better faster, I promise. But today, especially, I need to get some sleep. Please just take care of things today."

He walked to the side of the bed, squeezed my hand, and kissed my forehead. His face collapsed in relief—he didn't have to actually take care of me. He took the phone off the hook, shut off the fax machine, and left a note on the door requesting flower deliveries be left on the porch without ringing the bell. That was the last time I saw him until dark. In John's dictionary, the word "empathy" is missing.

Later that same day, I woke hungry. The yard workers were gone and it was dusk. I kept calling for John, but he didn't answer. He couldn't hear me two stories below in the basement where his motorcycles had captured his complete attention. *What sick wife?*

Although forbidden by Dr. Chang to walk stairs, I gingerly made my way down the steps to the kitchen and made the dinner I had left for John to prepare. When it was done, I went to the basement door and called for him to come to dinner. To give him a modicum of credit, he was embarrassed. I just had major surgery that morning and was serving him dinner that evening. I learned not to expect a lot of support, but this was reprehensible. I ate every bite with intentional tears streaming down my face, hoping he would feel miserable at the sight of pitiful me.

I should be ashamed to tell you that I took a small amount of pleasure in his discomfort, but I'm not and I did. I wanted to kick him in the crotch and bring him to his knees actually, but I didn't have the strength. It made for great comedy, though, in later years when the pain seemed more distant.

CHAPTER 23

My mother was a case study in bad parenting. In spite of that or because of that, I'll never know which, I have known since very early childhood that her welfare would always be my responsibility. Rather than resent it, I accepted it long ago. Because of her fiscal irresponsibility and her emotional instability, I had been taking care of her for several years even before John and I married. This sense of duty affected only me, the youngest of her three children.

I forced John to buy her a condominium in Orange County and pay what debt she had to avoid bankruptcy in Hawaii. I purchased and remodeled the condo for her, bought all new furnishings, bought her a car, and moved her from Hawaii to California while fighting, almost to the death, with John. It was his money I spent and it was one of the largest battles ever waged between us.

"If I had known I'd have to support your deadbeat, irresponsible mother before I married you, I probably never would've married you."

We had recently celebrated our tenth wedding anniversary. John was in a tirade, upset that I was demanding more money for my mother's upkeep. I was still in my robe, cleaning the breakfast dishes before John left for work.

"I married *you*, Roberta, not your mother, your drug-addicted brother, or your lazy sister. I have no obligation to them. The answer is no, Roberta, no more money. You're not an only child – ask your siblings to help, or I will. There is no reason I should have to pay for everything."

My fury matched his in spades. "John, we've been married ten years. I work my ass off for you and do it for no money. Consider this my bonus. Everybody else at Wendall Industries gets a bonus. What do you think I should do, John, let her live on a park bench? You know neither Scott nor Sheila have any money, but certainly, John, call them. Let's see if you can get blood from a stone."

"Fine!"

The conversation was becoming circular, no resolve in sight so it was time to switch tactics. I calmed myself and lowered my voice. "We have the means, John. What is the big deal? The condo is in your name only and she'll most likely be there long enough for it to appreciate in value. You'll probably make money, John. Think about it."

"That's *I*, Roberta, not *we*!" he screamed. "*I'm* the one who makes the money, not *we*. *I* have the means, not *we*."

His face was so contorted I barely recognized him. The sunshine streaming through the kitchen window illuminating his puffed up cheeks made him appear positively unearthly.

"Fuck you, Roberta, fuck your mother, and fuck your whole damn family!" He slammed the door behind him and left for work.

He relented a few days later, not because he'd reconsidered or because he'd suddenly found some empathy, but because the posse told him he must. He was furious the group took my side, but from that point forward, I called Raymond, the vice-president of finance, when I needed more money for my mother. He sent the checks straight to me and I never asked John directly for money on behalf of my mother again.

My mother and I did not enjoy a close relationship but I felt a sense of obligation, instilled in me by my grandmother years ago. Knowing me to be the responsible one, she'd prepped me early. It was not a sentiment that either of my siblings shared. When John asked my sister for financial help in moving my mother, she said no, without hesitation. Good thing Grandma had prepped at least one of us.

*

Anger started to mask my growing sadness. It was the slow burn kind of anger. I was married, but alone. Being alone with someone is lonelier than being alone by yourself. It's an overwhelmingly heartbreaking feeling to be lonely in a marriage. I was responsible for the care of so many things. We never had a roof leak, a water heater break, or a frozen pipe burst when John was in town. I don't remember a major crisis in any house that happened when he was available to handle the consequences. In addition, keeping John happy by continuing to pump his ego was a never ending, non-stop function of my job and this job was twenty four/seven. Not only did my husband neglect me, managing so many things led to me neglecting myself. Self-neglect enabled me to avoid looking at my situation and evaluating it more closely.

A seed was germinating. I suddenly didn't feel so confident, and I couldn't solidify one thought pertaining to the next steps I needed to take. When it came to any business venture, I was two steps ahead of the next guy and I always had a Plan B. If Plan B proved problematic, I could formulate Plan C on the spot. Why couldn't I now solve the problems in my personal life? Why hadn't I thought to drop some crumbs along the way so I could find my way back? I thought I had been protecting myself by rationalizing away John's behavior but now I was beginning to feel lost—from myself. I found myself searching for mere crumbs of my old confidence and the way back to the sassy broad who wouldn't take shit from anybody. Memories of that woman were fading and I could barely remember her.

On one especially introspective day, the word "abuse" popped into my head. I shouted it down with all the mental muscle I could muster. So averse to being victimized by anything or anybody, I could not accept or even entertain the notion that my husband was abusive. *Not me*, I screamed silently. *Nobody will ever do that to me. I can take care of myself.*

I thought I was. I truly thought I was.

*

Did I mention I'm a happy person? I am. I balance hope and happiness with grief and sadness like a milkmaid carrying two buckets on a yoke across her shoulders. Thankfully, I am mostly very upbeat, always optimistic, and am quite often asked, "Are you ever down?" I reserve my sadness, most of the time, for my solitude, when I can examine, evaluate, and dissect it.

Like most women, I think every life issue to death in an effort to resolve it. It makes no difference what the issue is; the onerous thought process is the same. Mostly there is never absolute resolution. I just find a way to live with any given situation until I can find a way to make it better. I do make an effort not to burden too many others with the full weight of my emotions.

If overwhelming sadness or guilt is hard for me to bear, to ask a friend to share that grief would be an unfair burden. As for happiness, I don't fake it, truly. I am happy. Ok, not every moment, but happiness is a choice I make. I told myself how happy I was a great deal during those years. Not wanting to burden others by confiding my desperate unhappiness led to a skewed analysis of the situation and me. It should be illegal to self-analyze. I don't know anyone who has had a positive result. Analysis belongs to trained experts, yet recognizing the need for an expert requires clarity of thought. Impossible, at least for me at that time.

*

My job as a corporate slut was no different from before. I broke it down, set goals, decided where and what to tweak and resolved issues satisfactorily. I chose to be happy in this role and a good deal of the time, I was. I was also beginning to see the roles of corporate slut and wife morphing. They were becoming increasingly distinct from one another.

As John's wife, I was losing the self-assurance I hadn't been without since I left home at age seventeen. He could crush me with a look or send me reeling if he didn't like my dress. I was powerless to fight back when he threw a cruel remark in my direction. I didn't slander him in return and I didn't outwardly cringe or cry. I handled it just like I did when I was a kid and my classmates made fun of my stuttering—I laughed. I made a joke of things and my laughter made him appear funny and made me appear strong and impervious to his insults. I thought it was a win-win.

I can't tell you the countless praise I garnered for being able to handle John. "You're the only one who can handle John," people said. Or, "Gotta hand it to you, Roberta, it's remarkable the way you handle John." Or, "Let Roberta ask him, she's the only one who can handle him."

I was the only one who knew I wasn't handling John at all.

At a very formal dinner party in our home, a guest complimented me energetically on the meal I spent hours preparing. Before I could say thank you, John responded from the other end of the table, "Next time, use a little more basil. It definitely needs more basil."

When all eyes turned to me, I let out my famous, bawdy laugh. What else to do? In reality, that remark crushed me where in years past it wouldn't have fazed me.

I was now either a corporate wife or a corporate slut. A two-headed creature, my husband addressed each one separately, depending on his need or impulse of the moment. "This meat is overdone," he might crow to a dinner table full of guests. After their departure as I was bent over a sink full of dirty pots and pans, his arms would circle my waist. Playfully, he would lay his head on my shoulder, nose nuzzling my neck, hand provocatively creeping upward to fondle my breast as he whispered his urgent and impassioned plea. "Baby, can you help me with some marketing ideas for the new toaster? Please, baby." Segueing seamlessly from one role to the other had me wondering at times if my sanity was slipping.

Occasionally the roles combined. I could prepare a six-course dinner, arrange the flowers, set the table and light the candles with a telephone precariously perched on a hunched shoulder, chin anchoring the mouthpiece as I closed a deal complicated by shipping concessions or blanket purchase orders.

John purposely chose to demean the wife, but the corporate slut could still intimidate him. The wife had forgotten how to fight back and became vulnerable. He subjected the wife to very personal criticisms, but he rarely questioned the corporate slut and continued to defer to me in that role. Confidence belonged to the corporate slut alone, and emerged only when dealing with the business. I still was very much a part of his decision-making processes as they pertained to Wendall Industries.

The lack of compliments or praise for the wife was taking a toll. Our life was about the business and being the corporate slut was about the business. I wasn't so sure about the wife stuff anymore. There were times I did think about leaving, yet not enough to find my prenuptial agreement. I began to imagine life without John. Never for more than a few moments, however. It seemed as if that musing was some illicit fantasy. Then, as it is apt to do, shit happened, accidents happened and life happened-in a very big way.

CHAPTER 24

The next five years were remarkable for the frenetic pace, the tragedies they produced, and the cumulative effect on me, the marriage, and the business relationship between my husband and me. The retirement dream house was under construction, the restaurant being built, and the traveling becoming more extensive with the expansion of the international division. Nobody leaves when they are too busy to leave and the list of tasks was infinite. Deliberation of a failing relationship or a crumbling marriage never visits a busy mind. In the midst of all of this chaos, the tragedies started.

*

It began with Emily, John's stepmother, becoming ill. Emily's advancing age was exacerbating all of her chronic conditions. She lost her ability to swallow as her esophagus became rigid. And when blended food became difficult, the doctor insisted on inserting a feeding tube. Because we lived next door, it was easiest for me to care for her when we were in Door County.

I embraced the task because I loved her. Over the years she had provided me with so much history of John and his father and helped me gain insight into John's character, or lack of it, and the reasoning behind some of his behavior. She helped to soften me at times when I was scrounging for the key to the gun cabinet, intent on wearing widows black the very next day.

John had been good to her in many ways and chief among them was keeping her property in good repair. Understand that John owned this property and it was in his best interest to maintain it, but Emily chose to believe he did so because of his sense of duty to the family. He had no such belief. I have always believed his poor upbringing prevented him from attaching to anything resembling family. This included me, of course.

Emily ruled the family – her three children, their spouses, and her grandchildren. John, as her stepson, was included. Her word was law and noncompliance would never be considered. If you did defy Emily's wishes, you'd suffer the consequences. It wasn't anger, it was coldness. And it didn't feel good when Emily froze you out. The length of time depended on the infraction. Age has a direct effect on flexibility and Emily became less flexible the older she became. She deserved to have things her way and she carried no guilt with that.

One afternoon, I was keeping Emily company. She had become more ill and we were sitting in her bedroom, her in bed, me in the wingback chair, watching her favorite soap opera. It was a dreary fall day in September, cloudy with intermittent sprinkles of rain. The brightness of the fall tints had dulled for lack of sun. The trees, normally alive with color this time of year, looked plain dirty.

She suddenly muted the volume on the television and began speaking to me in a weak voice. "Roberta, I don't want to live like this any longer. I have no quality of life. I don't enjoy going out to eat anymore because I can't eat, and my hearing has gotten so poor I can't hear conversations. I want to move on to the next life. I want to see Gabe again." She reached for my hand, and with a slightly stronger voice, told me she needed my help.

"What...what exactly do you need me to do?" I said. I patted the pillows behind her and helped her sit up.

"I'm not sure yet, but I do know I can't deal with my own children about this. They won't understand my desire to die. Promise me Roberta, this is between the two of us."

I swallowed hard. "Emily, they've published several books about this. Before you make a decision, let me get some of them. We can read them together, talk about it, and then you can make up your mind. How would that be?"

She nodded her head, patted my hand, and drifted to sleep. But not before she whispered, "Thank you Roberta, I love you, you know. I really do."

The next day I brought her the books. She read the material, found merit in the reasoning and method, and began collecting her sleeping pills as instructed. She wasn't sure when she would execute her plan, but she was ready. I promised her I would help when needed. I believed in her right to make the decision and didn't tell John, per her instructions. It was a burden, this secret, as one can imagine. I could handle just a little more stress. Sure I could.

*

I couldn't be in Door County all the time – John was too demanding for that–and as with most families, Emily's own children didn't or couldn't accept how dire her condition was. It's easier to deal with these situations when it isn't your own mother. Emily's care fell to me. Her feeding tube required cleaning every morning and evening and she was uncomfortable doing that herself. I did it most days and when I couldn't, a friend or sometimes a county nurse would be there.

I began insisting that we look for a paid companion for Emily. Her daughter was not in Door County full time, her oldest son was in Toronto and her youngest son in Chicago. She had a granddaughter in Door County and Jemma did all in her power to be there as often as she could. Given her time demands, she was remarkable. She owned a retail clothing store and had two young children at home, both born very prematurely and in need of care, and still she managed to spend a great deal of time with her grandmother.

I contacted an agency in Milwaukee that specialized in such companions and began interviewing. I wasn't blood family, and I was careful to dance around the toes I might stomp by being involved. I did not want to upset her children, my in-laws. Emily herself was open to the idea of a companion, as it was her desire to remain in her own home and she could afford to do so. She helped convince her children that my involvement was at her bidding. I promised the family I would work with the agency, conduct initial interviews, and only bring them what I thought to be viable candidates. It was very time-consuming but I finally found a companion who met the approval of all her children, including John. I moved Emily's new companion, Freda, from Milwaukee to Door County myself.

It couldn't have happened at a better time. Emily became weaker and more ill and was hospitalized several times in the next weeks. She reminded me many times of my promise not to let her linger and aid in her exit if needed. In turn, I made her promise to delay that exit until John and I returned from Italy. We were scheduled to leave in a few weeks, and we had to make a trip to Orlando prior to that. My intent was to give her a purpose to live a while longer and I wanted to be sure her desire to die wasn't solely depression, a treatable illness.

*

The evening before we left for Orlando, John and I were having dinner in the lake room.

"John," I said, "I think I should stay here while you're in Orlando and be with Emily. She's getting worse and I'm worried. The last few times we spoke, she was complaining that Freda was becoming less attentive."

It was nearing the end of daylight savings time and the days were getting shorter. The shadows making their way through the lake room made John's profile appear as if in silhouette.

"For God's sake, Roberta." He rose to put his dinner plate on the counter. "You're the one who hired Freda, told all of us you *loved* Freda, and now suddenly you don't trust her?"

"I don't know, honey. Emily's not a complainer. I feel so uncomfortable leaving…it's a gut thing, ya know?"

Unexpectedly the wood floor bounced and the noise from his pounding shoe made Porsche, my kitty, leap from her perch in alarm.

"Roberta, you are not staying home with Emily! We are paying a companion, for God's sake. That's the point, remember? You are coming to Orlando with me, period."

"John, it's only a three day trip…you can do without me, can't you?" I made my voice soothing, hoping to calm his rising anger.

"No, Roberta, I can't, I *won't*. If you don't go, I won't go." He was in full pout.

"Honey, you have to go. You're on the Board of Directors and this is the annual Board Meeting. They need you."

"And I need you, Roberta. We have a suite and we're having a cocktail party after the Board Meeting. This is what you are supposed to do, Roberta, as my wife. This is my first year on the Board of this organization and we're a team, remember? Everybody expects to see you there. I don't want to do this one alone."

The tone of his voice was demanding in a vulnerable way, like a child unwilling to surrender his binky. That vortex of need always drew me in, like a penny sucked into the car vac.

God I was tired. I was surely too tired to fight with him. I called my sister-in-law from Chicago and asked her to go to Door County, and although hesitant, she complied.

We left for Orlando, checked into the hotel, and within hours got the call to come home. We were told that Emily probably wouldn't last another day. My instincts had been right and I felt compelled to remind John of that on the flight home. I reminded him several times. The "I told you so" didn't provide the comfort I intended, however; I had never been so sorry to be right. We arrived in time for me to retrieve the pills she had so carefully hidden from all but me, and Emily died peacefully surrounded by her family. The promise and its fulfillment stayed between us only, exactly as she wished.

The funeral was two days later and we spread Emily's cremated ashes over the water behind the houses. I always did love her presence there, floating in that water. Once in a while on a very calm day, I would dangle my feet in the water while sitting on the dock and her face would float up at me with those blue eyes still twinkling. I knew she was content to be on the other side and I was pleased to have been of service. At the time, however, I felt this sorrow deeply. Emily in many ways was the mother I would never have. She was a compatriot, keeper of secrets, a teacher and a mentor, and she loved me without hesitation or qualification.

Conversely, John had to invoke his sadness. I could see that it was an effort. We left for Italy a week after the funeral and John was business as usual. He was impatient with my grieving, so I tried as hard as I could to hide my sadness. To him, when you're dead, you're dead – just move on and forget about it. John's reaction to any death was abnormal. He thought it best if he could make everyone laugh, but his humor rankled of impropriety, bordering on the macabre and rarely drew laughter. He was a mess at a funeral. However, this particular death and his inability to grieve, or allow me to grieve, astounded me. If he even saw a tear, I received a look that would make me wither. *It's over,* he was silently saying, *get on with it.* Bearing this sorrow in solitude was easier than dealing with his irritation at my sadness.

Backward glances net the most insight, and from this distance I can now see that at this juncture it had become terribly important it to please him. I'm not sure it was the pleasing as much as the avoidance of conflict. I was becoming less willing, on a personal level, to fight for me, the wife. Peace, yes peace, was becoming important.

Maybe it was the hormones again, longing to rest after decades of being so active. Maybe it was just getting older and wanting the serenity age seeks. Maybe I was just exhausted, unwilling to wage a battle for small victories, or risk losing a war at the cost of my feminine pride. At any rate, I had never given much thought to peace before. We were volatile. Our marriage was volatile. Peace wasn't something I sought, or felt I needed until now. My greatest joy became Sunday afternoon in Freshwater Falls when all the guests left. I would sit on the massive screened porch, both my cats curled peacefully beside me, the Sunday paper in my lap, and the beautiful water sparkling before me, sailboats gliding by. I would not even allow John to play music. That Sunday silence became the most beautiful sound of my life.

Yet on the business level, the corporate slut was in the mud daily, fighting for the success of the company. I had no problem calling John on any move I judged inappropriate. I was comfortable in this arena. I knew how to do this, how to coerce, pinch, or firmly state an issue to elicit a positive response from him, or a change in action. He was equally submissive and combative, depending on his mood, but backing down was never an option for me. I won most of those battles and was applauded endlessly by his posse and employees alike, but always out of his earshot.

It never occurred to me to call them out or use them to back me. I was capable of standing on my own, and I knew the cost to them would be intolerable. They could lose their jobs.

Again, being results-oriented, I didn't mourn the battles I lost. I merely put them on a shelf for another day, another mood, when I knew victory could be assured. I had come to love this company and its people and I fought for its success and their happiness. I felt duty bound but can't recollect when that started happening. I marveled at how these people, these employees, these friends had such fear of John, and I used to ask them repeatedly, "Why are you so afraid of him? Tell him to go blow."

Their response was always the same. "Yeah, that's easy for you to say because he can't fire you."

That's what I thought, too. I never thought of John as a powerful man. Everyone else did, ergo their fear, but I didn't realize until much later how much power he truly wielded. I'm not sure that if I had paid more mind to that power it would have changed things, but I think not.

CHAPTER 25

Spring of the following year brought the completion of our new home and the completion of JR's On the Bay, the restaurant. I knew little of the restaurant happenings because I chose not to. The new house and other life issues had moved to the forefront.

It was the nineties now and the new feminism allowed that women couldn't do it all or have it all. This of course, did not apply to my situation. As usual, I was disharmonious with the movement because I wasn't trying to balance a career and children. Then again, maybe I was. Who was a bigger child than John? He was a kid dressed in a navy blue pin-striped suit, and managing him was the most difficult job of my life. I was silently seeking affirmation from a non-existing peer group.

Chief among the life issues was my brother's diagnosis of stage-four lung cancer. I flew to California early that spring to meet with the oncologist and my mother and brother. We were told he had a year on the outside, if he elected to undergo chemotherapy. He chose to do so. He was forty-six years old and lived in Orange County, California, close to where we had recently moved my mother. He and his second wife, Randi, had two young children. In addition, Scott had an older son from his first marriage, Sam, who still lived in Cincinnati.

Family responsibilities always fell to me, even though I am the youngest. My mother had passed maternal duties to me years ago. It was left to me to coddle, cajole, decide, and generally keep the peace.

My brother's wife and my mother hated each other openly and it fell to me to remind them that it was about Scott and not their petty power struggles. As always, I was the pooper scooper.

*

It was later that spring, after arriving in Orange County that I chose to rent a car and drive to my brother's home. It was to be a short visit – two days – and my mother didn't like driving to the airport to retrieve me. I could hear them screaming at each other as I parked the rental car in the driveway. I hurried through the front door, hoping to diffuse another confrontation before it became unmanageable. My mother was standing in the middle of the living room. It was wall to wall clutter with newspapers strewn everywhere, toys overturned all over the floor and ashtrays that must not have been emptied for days. The windows were tinted brown from the build-up of nicotine. My mother was wearing the look that had grown so comfortable resting on her face—contempt and condescension tied up neatly in a sneer—and she was waving a stack of bills at Randi.

"I did *not* raise my son in a pig sty, and look at how you make him live!" she yelled. "This is deplorable. And look at these bills. You don't work! He's sick, Randi, or have you forgotten? Get off your fanny and pay these things before they turn off the electric or phone. He can't do it right now. *You* have to do it. What's wrong with you? I swear...I can't figure you out. You should be ashamed."

Randi's face was stone-like, as though she had lost her hearing, but I knew that behind her mask was an unleashed fury. Her bleached platinum hair was showing more dark roots than normal, for lack of attention. I wasn't used to seeing her void of any makeup and the effect was startling. She looked exhausted. Before she could answer, I jumped between them.

"Mother, stop." I held up one arm to her and another to Randi. "I'll help clean. Let Randi be with Scott and I'll look at the bills and organize them so she can pay them later. It's not a major deal. The two of you are only making the situation harder for Scott. He's dealing with enough right now...can't you call a truce for a while? Aren't you both taking your eye off the ball here? This is about Scott. Mom, stop screaming about what needs to be done and help do it. Randi, stop giving her so much shit to scream about. Is everybody clear here? Do we all get it?!"

This was a common occurrence and I found myself standing between them, arms held out, being the stop sign more times than I care to remember.

*

I flew to Orange County at least once a month, sometimes more if needed, and again began neglecting my duties as the corporate slut. John could not understand the stress I felt, or he chose not to, and he had no patience for my sadness. I began crying frequently over minor things that had little or nothing to do with Scott and it made John crazy. He felt that Scott was a drug addict so his loss would have no adverse impact on the world and, therefore, it shouldn't have such a great impact on me. When he verbalized that thought, thinking I should agree with his logic, I was rendered speechless.

My big brother was three years my senior and we were close growing up. In fact, I idolized him in all the ways that little sisters can. He was big and handsome and smart. He loved me and protected me until cocaine took over his life. It's difficult to know how or when his train left the tracks. His adult years as an addict now outnumbered his youthful days as a loving big brother, but those youthful days were all I could remember. Some of my tears were for all those things that could have been had our lives moved in a different direction. We have all shed the "what if" tears, even though we are powerless to change the past or the current outcome. I couldn't stop thinking about how sad it was to die with so many regrets. Even with no conversations regarding those things, I knew Scott had many regrets.

*

It was shortly after Scott and his first wife Lucy had decided to divorce in 1979, when one Saturday night around midnight I picked up the phone to hear Lucy crying hysterically. Scott had taken Sam, his two-year old son named after my father, for the night. When she called to check on them she could tell that Scott was high. Afraid to go herself, she asked me to please get my nephew and bring him home.

When I arrived at the house Scott was renting, I saw Sam, not quite two years old, lying on the floor asleep in front of a blazing fire from a fireplace with no screen. There was an overturned bowl of cereal at his side. A log could have rolled out of the fireplace and injured him. And he was given cereal for dinner? I unwisely lost my temper. Scott was so stoned, he could barely stand. I was screaming and yes I do mean screaming at my brother, sorely distressed at his lack of responsibility. As I turned and saw his face, I began regretting my outburst. He was heading towards me in a rage, and I knew I could not physically defend myself. I knew what was coming.

I let those blows rain on me. Again, I had to stand proud and pretend it wasn't raining. To fight back would have enraged him further.

He hit me so hard on the back of the head I fell forward to the floor and broke my eyeglasses. I stayed there, rolled into a ball, as he continued to kick me. When he tired of that he got down on the floor on top of me and pounded my back with his fist until he finally broke his wrist. Had he been sober, he might have killed me. Worn out finally, he passed out and I picked up my nephew and drove him home. Sam never woke, thankfully. I would hate for him to have that memory.

The following day my brother phoned in tears, full of apologies with strong professions of love. He had just returned home from having his arm put in a cast. He couldn't remember hitting me that hard, he explained. I told him that I was out of his life forever if he did not agree to go to rehab. He agreed, I made the arrangements and I checked him in later that same day. I did the intake with the counselors; I agreed to go to A.L.A.N.O.N. and attend any support meeting where a family presence would be necessary or helpful. It was a thirty-day in-house program.

When I called to explain the situation to my mother, she said she was sorry to be so far away and to give the counselors her number in case they wanted to ask her any questions. I was taken aback at her detachment. Apparently, I was in charge. My sister adopted the same attitude. She didn't need to come to any meetings, did she? Wasn't I already doing that?

*

Scott was never able to fully embrace sobriety and as a result, our adulthood relationship was more estranged. We didn't speak at all for a few years, but had reconciled when my mother finally moved from Hawaii to California to be near him. John only met him once and spoken to him very little. John's coldness came from ignorance of my brother, and intolerance of anything outside his profession or company family.

I had to convince John to allow me to invite Scott and his wife to our new home in Freshwater Falls for a long weekend. It meant bumping some company guests to make the accommodation. He may have thought my tears would decrease if he finally caved to the request so he finally did. He deeply resented paying for the tickets, though. I had to raid my milk money.

Scott was already undergoing chemotherapy and was sick, but it remains one of the most memorable weekends of my life, bittersweet, as one might expect, and filled with memories and tons of laughter. My brother and I knew it would be one of the last times we could be active together. We took full advantage by doing everything physical we could – jet skiing, boating, biking, tossing the football, even wrestling, and the playful jabbing that all siblings have mastered over centuries. We were the kids from Pittsburgh, in the street playing kickball again. Nobody cried that weekend and John, to his credit, made no demands of me, apparently relieved that I had stopped crying. The day after Scott left, it was business as always – no dallying. He had given me my weekend off with my brother, but it was time to get back to work. We had company coming.

*

It was a few months later and I was scheduled to leave for Orange County in a few days. After my return, we were scheduled to leave for Paris to attend a conference. My freezer was empty and it was my day to batch cook. It was in this way I could accommodate John's last minute dinner guests - the two o'clock in the afternoon call saying "Rick or Lou or Mark or all of them are coming for dinner, ok?" and make sure we had homemade food when I was too busy to cook from scratch.

I batch cooked every three months or so. I started at the grocery in the morning, and spent the day cooking multiple items to freeze and cook at a later time. These usually consisted of a few lasagnas, extra meat sauce for spaghetti, linguini, or stuffed shells, navy bean soup, Carolina chicken stew, wild rice soup, a few meat loaves. Point being, it was a lot of food.

This had been a particularly demanding day. I had been trying to cook and my mother and sister-in-law, Randi, had called a dozen times for me to settle whatever quarrel they deemed important at the moment. My brother attempted to rip out his catheter, my sister-in-law did not want to diaper him, and my brother didn't want my mother to diaper him. He was urinating from his bed onto the wall. Get the picture? I was in the middle, but thousands of miles away; there was yelling, screaming, crying, accusations flying, and I was trying to cook, referee, take calls from John in between, and maintain my judgment. When John arrived home, there was not one pot or pan or cooking utensil clean in my kitchen. There were cooked items in containers, some not, some still on the stove and I was sitting on the floor in front of the kitchen sink, head held in my hands, crying convulsively and unable to speak.

He took me by the arms, lifted me from the floor, carried me upstairs, undressed me, and put me into the bed. Not a word was spoken. I fell immediately into that deep sleep only depression can bring.

When I awoke in the morning, John had left for work. It was rare I did not see him off in the morning. I walked downstairs and beheld a spotless kitchen. He had done it all. During the course of our marriage, this was the greatest and most precious gift he ever bestowed upon me.

These were the times that made me stay. If he could do all this, clean up my mess and not blame me or complain, he surely did love me. He must. As long as he loved me, I had reason to stay.

Between Scott's visit with us in August and his death in January, there were many trips to Orange County. I broke up many a brawl between my mother and sister-in-law, and the holidays that year were particularly poignant with all of us together in Scott's home. In between, there wasn't any time off. John always had a list of things that I needed to get done, trips to make, dinner parties to hold. Stress became *STRESS*.

When my brother passed away, John gave a comical eulogy and dubbed it a celebration of Scott's life. The term was trite and the eulogy was tripe. John was drunk. He drank through the funeral and offended a few of my brother's friends, and outwardly ridiculed my sister-in-law's family in that obnoxious way he was beginning to trademark. I was too busy to care much. Between the funeral planning and organizing, and standing between my mother and sister-in-law in my role as stop sign, all of my time was occupied.

CHAPTER 26

In May, there was to be a pre-grand opening for the restaurant, followed on the same day by an open house at our new home for industry people only. The following morning we would leave for Chicago to attend the annual National Restaurant Association trade show over the weekend and then return to Freshwater Falls on Monday for the public grand opening of JR's that evening. There would be a ribbon cutting ceremony with the mayor, the press and thousands of local people invited for free food and drinks.

My emotions were in shambles. My brother had been gone a short three-and-a-half months, and I was dealing with my mother who called daily so that I might share in the loss of her son and comfort her accordingly. She forgot he was my brother—reminiscent of the time after my father's death, the loss belonged to her alone. My sister was no help. She actually compounded the situation by not taking any of mother's calls. I wasn't given any time to grieve because mother was so hard to manage and our lifestyle didn't allow it.

Because of all my family difficulties and the upcoming frantic summer schedule, made more frantic by the opening of the restaurant, I asked John if I could be excused from working the show this year. He refused. People would miss me; people would ask for me. He needed me in that booth. There was no sick leave for the corporate slut, no personal days.

I graciously stood at the pre-opening of JR's and dutifully thanked everyone for helping make my husband's dream come true. I looked the part, said the right words, and then did the same when one hundred and twenty people toured our new home. I conducted tours, served drinks, told the jokes, hugged my husband, looked proud, and did my job. I worked the booth that weekend for the company, manned the hospitality suite for employees and customers and then rushed back to Freshwater Falls where I was photographed with my husband cutting the ribbon for the opening at JR's, and having a conversation with the new chef and the staff. People started arriving in droves – not many can resist free food and drinks, and a fireworks show. We had approximately eight thousand people, the newspaper said, in a town of nine thousand. I made the rounds introducing myself, wore that smile, laughed as expected, never sat down, and never ate.

Suddenly it became apparent that I would no longer be able to shove a baseball cap on my head Sunday mornings so I could get pastry at the bakery. My days of relative anonymity were over. The entire town knew John, but I intentionally kept a low profile in Freshwater Falls. I wanted to avoid being like the bearded lady in the circus with people always asking, "Can we see her…the woman who married John Wendall? Is she normal in every other way?" The most distressing revelation of the evening was the realization that my role had been suddenly expanded without my permission.

As John's wife, I was angry. I wanted no part of this new venture, much less publicly, and I was hurting terribly because of my brother's death and my mother's craziness and my sister's ambivalence. I had given up looking for my knight, knowing he was non-existent, but my knees were beginning to buckle just a little from bearing the weight of my own burdens alone.

All the same, the corporate slut would never consider not doing her job to the absolute best of her ability. When John insisted I work the show that year, I was disappointed but didn't argue. I never even considered fighting for the requested time off. I would work it all in and do whatever had to be done for my husband and his companies. I had a smile on my face and a ready handshake, always, for my job. Give the man credit, he had trained me well and I had shown him exactly how to do it.

*

Something prevented me from leaving. The rare moment I had time to think about the possibility of leaving, it was in general terms and not in a serious way. Looking back, I see that I wanted to punish John, not leave him. *Let him see what his life would be without me...hah! He has no idea what an asset I am...he can't possibly do this without me.* It was rather childish thinking, like making your parents pay by running away because they wouldn't allow you dessert after dinner.

I couldn't leave tomorrow, because tomorrow I was having company, or we were having a big party next month, or the holidays were coming, or we had guests for the next few weekends. I had no answers for the flurry of pressing questions. When was the right time? Would there ever be a right time? Where would I live if I walked out the door tomorrow? Should I move back to Cincinnati? What would my life be like? What would I do? What about my friends here? Should I stay here? I'd miss all my friends and the summers in Freshwater Falls. Would I miss John? *Could* I miss him? Tough as he was, I think I probably would miss him. He needs me too much. Wouldn't that be comparable to taking a dog into the woods and abandoning him? I can't do that. Can I? No, I can't. Can I? No...

As if he knew what I might be thinking, there would always be something to remind me of why I fell in love with him and how acutely he depended on me. It could be an undeserved slight directed at him that made me run to his defense like all mothers protecting their defenseless children. Or the surprise fortieth birthday party, when I fell in love with him again, or after an especially lavish or considerate gift-such as the car I wanted that just showed up in the driveway with my name on the title. There was always a good reason to stay, and never a good time to go.

CHAPTER 27

JR's had been open just four months. I paid it little heed, with the exception of eating there. It provided me respite from always cooking for our guests, and we regularly hauled our weekend parties there for dinners. But I never entered JR's with my restaurant eye – the eye trained to notice everything about any operation. I purposely kept that eye closed.

On one of my cherished Sundays when the guests had all gone and I was so enjoying the silence, John marched in with a parade of business associates. They announced that JR's was alarmingly in the red. After asking, consulting, and discussing the issue with several industry people it was decided that "Roberta should get involved."

God I hate that term – get involved. With John, it always meant running something, bailing him out of something, or taking the blame for a poor decision. (The only decisions I got credit for were the ones that didn't work out.)

At this point when I thought about the word involved, I hoped it might mean involved in an affair with another man. The wife part of me was craving some positive attention. I had given the idea some semi-serious thought, finding it so pathetic I had named my vibrator in an effort to get more personal with my lover. An affair didn't happen then, or ever. I never could find the time. I got involved with a restaurant instead.

I opened the books – what a mess I discovered. Food costs, paper costs, labor costs, were all reeling out of control. I packed up the kids (my two cats) and moved to Freshwater Falls full time. John joined me on the weekends, when I had to quit working long enough to work—entertain, that is. I left for the office by six-thirty in the morning and returned around eight o'clock in the evening. I had a full-time housekeeper who arrived at the house daily at seven in the morning and I didn't see her for a month. I ran two o'clock in the morning raids to see if the kitchen had been shut down properly and take random food inventory to detect theft. I conducted employee meetings, fired the chef, fired the manager, and went about the business of running a restaurant. Having been involved in operations early in my foodservice career, I already knew I hated it. I really hated it. John knew I hated it, but as always, I gave two hundred percent to this new job. Somebody had to do it and John had neither the time nor expertise. Corporate slut expanded. No raise. And worse, no time off.

The weekends were still booked with company and although I cooked fewer dinners, I still cooked most evenings, still did the shopping, and still hauled wives to every quaint Door County shop on the Peninsula. I still had to smile before my morning coffee, comb my hair before I left the library where I slept, and always be "on" in addition to being "on it."

*

It was six o'clock on a Saturday evening and the plan was to dine at home. There were ten of us. I was just starting to prepare the meal and set the table when the phone rang.

It was Daryl, the assistant manger. There was a crisis at JR's.

"Roberta, sorry to bother you at home, I know you have company," he said, "but Roberta, I quit. You'll have to get somebody to cover my shift tonight. I've had it."

I could hear John and our guests on the screened porch explode with laughter. Somebody must have told a joke. What I would've given to be in a room full of friends, laughing at a good joke.

With the phone resting on my left shoulder, I began rubbing my eyes with my right hand. All of a sudden, I had a terrible headache. I reached for a cigarette, lit it, and inhaled deeply.

"What happened, Daryl?"

"Roberta, I can't talk about it on the phone. Can you just meet me for a few minutes at The Perk?" This was our local coffee shop downtown.

"Sure Daryl, no problem. Give me a second to tell John and I'll be there in five minutes."

I hung up and walked to the porch. "John, that was Daryl on the phone. There's been some kind of snafu at the restaurant and he's threatening to quit, right this minute. I have to run and meet him at the Perk and see if I can defuse the situation. I haven't got anybody else to work his shift tonight, unless I do!"

"Really?" John turned to me, still laughing from the last round of jokes. "I guess you need to do what you need to do, Roberta. I'm sure you'll handle it. Take your time...you guys aren't starving are you?" He raised his glass, brimming with scotch.

"No, no problem," they said, almost in unison.

John returned his smile to me. "Hey Roberta, do me a favor and cut up some more cheese and sausage. That should hold us until you get back. Thanks, honey."

It took about two hours to talk Daryl down from the ledge. I don't even recall the source of his upset, it was so trivial. He did return to work that evening and was with JR's for a long time after that emergency. One of the reasons I so dislike operating a restaurant is the level of drama always present in its personnel.

It was eight o'clock before I was able to return home. I found the state of my kitchen and meal preparation exactly as I had left it. John and our guests were still having cocktails and didn't really care – they were all drunk by now. We finally ate at ten o'clock and I was overwhelmed with fatigue, but still laughing. The most important point was our guests and John had a fabulous time. *Job well done, Roberta.*

I was in Freshwater Falls for nearly eleven weeks without returning to Milwaukee. I needed to get home even though the restaurant was still on very shaky ground.

JR's was now firmly in my To Do column. If I wasn't physically there, I spent hours on the telephone with the restaurant personnel, the manager, or the chef. I was frustrated with what I assumed was my inability to get this operation out of the red.

Luck or talent, or a combination of both, had yielded success for me in the past, so failure in a business venture was uncomfortable for me. The monthly financial meetings were dismal. I seemed to take this to heart more than John. His response to all who asked was a chuckle and the comment, "I'm driving a Porsche into the lake every day."

I was puzzled he thought it was funny, and embarrassed he felt a need to disclose just how much we were losing. I skipped a few scheduled Wendall Industries business trips with John and, unlike the past, he didn't seem to mind. I was tending at least one of his businesses; therefore I wasn't taking time off, so to speak. The corporate slut was fulfilling her duty.

CHAPTER 28

It was the Millennium, New Year's Eve, 1999. It was to be more than just a party for all of our friends; it was a PR event for JR's. I was looking for business, predominantly private party business, as a way to increase sales and see some black ink. We closed the restaurant to the public and hosted our annual celebration there instead of our Milwaukee home. In addition to the usual Milwaukee crowd, local dignitaries from Freshwater Falls had accepted the invitation. We invited the mayor, the city council, and the leaders of both the Republican and Democratic parties. Any socially prominent person from the area was planning on attending. My friends from Cincinnati made the trip along with my nephew Sam and his future wife Alice. Lola and Trevor, usually in Florida for New Year's Eve, agreed to help us welcome 2000.

The celebration was a year in planning, with every detail meticulously attended to. I wanted to show the local powers that we could transform this restaurant into an elegant banquet room. It was a black tie event. I imported the florist we dealt with in Milwaukee to decorate not only the restaurant but our home. He erected a twenty-foot poinsettia tree in the foyer of our house. The back screened porch was transformed into a snow covered forest complete with pine trees and lighted deer.

It was magnificent. In addition to the New Year's Eve party, we were hosting a walk-through brunch New Year's Day for seventy-five of our dearest friends.

We couldn't accommodate all of our guests even with the three houses, so those staying in hotels were given, at check-in, a gift bag personally assembled by me. It had JR's coffee mugs, instant coffee bags, and tea bags, along with an immersion element to warm the water for their beverages. There were muffins, granola bars, and fruit. I threw in some Alka-Seltzer, aspirin, and Pepto-Bismol just in case. This would last, I thought, until they could arrive at our house for brunch.

I arrived early and alone at JR's to make sure all was in order. The place was a sea of gold lamé and royal blue and pine boughs wrapped in tiny white lights. Everywhere I looked my eye fell upon stunning flowers. The outdoor dining room, void of furniture in the winter, was filled with lighted deer.

I walked downstairs to check out the bar, which was to be the scene of the party after our very formal dinner. Balloons waiting in nets secured to the ceiling would be released at midnight. I picked up one of the engraved menu cards.

New Year's Eve Menu
December 31, 1999

≈

Acorn Squash Soup with Whipped Cream and Maple Walnut Praline

≈

Cold Poached Lobster with Smoked Tomato Oil, Frisee and Black Trumpet Mushrooms

≈

Fruit Sorbet

≈

Grilled Filet Mignon
stuffed with Roasted garlic and Chevre Cheese
Rosemary Roasted Potatoes
Baby Vegetables

≈

Salad of Bitter Greens with Toasted Hazelnuts,
Maytag Bleu Cheese and Caramelized Apples
with Door County Cherry Vinaigrette

≈

Chocolate Kahlua Soufflé with Liquid Center
served with Oven Roasted Fruit

The meal was going to be perfect. It was gourmet with a capital "G," unlike anything Freshwater Falls had seen.

*

As nighttime approached, one hundred and seventy-five guests began to arrive. I smiled at everyone as they came through the door. "Welcome and Happy New Year!" I said. "Please have a cocktail and we also have a vodka and caviar bar for your pleasure. There's a gift waiting for you at your place setting when you find your seat." Each guest received a custom-made service plate and champagne glass to commemorate the occasion.

I caught a glimpse of John wandering through the crowd, drink in hand, with a huge smile titivating his face. With every compliment, he beamed with pride.

Lola took my elbow from behind and whispered, "Roberta, this is simply gorgeous. You've outdone yourself this time...you'll never be able to top this!"

I smiled as I squeezed her hand and turned towards the kitchen. "Excuse me Lola, I need to check with the Chef. I have you sitting at our table, so I'll see you shortly."

I took a short detour to check the Cuban Cigar Bar and make sure they were keeping the caviar stocked. It was going quickly. I wanted everything to keep running smoothly.

Shramsburg Blanc de Blanc had long been our champagne of choice and was notable because President Nixon had presented this California champagne to Premier Zhou En Lai of China in 1972. John was the largest single private buyer in the country. Any really good champagne was in short supply that year and even JR's wine supplier couldn't procure Shramsburg. John only made one phone call and we were assured ample supply. *Hmmm,* I pondered, *testament to his power, or his drinking problem?*

The meal was a huge success and dessert and coffee was just being served when Grant and Marie approached our table. With a gentle touch to my elbow, Grant signaled me to stand. He put one arm around me and the other around his wife and leaned into the microphone perched over my shoulder.

"Ladies and Gentleman, could I have your attention…" he began. The string quartet, playing during the meal, stopped. "My wife Marie and I have known Roberta since she was eighteen years old and that's a long, long time."

I punched him playfully as the laughter ran through the restaurant like "The Wave" at a football game.

"We've attended many events that Roberta has planned, both of her weddings included." There was more laughter as I punched him again.

"This is sincerely the most beautiful function we have ever attended. The food is unbelievable, and this décor, the flowers, everything...

Roberta, here's a toast to you. This entire event is spectacular, and we're flattered and honored to bring in the New Millennium with you."

Everyone stood and as the applause grew louder, I reached over and pulled John out of his seat. I quickly put my arm around him so he might share the praise.

John took the microphone from Grant and with real genuineness said, "I want to publicly thank my wife for this beautiful beginning of a new era. You have no idea how hard she worked on this party. It was worth it, Roberta; you've done a spectacular job. Because of this…" he gestured all around the room, "…everyone here will always remember where they were when the clock ticked over to 2000. Everybody, a round of applause for my wife, please." We turned to each other and exchanged a kiss for all to see.

It was probably the most elaborate, expensive and detailed party I ever planned, and it was flawless.

Unlike the New Year's Eve of 1990, John and I were holding hands this midnight, and I was the first person he kissed as the fireworks started out over the water. He looked at me and his eyes shone with pride. This was a superb event and he had publicly acknowledged the work it took to attain its success. *He loves me*, I thought.

It was moments like this that rekindled my belief in happily ever after. I equated John's pride in my work with what I thought was his love for me. I thought achieving one might assure the other.

In reality, I planned a mostly corporate event aimed at bettering the image of JR's so we could increase sales. It really was that cut and dried.

The wife wanted some affirmation, but she wasn't so blind she couldn't see what was what: the pride John had was for his corporate slut, the woman who'd worked to achieve his goals and fulfill his dream. That night I had done an outstanding job.

And that night, John went to the master bedroom and I lowered the Murphy bed in the library, as usual. The sheets were very cold, the room was very empty, and I was sad...very sad.

Not for long, though. I had to be up in a few short hours to prepare brunch.

CHAPTER 29

John and I began spending more time apart as his international travel increased. If his itinerary called for ten cities in as many days, I elected to stay home. I relished his absence and the peace in the house. It was a refreshing lack of drama. There was less entertaining and fewer orphan dinners, although I was still lunching and conversing with Wendall Industries friends and personnel. I had a little time to think, to read, to prioritize issues, rather than have them prioritized for me.

I had time to play with my cats. John was so demanding of my attention and so jealous when he felt it wasn't adequate he would lie on the floor, roll over, and imitate purring. It was his not so subtle way of telling me he thought I paid more mind to the cats than him. Maybe I did.

We had been to visit our close friends Lola and Trevor in Ft. Lauderdale, as we frequently did, and for the past two years had witnessed a beautiful high-rise condominium building being erected across the street from them, directly on the ocean. One rainy afternoon after viewing the models and liking them, we looked at some units for sale. I fell in love with one particular condo.

Quite spontaneously, while standing on the twenty-third floor balcony with the beautiful ocean spread before me, I envisioned a way to simplify our lives. John was soon to be fifty and our plan had always been for him to retire at fifty-five, purchase a home in Florida, and establish residency there. Then we would sell our house on Lake Michigan in Milwaukee and buy a condominium there instead, and continue to spend our summers in Freshwater Falls. I wanted to accelerate the process. I didn't want John to retire, just get ready to retire. The five-year head start would give us a chance to adjust to Florida, establish ourselves, and make friends. I didn't exactly confide that I saw a way to escape occasionally, like a kid running to a tree house.

*

It's baffling to me that couples continue to act as couples when, for all intents and purposes, they are not. We were no different. At this stage, our marriage wasn't a happy one, but like most couples, content or not, your hands sometimes lock together when walking down the street, and once in a while, your eyes meet with a shared memory.

There was still the kiss hello, the kiss goodbye and the always-important kiss goodnight. Some continue to act as couples because among other things, children would make a break difficult. Our children were his businesses – Wendall Industries and JR's. More important, I knew John thoroughly. Even in our worst moments, disconnection was never total and because of this, I always felt a small flicker of hope.

As for John, he had lost his respect and, I daresay, his love for me as his wife, but the corporate slut maintained her value. It would be hard for him to explain my absence in either business when I had earned so much respect from each.

He approached a table of strangers one evening in JR's and while I was standing by his side, John took my arm a bit forcefully, introduced me as his wife and blurted out that I had not had sex with him for two years. He told them I possessed absolutely no passion.

Imagine this. These were total strangers and we were the proprietors of an upscale establishment, and John was in an obvious state of inebriation. Their mouths dropped. I had to act quickly, calling on my expertise now at defusing these embarrassing moments. I kissed John lovingly, donned my famous smile, and said, "Have you ever met a husband who thinks he's getting enough sex? Sorry about the interruption...We'll let you get on with your dinner, folks. And you, my darling husband...."I lead him away from the table.

A scant half-hour later, he was earnest in soliciting my approval for a new menu design. The demeaning sneer afforded the wife just a short time before turned to earnest importune regarding a decision needed from the corporate slut. I was starting to believe I even looked different with each role. The wife had a softer smile—or was it just a weaker one? Before I could respond to any question John asked, I had to ascertain who, exactly, he was addressing. Wife or corporate slut? What the fuck was happening here?

*

So now in Ft. Lauderdale I was gazing at the ocean, thinking of a future. I was unhappy in the present and I refused to look back at the past, fearing it could reflect my future - repetitive and unchanging. With my very special brand of reasoning, I rationalized that it was a volatile marriage and it always had been. Things got bad, but they always got better. It was bad then, but it was bad before and it would get better. We'd been through a lot together, raised these "children" together and we had reasons to make it work. We had a history.

If I turned JR's around, would his respect for the corporate slut grow to such an extent that he'd he'd love me as his wife again? Of course! It would come full circle. If he loved me as his wife again would that mean we could even start having sex again? Most definitely! Did he miss holding me as much as I missed feeling him wrapped around me in bed? I'm sure, no I'm positive! Does he love me? He has to love me. He just has to. I also realized that it was easiest when I asked and answered all the questions myself.

My suggestion we accelerate the purchase of a home in Florida was met with resistance. Actually, it was an emphatic no, and for the first time since I had known him, John told me we couldn't afford it. I was dumbfounded. I thought we could afford anything—or was it just anything John wanted?

He had no fewer than twenty-seven cars—seventeen of which were Porsches—eight boats, and seven vintage motorcycles. He had four houses in his name only and together we shared two, for a total of six houses. The restaurant and liquor license, worth a small fortune, were in his name.

As for me, I had an entire closet full of shoes. Okay, there were a few Manolo Blahniks and Jimmy Choos mixed in, but by comparison... well there was no comparison. John had enough toys for ten men and I had a few consolation prizes. I wanted something significant and substantive for *me*—there was no question I'd earned it. I used all of my sales experience from the past, my best persuasive powers, and I even threw in a blowjob, but to no avail. The answer on the Ft. Lauderdale condo was still an emphatic no.

The upside was that he couldn't say he hadn't had sex in two years. It was only me who hadn't had sex in two years, and of course, I would never say it out loud. Not then, anyway.

*

I was sitting in the Lake Room at our home in Milwaukee. It was an exquisite, sparkling Easter morning and only three months since our visit to Ft. Lauderdale. I was sipping coffee, petting the cats, and reading the paper. I sensed John's presence before I saw him. I looked up, and there he was, holding two small gift-wrapped packages in the palm of his outstretched hand. He looked extremely pleased with himself. I had to smile. Even then, when he put on his impish, playful face, it softened me and made me feel tenderness for him.

"Go ahead, Roberta, open them!" he said anxiously. He was so excited he could barely contain himself. He plopped down next to me on the couch.

"John, an Easter present? Since when do we give presents for Easter? I don't have anything for you...you should have told me so I could get you something." I was grinning, teasing him by delaying the opening.

"Roberta, just open them...come on...hurry up!" He was squirming in anticipation.

I tore the paper from the smaller box, opened the lid, and saw a key attached to a small seashell ring. *Could it be,* I thought, *did he really buy that condo in Ft. Lauderdale?*

"I don't believe it, John...is it really..." I was almost stuttering.

"Believe it, Roberta – yep honey, it's the condo. You know how much I love making you happy." He couldn't possibly be more proud of himself, his chest puffed out, his arms stretched in front of him, waiting for me to throw myself into them. I obliged by doing so, and did so gladly.

"Open the other one," he prodded.

I hurriedly tore the paper from the other package and beheld a model airplane. I looked at him, puzzled.

"That's for a trip to Hong Kong," he said. "I want you to either buy the furnishings there or have them custom made, whichever you like. I want you to make this condo everything you ever wanted. Happy Easter, Roberta. The condo is yours…from me to you, honey."

Later the same day, over Easter ham with our friends, he boasted loudly to the group of Wendall Industries employees and their wives. "Yeah, I gave my wife a one-point-three-million-dollar condo on the ocean in Ft. Lauderdale and a trip to Hong Kong to buy the furnishings." He was the perfect husband. Should there ever be a doubt, feel free to seek his confirmation.

Oh yes, another reason to stay. Nothing says "I love you" like a one-point-three-million-dollar, four-thousand-square-foot condo on the sandy shores of the Atlantic Ocean.

I saw a way to spend time in Florida alone to regroup. I would have time to think of how I might put it—my marriage, my self—all back together.

The condo was designer ready, which in Florida means dry wall, concrete floors, bathrooms and a kitchen. Finishing it was a project I relished because it meant eventual breathing room for me. I declined the trip to Hong Kong as I felt time demands with JR's wouldn't allow it. We were still losing money. I flew to Ft. Lauderdale to interview designers. I wanted to start construction yesterday. I wanted my hideout, my tree house, my own space and I wanted it as fast as I could make it happen.

CHAPTER 30

Less than one month later, I was sitting at the kitchen counter in Freshwater Falls, alone. Per our usual routine, I had motored north a few days early to prepare for our weekend guests and John was still in Milwaukee. In addition, there was a National Sales Meeting for Wendall Industries in Green Bay the following week. This was an every five-year event that required a year's planning. It was major. My presence was expected, as it always had been. I loved seeing all the reps, and I was looking forward to the week of events. One of those days, buses were to bring two hundred people to Freshwater Falls to tour the factory, and then transport the troops to our home for cocktails. I was enjoying the calm before the chaos.

It was early evening when the phone rang and it took me a moment to recognize my mother's voice. She was sobbing uncontrollably. She had been diagnosed with stage-four stomach cancer just an hour earlier. I was shocked because she hadn't confided she was ill. Her prognosis was six to eight months. I calmly told her I would be in Orange County as soon as I could get there and we'd sort everything out together. I replaced the receiver, picked it up again, and dialed my husband. I shouldn't have been surprised not to find him. He seemed never to be around when I absolutely, positively, without a doubt needed his support. He had an incredible flair for not being there.

I found June, my niece, in Freshwater Falls visiting her mother (John's step-sister) and within minutes, she was sitting at the counter in my kitchen with my head on her shoulder and her arms around me. She just let me cry. I couldn't stop crying knowing what lay ahead.

I quickly made arrangements to leave, got everything covered for JR's and stopped there to speak with my nephew, Sam. He was in Freshwater Falls for the summer to work at JR's as a server as he had done the summer before. This was his grandmother, and although they weren't terribly close due to distance, he was very fond of her and felt attached. My mother kept in close touch with Sam and maintained as grandmotherly a relationship as distance and her nature would allow.

I drove back to Milwaukee while John drove north to Freshwater Falls. My flight was the following morning. Rather than cancel the guests because of my absence, he elected to entertain on his own. I had cooked the majority of the food ahead, so why not? There was no need to accompany his wife for support, of course!

The trip was fraught with anxiety. After we spoke with the oncologist together, my mother resolved not to seek treatment. She didn't want to experience the agony she had seen firsthand with my brother. The memory of watching him die slowly had already determined her course of action.

That evening I called John to tell him I wouldn't be back the next day. In spite of my mother's decision, I wanted to check with UCLA for possible alternative treatment and would be returning a day later.

In all our years together, I had never heard John so drunk. I was even more alarmed when he put Sam on the phone and Sam was totally unintelligible. I didn't even recognize his voice, and had to ask whom I had just spoken with.

"John," I said, "do *not* let him drive. Make him stay at the house tonight." I gave him my new flight information and hung up the phone in disgust. John called in the morning to confirm my flight arrival for that day. He had no memory of my call the night before or any part of the conversation. He didn't recall that I would be arriving a day later.

The conversation made me nauseated. And afraid. I knew what lay ahead, and I was very afraid for my mother and what she would have to endure, and for myself and the price I'd pay for bearing witness to her suffering. Knowing I couldn't count on my husband filled me with dread.

*

Southern California sun brightened the kitchen, as if to disallow the darkness of the recent news. Mother and I sat looking at each other across the glass kitchen table.

"Mom," I began, "I think you should come back to Milwaukee with me now. You don't want treatment, so there isn't a need to stay. All we need is a primary care physician and you will love Dr. Rah."

Her face was serious, her voice matter-of-fact. "Honey, I will, I will. I will come to Milwaukee, I promise. I just think I can hold off for a while. I feel fine, honestly...look at me."

She stood and did a little twirl in front of me, smiling, her blue eyes lively, as if this cancer talk was mere rumor.

"Let me stay for as long as I can. I have friends here, the grandchildren are here, and I honestly don't know anyone in Milwaukee. I'm not housebound yet, and I still feel good."

I was torn. "What about hospice?" I asked.

"I'll tell you what. Why don't we agree that as soon as hospice needs to get involved—and it isn't yet—I'll let you know and that's when I'll come to Milwaukee with you. Fair?"

We agreed. She sat again, only this time she chose a chair next to me at the table. She took my hand in both of hers and looked me directly in the eye. "Roberta, you and John have been so good to me all these years. I know it's a lot to ask, but I have to. Promise me Roberta, please. Promise me you won't let me die in a hospital. I don't want to die in a hospital."

I was struck by the child-like pleading in her voice, and on her face. Suddenly, she became me when I was a kid in Pittsburgh, standing by the ice-cream truck pleading, "Can I please have an ice cream cone Mommy, *pleeease*!" You read about the role reversal of parent and child, but reading is not good preparation, really. It wasn't supposed to happen so quickly and with so little warning. Was I really old enough to do this?

I was abruptly overwhelmed by a sense of responsibility. I knew I would be the ultimate authority for the remainder of Mother's life. There were no siblings to help – Scott was gone and Sheila...well there was no possibility that she'd come through. Not even this time.

And all at once I decided it didn't matter—I would do what I had to do, with help or without, and I certainly had to do this. In spite of everything she wasn't as a mother, she was still my mother.

I promised I wouldn't hospitalize her and I would come to Orange County every three weeks or so until it was time to move her.

*

After a long flight to Milwaukee, I drove to Freshwater Falls with the intention of driving to Green Bay the following morning. Corporate slut attendance was required for the National Sales Meeting. Soon after my arrival in Freshwater Falls the housekeeper let slip that Sam had been given a DUI the night I had spoken with him. John had allowed him to drive home.

I was in Green Bay a scant hour later (it's an hour and a half drive) and when I walked into the hotel where the meetings were being held I spotted Paul.

"Paul, go get John. *Now.*"

Paul looked puzzled and a little frightened. "John's in the middle of a training session, Roberta, teaching the reps about our new Cook and Hold Oven. Can I help?"

"Do I look like I give a shit what's he's doing, Paul? Get him or I'll knock on every meeting room door until I find him. I want him now and I mean *right now.*"

Having always regarded Sam as though he were my own son, my face bore the rage any mother would feel when her child has been needlessly harmed by an adult who should have known better. I looked demonic and Paul literally ran to retrieve John from his meeting.

I can't recount all of the conversation with John but I know I started with, "You motherfucker."

"Roberta, I am in the middle of a National Sales Meeting!" John was nervously running his hands through his graying hair and carefully avoiding my glare.

"I don't give a damn *what* you're in the middle of. How *dare* you allow Sam to drive in that condition? *I can't believe you*! Are you a total moron, have you lost your mind? Why would you even drink like that in front of him? *You* are supposed to set the example, John. *You are the adult.*"

I didn't care who heard me. My voice, ordinarily low in pitch, had turned into a piercing shrill, rebounding off the stark white walls of the narrow hallway.

"I *told* you not to let him drive, I told you—"

"Roberta," John said. He reached for my hand in an effort to calm me, but I had taken a swan dive off the high board of fury and there was no turning back. I jerked my hand away.

"You bastard! You rotten son of a bitch!"

"Roberta, Sam is a grown man. I can't *make* him do anything. He knew the risk when he left. I told him not to, but *no*, he had to get back to the condo. It was *his* decision." His face was a mixture of defiance sprinkled with a small amount of knowing guilt.

"He was drunk John. He was in no state to evaluate the risk. Are you saying that you had *no* responsibility in this John, none?" I put my hand up, palm facing him, in a gesture that shouted, *don't talk to me, talk to the hand.*

I turned and walked quickly away from him, feeling the tears starting to come. *It's too much*, I thought. *What am I supposed to do with all this?*

He ran after me, catching my elbow and said with mock sincerity, "Roberta, we'll take care of Sam, trust me." Now concerned, he continued, "Where are you going? The meetings are almost over and you're supposed to be at the cocktail hour and banquet tonight. It's Casino Night, remember? Where's your bag? I'll have Paul put your suitcase in the room."

I stopped so abruptly John ran into my back, pushing me off balance. As I grabbed his arm for support, I stared at him in disbelief. "Are you serious, John? You think I'm going to stay and support *you*? When have you ever supported me, John, when? I just fly in from L.A., my mother is dying, now Sam has been arrested because of your flagrant disregard, and you honestly expect me to stay at this meeting and play hostess to all of your reps? Kiss my ass, John. Maybe it's time you got a taste of what it feels like to never have your spouse around when you really need them."

I pulled my arm from his grasp and flew out the front door. I reached my car as the tears started an uncontrollable flow. I could feel the mascara, already gritty, on my cheeks. I didn't have any idea what I was going to do.

Instead of taking the exit for Freshwater Falls I kept driving, wiping tears, until I reached Milwaukee two hours later. I did not attend the remainder of the three-day meeting, and when two hundred people stopped by the house for cocktails, my absence was conspicuous. John blamed my inability to handle my mother's illness so soon after my brother's death, and did it in a way that made him appear sympathetic. In reality, he was seething – the corporate slut had been a no-show.

I found counseling for Sam. I demanded John obtain the services of the same attorney he had used for his own DUI the year before. He was the best money could buy. He yielded this time, confronted with the rage I couldn't seem to lose. Apparently, I hadn't lost the demonic look.

CHAPTER 31

It was somebody's birthday, I've forgotten whose, and the party was in our home in Milwaukee. John started to regale friends with his tale of woe regarding his cold wife and his lack of sexual fulfillment.

"You know what I call our bed?" he started, sipping his fourth or fifth scotch. "I call it the dead sea. I have to wear those pajamas with the feet in them because our bedroom is so damn cold. I checked all the windows for leaks, before I figured out it was Roberta. She's so frigid it almost snows in our room."

Ok John, I thought, *you want to play? Well let's play asshole. You think I've forgotten how?*

I suddenly blurted to the room full of guests in our living room, "They say practice makes perfect, but that hasn't been the case for John. We've been practicing for years, but even now, when he's done he just rolls over and starts snoring. How many years it is it now, John, since you took care of me? There's a reason God made vibrators." My mouth was laughing, even as my eyes flared with anger.

"Here's the key, John. If you want to get laid, you have to get it up…at least take care of that little problem, 'little' being the operative word."

I couldn't stop myself. Our guests' laughter just egged me on.

"You want to get laid, honey? Not to worry. The second you get a hard-on, wake me up. When you're done, if I've fallen asleep, and we both know that's happened before, just pull my nightgown down."

John's face, so often the dusky red of heavy drinkers, was now the color of a beet.

"Sure John, I'll give you a blowjob – what's one minute out of my day?"

The air was charged with laughter. I had my mojo back and it felt good to finally get a gotcha myself. John was the only one in the room not laughing. I relished my victory.

I didn't forget it. The next time he was critical of my cooking in front of guests at a dinner party, I came back quite loudly with, "If you can do a better job, for our next dinner party get your ass home and do it yourself." Everybody laughed but John.

I was even getting a sense from time to time that some people were silently supporting me, as if to say, "Way to go, Roberta."

*

It was the one hundredth anniversary celebration for Harley-Davidson and John had invited a bunch of biking buddies from out of town for the weekend festivities. Although they were to stay at our other house in Milwaukee used for corporate guests, he informed me that we would be hosting them for a BBQ rib dinner at our home. I was to make the ribs he so favored. I did an unprecedented thing.

John stood staring, incredulity all over his face. "What did you just say, Roberta? *No?* No, what? You won't make the ribs?

"You heard right, John." I continued working on my computer, doing the daily web page update for Wendall Industries. Without turning, I continued. "That means no to everything, John. I will not cook for you or your guests, I will not clean up, I will not serve hors d'oeuvres, and I won't buy the food, the booze, or even the nuts. If you want them here, call a caterer and make sure they are a full service caterer who will shop, cook, and clean. I'm not available, and you won't see me downstairs."

He was dumbfounded and speechless. A few moments later, I heard the garage door close as he left for work.

They dined out. And for the first time, I wasn't invited to join the guys. Although he had used the term for years, he refrained from calling me his biker bitch that particular weekend. He was starting to realize that an insult hurled my direction might possibly be returned in the same fashion. The wife had found her voice.

*

A month later, my mother phoned to tell me her doctor had requested hospice get involved in her care. It was time to bring her to Milwaukee. I had approximately two weeks to get everything prepared and get her moved. I needed some help, and Sam and his fiancée Alice agreed to fly to California and help pack and ship the things she wanted them to have, haul the rest to Goodwill, and have what would likely be her last visit with them alone. I was grateful for the help.

I checked the schedule and could see that I had two weekends to cover when I wouldn't be able to be home to care for her.

One of those weekends involved corporate guests we were entertaining in Freshwater Falls. The deal on the table was a big one and required my attention. The pooper-scooper had increased in size as John's behavior had become more mired in alcohol and his inflated sense of self-worth.

"Don't you know who I *am?*" John was addressing Henry, an important customer via phone conference, arranged by Bernie the Vice-President of sales. "I am the CEO of Wendall Industries, Henry. If there is a change in the production schedule, it will be at *my* direction, not yours. What do you think… you're my only customer?" Henry wanted to procure several hundred holding cabinets but John was balking at the additional costs required in setting up another production line needed to accommodate Henry's desired delivery date. The story had been related to me by Bernie as he made it clear that under no circumstances could I put down the pooper-scooper. The stakes were high and under no circumstances could I miss this meeting. The corporate slut had to be there with her PR smile, hearty laugh, and pooper-scooper.

The second was a three-day trip to Ft. Lauderdale to start the process of finishing the condo. After the initial meeting with the designer and construction people, I could handle most of it by phone, fax, mail, or computer, but my need for that hide-out, that tree house, had increased threefold. I would not miss this trip.

*

I invited John to join me in my office shortly after he arrived home from work. It was a first, with me behind the desk and him in front. It made me feel powerful.

"John," I said, "after Mother gets here I'm afraid I can no longer fulfill my duties at JR's. No one can predict how long she's going to be with us, but my time will be spent caring for her. I won't take phone calls, I don't want emails, and I won't be attending any financial meetings. I guess, in short, I quit. Under the circumstances, John, I have to."

He said nothing so I continued with my matter of fact delivery. "I can still do the Wendall Industries work from home pertaining to the web page, but the entertaining stops now, with the exception of my mother's friends from out of town who want one last visit with her. I will not be going to Freshwater Falls."

I leaned over the desk, my demeanor begging him to look at me so he could see the sincerity in what I was about to say.

"John, I need you. I love you. This is going to be tough and I'm not sure I can handle it by myself. What happened to us, John? We were happy once, and it wasn't so long ago...right? Weren't you happy? I want our life back – the life we should be enjoying as husband and wife. Please go see Dr. Rah about your ED and get some help so we can start having sex again. I miss you so much, John, even when you're here. Do you understand that?" My tone had taken on a pleading quality. "This is going to be rough John, be there for me, please."

I wanted to come together as we should have from the beginning, a team, yes, but in every sense of the word. I wanted the vows – to love, honor, and cherish—to be reciprocal. I wanted to be his wife, not his corporate slut.

There was such a lack of compassion and caring in his eyes, I wondered if anything had registered.

"Roberta, I love you too, honey, and of course I'll be here. I'm just a little worried about JR's without you running the operation. Hospice will be here to take care of your mother. I'm not sure you need to step back from your responsibilities so completely."

He completely avoided my mention of seeing a doctor or having sex again. Something in me knew that his need or desire for a wife had died.

Avoiding for most couples becomes the standard and it was for us as well. I didn't mention the subject again. I had too many other worries and he obviously didn't want to engage in the conversation. I could have insisted, but chose to avoid instead because it was much easier. I had no thought of leaving now. How could I?

The following morning by eleven o'clock, I received calls from each member of the posse imploring me to convince John to close JR's and list it for sale.

"You could've had two penthouses in that building in Florida if it weren't for JR's," Michael said.

Even though I was not successful in turning the red ink to black, we weren't bleeding nearly as badly, and they felt without my contribution the losses would be too significant. They left it to me to get JR's closed.

So puffed up with a sense of importance once again and not realizing I was being used, I set about the task at hand. I would play the bad guy, as in the past, because I was the only one John wouldn't terminate. My approach had to be very cautious as John's ever-expanding ego was involved and I couldn't deal his self-worth a fatal blow.

*

On top of everything else, my oldest cat Porsche became ill. I took her to several cat specialists before it was determined that extracting her teeth might improve her health. She got sicker, not better, and I now had to feed her by hand. She was losing weight rapidly and her coat was becoming dull. I was in a panic. My kids, my cats, had always been two of my greatest sources of joy. I refused to think about losing her. I wasn't entirely sure I would be able to take that loss in stride, combined with the losses of the not too distant past.

CHAPTER 32

The next two weeks were busy making arrangements for hospice and getting Mother aligned with my primary care physician. She did not want a funeral or memorial but preferred her body be donated to the Medical College of Wisconsin. I made the arrangements. I flew to Orange County, helped her pack what she needed and made arrangements for an estate sale. I took care of her change of address, closed her bank accounts, obtained her medical records, sold her car, and sent the check to my sister Sheila in New York. I listed the condo John purchased for her (in his name) with a realtor. She said good-bye to her many friends with a series of cocktail parties we hosted together.

When we finally boarded the plane for Milwaukee we were both exhausted and she was already in a great deal of pain. I couldn't imagine what she must have been feeling, boarding a plane for the last time in her life, almost like having a one-way ticket to die. I held her hand all the way home. Melancholy enveloped us in its miasma the entire four-hour flight.

The guest room was waiting for Mother. I equipped her new surroundings with a mini-refrigerator, a TV with a headset, and a Bose stereo and CD player so she could play her favorite jazz. I brought, from the living room, a large easy chair with an ottoman for her guests.

She seemed pleased, but then she turned to me suddenly and said, "I don't know why you're doing all this for me...I wouldn't do it for you."

It stung, that slap, in its bone-jarring truthfulness. How very like my mother. I looked at her, my face quizzical, and thought, *what the fuck am I supposed to say to that? What kind of response does she hope to get from a statement like that?* This woman before me, my mother, was suddenly naked, out of the blue acknowledging her own weakness. Self-absorbed her entire life, she was admitting she hadn't been there for me or any of us, besides my father. Was she asking my forgiveness? My understanding? Did she expect to be punished?

"Mom, it's my pleasure, really. You're my mother. I'm happy you're here with us and I am happy to care for you. It doesn't matter...none of it matters anymore...everything is okay now."

It was an honest response. I moved towards her and grasped her in a hug wanting to assure her of my sincerity. She bowed her head, not knowing what to say, and began unpacking her bags.

John and I left for the corporate weekend. I flew in Mother's friend, a nurse from Cincinnati, to care for her while we were away.

*

Our customer arrived. "Henry, welcome, welcome...it's good to see you...come on in...can I get your luggage?" John warmly greeted our weekend guest. I was preparing dinner and was just wiping my hands on a dishcloth so that I might join John in his greeting. Barely taking a breath between sentences, John's voice twisted from welcoming to sarcastic. "Holy shit Henry! What's with that goofy tie? It's an ugly tie, but it sure looks good on you!"

Quickly tossing aside my dishcloth, my feet moved double time as I almost slid on the limestone floor into foyer. My smile was extra bright and my laugh was extra loud.

"Henry! Hey there sweetie, don't you look great…it's been way too long." I kissed his cheek and hugged him. "I heard the remark Henry – it's a euphemism for 'I love your tie'…that's what he really meant to say. If he *didn't* like it, he wouldn't say anything! Drink Henry? Scotch if I remember, right? I hope you like beef tenderloin, because I've made a mountain of it for dinner…rare, right? And I remember that you like my homemade whipped horseradish sauce, so I made extra for you." As I led him into the bar, I glanced back at John. He was becoming all too familiar with the look. *"If you can't say something nice, shut the fuck up, asshole!"*

*

The weekend went well; the big deal was consummated with less drama than anticipated. In other words, I hadn't had to scoop too much poop.

The next week Porsche got sicker every day. My sister Sheila was due in Milwaukee Thursday so that John and I might go to Florida and finalize the arrangements for the condo. The night before we left for Florida, Porsche was curled up in my lap as I watched TV. Her weight was down from thirteen pounds to eight. I had taken her everywhere and nobody could determine her ailment. She woke, rolled to one side and her blue eyes, normally alive with color, now dull from sickness, met mine. She let out the smallest, weakest mew and I knew that moment, as she stared at me, that she was asking me to let her go.

The following morning, I held her while the vet administered the lethal dose. We cried together, the vet and me. She was the very first Ragdoll kitten he had seen, twelve years ago when I brought her there for the first time. He had been treating her since she was eight weeks old and his nurse confided, long ago, that Porsche had been his favorite patient.

The tears flowed freely, but I did not really have time to mourn her loss. My mother was at my house dying, and I was worried that Harley, my other Ragdoll and Porsche's little brother, would be desolate without her. I had to pick up Shelia from the airport and get back to meet the hospice nurse. And I had only a few hours before John and I were scheduled to board our flight to Ft. Lauderdale. I thought that maybe it was best to be so consumed. If I did not have time to think about Porsche, maybe the pain would be more like a broken arm, rather than the agony of open-heart surgery.

In Ft. Lauderdale, we chose the design and most of the décor in a few days. I was always decisive when decorating but I worked doubly fast here. I called home two or three times a day to check on Mother and see how Sheila was handling everything. All appeared well.

We took both cars to the airport. Upon our return, John drove directly to Chicago for meetings.

*

I called Sheila on my way home from the airport to ask if they needed or wanted anything. She was frosty cold when she said no. Upon my arrival, I checked on Mother and Harley. They were together in Mother's bed and appeared content with one another. Sheila left the room as I entered. "I don't know what's wrong with her," Mother said. "She was fine until you got here."

I followed my sister downstairs to the kitchen. "Sheila, what's wrong?" I said. "I haven't been home long enough to piss you off." I laughed, thinking she might do the same.

She looked me in the eye and said, "Oh, it's nothing you've done, Roberta, it's who you are." I shook my head thinking I hadn't heard her properly, and asked her to repeat the statement. She did.

The remark made me lose my breath, actually. Our mother was upstairs dying and my sister was telling me she hated the person I was. Not knowing how to respond, I retreated to my room and unpacked my bags. I joined my mother and Harley and played gin rummy with my mother until bedtime. I didn't confide the statement to my mother. It wouldn't have changed anything. Sheila didn't spend her last evening in Milwaukee with mom. She popped her head in the door to say goodnight and withdrew to her room.

The following morning I was driving Sheila to the airport. Ignoring the comment from the evening before in the light of our current circumstance, I said, "Sheila, I will send you tickets as often as you want to come. No matter who is here, you are always welcome in my home and I will always make room for you. She's your mother, too."

She never turned her head to look at me, but said, "Just let me know when she's about gone. I might come back then." I shouldn't have been surprised. She didn't attend my brother's funeral either.

Not another word was spoken until our arrival at the airport fifteen minutes later and when she exited the car, she snapped a terse "goodbye" in my direction and slammed the car door. It was the last time she saw our mother. She never came back.

We are fourteen months apart in age, Sheila being the older, but were never close. Our personalities were different and we could never breach the gap of those differences.

She was a studious kid, and I was not. She was the girlie girl and I was the tomboy. She liked dolls, I liked to climb trees. She would be playing piano; I would be playing kickball in the street. I lived on my bike, and Sheila rarely rode hers. She was book smart, always earned good grades, but I worked for mine. I don't recall us ever playing together, really. When we were at my grandfather's farm, if there were no cousins around, I could sometimes convince her to go to the creek with me and catch salamanders. I played the boy stuff with my brother, but Sheila rarely joined us.

Sheila went to the beauty shop, with her beautiful long carrot red hair. My father took me to the barber with my brother. I don't think Mom wanted to deal with the hair of a child who was tumbling all day – better to keep it short; Sheila got the rollers. Sheila had a proclivity to untidiness. I was, even as a child, exceedingly neat. We shared a bedroom in Pittsburgh, but when we moved to Minneapolis we each got our own room. Not dealing with each other in a shared room furthered our distance from one another.

She did instill in me however, a lifelong love of classical music. She earned her Master's degree in piano from The Cincinnati Conservatory of Music and remains a talented pianist, if not a working one. I never realized how much I loved her music until I left home and nobody was playing the Rachmaninoff I found so comforting.

I will never understand her indifference or her disdainfulness for all that I ever was or have become. Over the years, her refusal to enter a dialogue regarding our relationship created a mystery that captured my contemplation. But resolution is impossible without participation by all parties, and her remark burned such a large hole in my heart, the mystery no longer warrants my attention.

I felt panic start to settle in my chest, like pneumonia. It was hard to breathe. John didn't know how to be there for me and now my sister had jumped ship, too. I felt like I was running through a paintball course, the lone unprotected prey, being pelted and bruised. Every direction was another obstacle. My mother had a best friend from Hawaii who she adored and so did I. They enjoyed a wonderful sibling-like relationship. He was a natural caregiver who cared for my grandmother in her last days in Hawaii. I called and pleaded with him to come and help me. He hadn't left the island in fifty years. He agreed to come, but he couldn't be there for two months. That was okay, I could manage until then. I could breathe again; Pete was coming and my mother was thrilled, too.

CHAPTER 33

The two months I cared for Mother alone seemed never-ending. The only hospice service available at the time was a terrible disappointment.

The nurse assigned to us was more concerned with telling me about her dogs and dates than checking medications or Mother's condition. After doing without pain medication for two weekends in a row, I tracked it myself and made the requests in a timely fashion. I also reminded the nurse to take Mother's blood pressure.

An aide was supposed to help bathe her and give me a break every now and again but she fell ill and there was no replacement available. I only saw the hospice aide twice.

The social worker was the best of the lot. She provided comfort and crucial information about the process of dying. When Mother was initially diagnosed, she spoke freely of her illness and impending death. The sicker she became, the more she denied her disease. When she started to vomit regularly, it was because I had cooked something improperly. When she started having diarrhea, it was because I gave her fruit and she wasn't supposed to have fruit. The task of helping bathe her became more challenging as she became weaker. I inherited my petite stature from my grandmother, not my mother. She was a big woman. I would sit her in the chair while I changed her bed, but I couldn't get it changed fast enough. When I opened a Pepsi can and it sprayed her accidentally, she screamed, "I can't believe you would do that to me," as if it was intentional.

The social worker explained that this behavior was normal, but one day after Mother said something particularly cruel, I left the room. I didn't want her to see me cry. I overheard the social worker scold her, saying, "You better be careful. If I was your daughter and you treated me like that, I would put you in a home to die." It helped for a while.

I told my mother to invite whomever she wished to visit and she did. We had her old high school friends from Pittsburgh visit, and her college roommate from Cleveland. They stayed in our home, so I was once again entertaining. It wasn't long before she didn't want more company. She was deteriorating.

John spent a lot of time out of town, and when he was in town he retreated to the basement every night after dinner to work on his motorcycles. Her illness seemed uncomfortable for him, but I was so tired after caring for Mother, there wasn't time to tend to his needs as well.

*

It was a Sunday morning and I woke early and found my way downstairs hoping for a little peace with coffee and the paper. Mother and John were still asleep. When I entered the kitchen, there was a terrible smell that seemed to be coming from the basement. My investigation revealed the basement was full of raw sewage.

I woke John. We called the emergency plumber and started the clean up and bleach process. It was a very large basement, at two thousand square feet.

I stopped long enough to run upstairs and check Mother. She was crying. She had suffered an accident in the bed. I bathed her, changed the sheets, and tried to comfort her.

On my way back to the basement, my foot slipped on something wet on the kitchen floor. It was cat vomit. Harley was sick. After cleaning that, I resumed helping John.

About a half hour later, I checked Mother again and she had another accident. It was back to the tub, and more clean sheets, my last set. I started the washer and made a run to the department store and bought two new sets for her bed. On the way back I stopped for adult diapers.

After I arrived home, I was putting sheets in the dryer when I heard crying from her room again. I went running. Another accident, but this time she tried unsuccessfully to make it to the bathroom, so there was feces all over the carpet in addition to the bed. I bathed her again, another fresh nightgown, and clean sheets fresh from the dryer. I scrubbed the carpet on my hands and knees. She refused to wear the diapers.

I was back in the kitchen to check on Harley. He had vomited all over the upholstered chaise lounge in the lake room. He looked horrible, poor thing, and I cleaned the chaise, covered it with a towel, and laid him back on it. It was his favorite spot. I would have to call the vet Monday morning if he didn't improve.

I went back to the basement. By now, the plumber had snaked the drain, but there was a whole lot of bleaching left to do.

Not long after, I took another break from bleaching to check on Mother and she had begun to vomit in addition to the diarrhea. She wasn't able to make it to the bathroom. More rug cleaner, another bath, another set of sheets and a new nightgown. I demanded she wear the diaper and she finally agreed. I put a bucket by her bed.

When I checked a half hour later, the bucket was half filled with vomit. I took it to the kitchen and as I emptied it into the sink, I watched her false teeth slide into the garbage disposal. It was two-o'clock in the afternoon and I had started the day at six o'clock in the morning. The paper sat on the couch unread. I hadn't taken a shower yet or eaten anything. My hands were raw from the cleansers, my cat was sick, my mother was very sick, and my basement, recently covered in raw sewage, wasn't yet cleaned properly.

I changed the bed I forgot how many times, and bathed my mother an equal number of times. My back was killing me and the washer hadn't stopped running all day. Now her false teeth were in the disposal and I had to reach for them through a sink full of vomit.

There was nothing else to do but laugh. And, I laughed a very long while before the tears started to stream. It was one of the worst days of my life. The next day, Mother wasn't much better, but Harley was, and because I had to be, I was much better, too.

*

As I became more housebound, the Wendall Industries family came to the rescue. I could call Sally, John's personal assistant and she would bring diapers or applesauce. Dana, director of international sales and my good friend, came by regularly to visit with Mother and the sales guys would sometimes stop by just to tell me the latest jokes and make me laugh. I didn't want to talk about business.

Being a corporate slut was the furthest thing from my mind. I was only occasionally reminded when Michael would call to jog my memory about convincing John to sell JR's. I hadn't been successful so far and at the moment it wasn't a priority.

Lola would drive up from Chicago with a fully prepared dinner so I could get a break from cooking. She would spend hours keeping my mother company. These were the many people who helped ease the very long days of Mother's illness. I didn't have a husband willing to help, but I had friends and I said their names in my prayers every night.

CHAPTER 34

My angel, Pete, arrived on September 21, 2000. It was not a moment too soon; I misplaced my coping skills and I couldn't find them anywhere.

The date is memorable because it was our fifteenth wedding anniversary. The original plan called for an elaborate cruise of the Mediterranean and Greek Islands accompanied by two other couples. Because of the circumstances, we all agreed to postpone the trip for another year. We would celebrate our sixteenth anniversary instead. We did plan an evening out alone for a quiet dinner. With Pete in charge, we left.

I had neither the time nor ability to get out of the house long enough to buy John a gift. Worse, I didn't want to. I was embarrassed when he slid a jewelry box across the table. I opened it to find a beautiful set of diamond stud earrings.

He said with much pride, "They're bigger than Lola's. They're just over two carats each." I was unaware we were in a contest.

I looked directly in his eyes and thought; *I would give all my many jewels back if I could have a husband who recognized what a meaningful gift was. It isn't two-carat diamond earrings. Talk to my mother, play a game of cards with her or take her for a walk on the days she's able, or cook a meal for us.* Again I was caught in a trap. What kind of a bitch complains about two-carat diamond earrings? Who could possibly have the impertinence to carp? I thanked him with as much appreciative expression as I could muster.

He didn't know how to be my husband; he only knew how to be my boss. Tonight, like every other night he was home, became a protracted conversation about JR's. This particular night, it was about the new manager.

My repeated response was, "Sell the place, John, I told you I'm not doing this anymore. No, I won't talk to the new manager. If he can't figure it out you'll have to fire him."

He was trying to nudge his corporate slut back into action, but I wasn't budging. It was nothing short of insubordination. The diamond earrings did not change my mind.

*

Pete saved me. I got up the first morning he was there to find breakfast made and dinner already started. He was a fabulous cook.

When I came out of the bathroom from bathing Mother, the sheets were changed and the laundry was started. He found the car keys and the grocery store by himself, without asking for directions. When the hospice nurse came, Pete wrote down any new instructions and took charge.

Most importantly, he made her laugh. He made us all laugh. I never asked Pete to do anything because he did exactly the right things, every day.

John, embarrassed by Pete's command of the situation, would stand in front of me as if to say, "Tell me what to do." I never could.

As Mother's pain increased, her lucidity decreased, but in a cogent moment, she told me she had procured a life insurance policy for one hundred thousand dollars and made the beneficiary John. She wanted to change the beneficiary to me because living with us for four months gave her firsthand knowledge of his controlling behavior regarding money. I told her no. If the reasoning behind the insurance was to repay him for buying the condo and paying her debts, she should stay with her initial plan. If I knew then...

She was in and out of wakefulness now, but her pain had increased so much that hospice decided to start the morphine pump. We all knew it marked the end and it would only be a short while now. One of the last things she said to me was, "Roberta, promise me the day I die that you, Pete and John will share a bottle of champagne. I want that to be the extent of your mourning for me." I promised.

Mother slipped into a coma and although I thought her passing would be quick, it wasn't. Her breathing was shallow, but she was still clinging to life. I sat in her room curled in the big chair most of the time. Pete would come pry me from it for meals or he would force me to take a walk. John came home every night and before he could loosen his tie, he would down a double scotch on the rocks. He chased it with another until he was drunk – every night. His standard question was, "Is she dead yet?" He repeated it several times a night, and laughed without exception.

It had been a week and Mother was still with us. On Sunday, Lola and Trevor arrived with a full meal of brisket, noodle kugle, vegetables, and potatoes. It was a beautiful fall day and their presence was a much needed break for me and for Pete, too. The food was outstanding and we would have enjoyed a peaceful supper but John's behavior was out of control.

"I never forget a face, but in my mother-in-law's case I'm willing to make an exception. How long is a person dead, do ya think, before you forget what they look like?" This was John's manner of joking as we all averted our eyes at the dinner table.

"Isn't stomach cancer supposed to make a person skinny? How come my mother-in-law is still fat? Jesus, Roberta can barely get her off the toilet! And I sure as hell won't do it. Yuk. I couldn't look at that." He actually laughed.

"Last week Roberta and I went car shopping, and the salesman asked if I wanted a car with an Air-bag. I said, "No thanks. I already have a Mother in law. Wait! On second thought, she's almost dead. Maybe I *should* get a car with air bags." He was drinking. His maudlin and shocking jokes might have continued all day, but Trevor pulled him aside. "John, your behavior is uncalled for. Can't you show a little compassion here? This is Roberta's mother, for God's sake. You're being awful. It's not right, John, it's totally inappropriate."

It was to no avail. John turned towards him, drink held high, a sneer spread across his lips and asked for the millionth time, "Is she dead yet?"

A new hospice nurse came that same day and Pete and I retreated to my office to speak with her. John was so unconcerned with what was happening in our own house that the hospice nurse believed Pete was my husband.

The first question she asked of me was, "How did your mother behave when she was ill?"

I told her that she retreated, wouldn't answer the phone, and wanted to be left alone.

She said, "Roberta, that's how she wants to die. Stop sitting in that chair all day and leave her alone to die."

She administered more morphine and left additional for us to administer later.

Pete was due to fly back to Hawaii on Tuesday and I was a mess thinking I would be alone to care for Mother. I came to depend on him so fully that the thought of his absence was terrifying.

Monday, her breathing was shallower and there was a rattle in her chest. In spite of the hospice nurse's warning, I continued to sit in her room as if compelled to do so, but then Pete dragged me from there and made me promise not to go back until bedtime.

I had to get out of the house for a while and Pete encouraged me to drive to a nearby park. It was a gray day and the waters of Lake Michigan reflected the dark, murky clouds. They were thick and rolling and even somewhat threatening. Winter was coming; I could feel it even in October. *She's a pain in the ass,* I said to God, *is that why you aren't taking her? Find my dad...maybe he'll take her...then again, maybe not...* remembering his mockery of her at times. *Find my grandma...I know for sure she'll take her. Oh Lord, please don't let her suffer anymore...even she doesn't deserve that. She tried, honestly Lord, in her way...she tried. Please take her home now.*

I endured another dinner and another evening with John's behavior. At eleven o'clock when I checked on Mother, I discovered she died. She was alone, as I guess she desired. It was as if she knew Pete was leaving and I might not be able to manage without him. I bathed her and changed her gown while we waited for the hearse to retrieve her body. I fulfilled her last request. Pete, John, and I opened and drank a bottle of champagne in her honor.

By the time it was all done, we didn't get to bed until two o'clock in the morning, but I rose at six o'clock anyway. Pete was already in her room, stripping the bed and emptying the bureau. He said he wouldn't let me clean out her room alone and he wanted to get it done before his evening flight.

We were working in silence when John appeared at the bedroom door, dressed in his suit, briefcase in hand. I looked up and asked, "Are you going to work?"

"Of course," he said, "what the hell can I do here? She's dead."

My body went numb. I sat down on the bed and my head fell into my hands. I sobbed like a child.

Pete followed John down the hall, down the stairs and into the garage. To this day, I have no knowledge of the details of their conversation.

Pete was careful to stay neutral during his visit. He did not defend John's behavior, nor did he jump to my defense. Better to steer clear and not be in the middle. When he returned, he sat down next to me, embraced me, and said, "Roberta, I don't know what to say, girlfriend. He's been a real asshole."

Pete left that evening for his home in Hawaii and there was a void in my life for a very long time afterward. We still talk and we still remain the closest of friends because of what we experienced together.

CHAPTER 35

John presupposed I would jump right in and assume the corporate slut role again. I had neither the intention nor desire. My mission was to get to Florida and finish that condo. It was November and I only had a short time to ensure its completion for the holidays. I wanted to be away from Milwaukee and all parties and festivities.

"Roberta, honey, with all due respect, cancelling the New Year's Eve party won't bring your mother back, and keeping our routine might make you feel better." How very John to temper a disgusting remark with a solicitous comment, like a run on sentence.

"As if you have the slightest idea what could possibly make me feel better, John. No New Year's Eve party. I am exhausted and I don't feel like it." I said. Cancelling our annual New Year's Eve party was sacrilegious. The fatigue I felt was more than just physical. I was more overwrought emotionally than even I knew.

After settling all those things you do when someone dies, I packed up Harley, the cat, and went to Florida.

I made John aware of the insurance policy my mother left for him. Her condo sold at a very large profit – more than enough to cover every dime he ever spent on her behalf, including the loan he repaid for her and wrote off as bad debt on our tax return. He kept the money.

"You must need the money, right John?" My voice was positively acidic.

No response, as he continued to write the deposit ticket for the bank.

*

Although behind schedule (welcome to South Florida), the condo was finished enough for me to stay there. John and I fought via telephone several times a day.

"Roberta, I know you're busy in Florida, but if you could just take a few minutes and telephone JR's—"

"John, *John*," I said, my patience now in shreds. "How many times do I have to tell you, I am *not* involved anymore? What is it going to take for you to realize that it's over? JR's is a failure, John. I know you aren't used to hearing the word, but swallow, John. Swallow hard and put up the For Sale sign. It is absolutely ridiculous for you to keep flushing money down the toilet because your ego can't admit failure. *Do not* mention JR's to me again. *Damn it, sell the place.*"

To admit total failure was horrific for him and I wasn't exactly successful in preserving his ego. Unlike years past, I wasn't overly concerned.

John finally caved to the demand to sell JR's when he became convinced I was dead serious about not running it. I think he hated me for it.

I just poured my first cup of coffee when the telephone rang. Caller ID revealed it to be John.

Sweet Jesus, couldn't I get a shot of caffeine before I had to deal with him? I lit a cigarette.

"Good morning, John. What's up?"

"Roberta, I have the greatest idea. Remember the antique ship's wheel you've been hiding behind the couch in the library in Milwaukee? I think we should make that our coffee table. I can have a carpenter put legs on it and get a piece of glass cut for the top. It will be perfect for Florida!"

"Absolutely not. I will not have a ship's wheel for a coffee table, or anywhere else in this condo. I will not have the typical Florida pastel palette either John, the last thing you suggested. I hate seashells and sea horses and I hate light blue. This time I'm doing it my way. Get over it."

He hated everything I chose but I bought it anyway. I selected a smart "Out of Africa" English style with mahogany furniture, leather topped tables, and a more neutral to caramel palette, with deep purple accents. The result was stunning. Whether he liked it or not was immaterial to me.

He didn't think I needed to be there so much and I wouldn't come home. I laid claim to the master bedroom. The first time he came to Florida, before he could even put his bag down I told him to take it to the guest room.

Although he never said so directly, he was furious that he'd lost both Robertas. His corporate slut flew the coop, and his wife no longer caved to his insults. I didn't care how angry or hurt he was, or that he suddenly was forced to fend for himself. I didn't say I would never be back anyway. I took an extended vacation and just didn't know when I'd return.

He called a few times while partying with friends at our house in Milwaukee, and on one occasion he told me Lu, our representative in Hong Kong, was staying with him at the house.

"Roberta" John said "I'm going to put Doris on the phone. She's here with Lu. They're best friends and she wanted to get away from Hong Kong for vacation. Because Lu had to come to Milwaukee for business, she came along. She's never seen snow! Maybe you could tell her where to shop?"

"Hi," I said into the phone. "Is this Doris?"

"Yes," a small voice replied.

"Hi Doris, I'm Roberta, John's wife. It's nice to meet you and I'm sorry I can't be there to welcome you personally. Wow, are you brave to come to Wisconsin in January! I would think there are lots better places to vacation in January!" I laughed, but heard no response, so I continued. "John says you'd like to shop while you're in Milwaukee. What kinds of things are you looking for? Do you want souvenirs to take back with you or clothing for yourself?

"Yes," the same small voice responded.

"OK, Doris." I sensed that Doris was either unable or unwilling to converse. "Maybe it's better if you put John back on the phone and I can tell him where to take you. Okay?"

"Hi honey" John's voice was saccharine sweet.

"John, you know where to take her to shop. Why did you want me to talk to her? Is English difficult for her? She didn't say anything but 'yes'."

"Her English is excellent," John said. "I think she's just tired. We were up half the night drinking and talking"

"Is she staying with you and Lu at the house, John?"

"Well, sure Roberta, what's wrong with that?"

"I'm not so sure it looks appropriate John. She's single."

"Roberta, don't start. That's ridiculous. Lu is in one guest room and she's in the other. Don't be such a prude. Nobody thinks anything of it, I assure you." John sounded disgusted.

"I don't like it John. I would prefer if you made other arrangements for her, that's all."

He made it clear he had no intention of doing so. I hung up the phone disapproving of John allowing Lu, his employee, and his single female companion, use of our home as a place to drink and have sex. My supposition at the coupling was totally inaccurate, but I didn't know that until much later.

John made an inordinate amount of trips to Hong Kong that year. Never connecting the two events, my assumption was that the Pacific Rim business was extremely good.

*

I spent so much time in Florida that I made several friends in the building. I was invited to dinner or the movies often, and I had become active in the politics of the building. A few people suggested that I run for the board of directors. I had to be the owner of the condo to do so, and it occurred to me that I never saw the title to my own condo, my Easter gift. I knew not to call John.

I called Raymond. "Is my name on the title to this condo, Raymond?"

A full moment of silence elapsed before he responded with a joke. "I think it's in my name, Roberta, because I did the closing while you two were out of town. I think the power of attorney is still in effect."

I didn't laugh, but went on to explain that I needed to vote on an issue in the next condo meeting and if my name was not on the title as an owner, I needed John's proxy. Raymond told me he would look into it.

I hung up thinking, here we go. It's Freshwater Falls all over again. When John called later and I explained, he said he didn't really know how the condo was titled. I knew he was lying. I didn't ask but rather demanded he change it and do it fast. I fought that fight once and won. I had no taste for the same battle. Every time after that and right up until the divorce, when I asked about switching the title to my name, he told me he was working on it.

CHAPTER 36

John was driving to Florida hauling a trailer full of motorcycles and artwork. We were invited to a party by people from the building with whom I became very friendly. I was about to introduce John to an entire group of people who only knew him anecdotally. He visited the condo only twice and never long enough to meet my new friends.

I loved these people. No one was Wendall Industries related; not one of them was required to like me because I was the boss's wife and all enjoyed equal or better net worth than John. They would not be beholden to him. His friends were bought and paid for – they all worked for him and were obligated to tolerate his bad behavior. My new friends would not put up with John's rudeness, so I believed he would behave himself and I would have my good John back. I sorely missed him these last years, but I remembered him.

I spoke little of our life in Wisconsin and the only thing my friends knew about John was that he was a manufacturer, traveled quite a bit and we had been married fifteen years. I referred to him as a nice guy, a generous man, with a great sense of humor. I told them he gave me the condo as a gift.

"How generous is that?" I would say at cocktail parties. "What a wonderful man. He's a bit eccentric, but very bright. I know you'll love him."

The evening of the party I sat John down before we left and told him, "Look John, I like these people, I know these people. They're great and they've been extremely good to me. I think you'll like them and I think they'll like you too. I am asking you *please*, do not over-drink tonight. Please do not get carried away, because it isn't pretty when you do. Nobody works for you here, John, and they won't dismiss it as readily as our friends do."

"Roberta, I am so sick of you telling me how to act," he said. "I am not three years old! I have no intention of getting drunk."

This was the wife he had no use for.

He forgot his intention on the short elevator ride to the penthouse. Within an hour, he was drunk, loud, unruly and rude. He cursed like a sailor and "fuck" was liberally sprinkled throughout his dialogue, no matter who he was speaking with. I wouldn't even stand next to him.

I looked over at the bar to see a woman desperately trying to free herself from his grasp. John was grabbing at her chest. When I saw her date head for John, I put down my drink and flew across the room.

I got there first. "John put your drink down *now* – we're leaving." I apologized to her (I never met her before) and humbled myself to my friend, the man who had brought her. I don't even remember what I said to him because I was intently pushing John toward the elevator at the same time.

The next day I went to the pool before John rose. I couldn't look at him. I didn't want to. His behavior was the talk of the building, and it mostly centered around the comment, "Can you believe Roberta is married to a guy like that? I would never have guessed that of her."

Even though technically no one person is responsible for another's behavior, it's pretty standard to be embarrassed if your spouse has been an ass, particularly when the picture you painted of him was contrary to the person they'd met. Part of the embarrassment is wondering if they could be right. What *was* I doing with a guy like that? What exactly did it say about me?

This was one of the few times the pooper-scooper didn't scoop so well. My alacritous explanations of years past were suddenly forgotten and my grip on the handle had loosened considerably. I had no plausible explanation for his behavior or my tolerance for it. The subject of my husband was politely avoided. We were never invited anywhere as a couple after that. It was only when he was gone that I began to receive invitations again, and they were for me alone.

*

I'm not sure when I began to analyze our married friends regarding their state of happiness. My awareness heightened, and I listened attentively to the bickering. I became an eavesdropper to every conversation that suggested they were less than content. I took note of rolling eyeballs from husband or wife, exasperated sighs, looks of boredom or frustration or apathy. I became expert in identifying my compatriots. Certain looks passed between us that acknowledged each other's unhappiness. That so many were unhappy gave my feelings some sort of credence, normalcy. Everybody's unhappy...so what.

Then I began to pay attention to the changes couples made to accommodate their unhappiness. They may not grocery shop together any longer, or they watched TV in separate rooms in the evening, or they vacationed separately under the auspices of keeping the marriage healthy by allowing each other space. Not to suffer each other's company was an intentional objective, reducing shared moments to social gatherings where they could be surrounded by many. The women especially were becoming permanently furrowed between the brows, faces caught in a scowl one time too many.

Do they think of leaving, I wondered, or was that my solitary fantasy? I wasn't comfortable asking, and in reality I didn't want to know, so I drew my own conclusions. *At least I wasn't the only one.* They were just like me. It's sad that I drew comfort and affirmation from such specious reasoning. It was sad that I needed to.

*

I still wasn't ready to resume my duties as a corporate slut. Finishing the condo was more of a project than I intended. After it was complete, the slower pace finally allowed me time to grieve for all that I had lost those last five years - Emily, Scott, Porsche and my mother. I knew I had to work through sorrow so I could emerge emotionally healthy again. It wasn't that I didn't want to take care of John; I just didn't have the strength. It wasn't that I didn't know how to make him happy; I was just too tired to rally.

There were times his overwhelming need sucked every last bit of energy out of me. He would come home from work and stand in the kitchen doorway with his arms outstretched. It was my signal to drop what I was doing and walk into his arms to deliver his welcome home kiss. I had to be the one who approached him, never vice versa.

Once, as a test, I turned at the kitchen sink and stood firm to see if he would come to kiss me. He waited for a long moment, and then went to the bar and made himself a drink. To avoid an evening of pouting, I quickly corrected my error and ran to kiss him. It got to a point that my teeth clenched when I heard the garage door. It became like the chore you hate the most, but you have to do it or you know you'll be punished. I was reminded of my father saying, "We all have to do things we don't like. That's just life."

If I were sleeping when John was dressing for work, he would wake me to choose his tie. I'd started this tradition myself and didn't mind his waking me. It was preferable to him leaving the house with a tie totally mismatched to his suit. John once asked why I cared so much about his appearance.

"John," I said, "when you walk into a business meeting wearing a shoddy suit and a tie that doesn't match, people never say, 'John has bad taste.' What they say is, 'How in the hell did Roberta let him out of the house looking like that?' If I have to take the blame, I'm going to assume the responsibility." From that moment in the earliest days of our marriage, I became his personal valet. The people at the office used to tease that it was obvious when I was out of town by the way John dressed. They asked if I could use some sort of Garanimal matching system to assist him in my absence.

I could no longer take such total dependence. The only way to help myself was to avoid John as much as possible. So it came to be that when he was in Milwaukee, I was in Florida or Freshwater Falls. If he called regarding a business matter or wanted an opinion regarding Wendall Industries or anyone involved with Wendall Industries, I told him I would think about it and get back to him. Most often, I didn't.

I became unavailable as his sounding board. I no longer offered an opinion, and I was completely devoid of any ideas. I knew he was unhappy, but I couldn't help him. I couldn't find a way to tell him how difficult it was to care for him; he saw himself as low maintenance. How could I approach that topic without incurring a sarcastic verbal whipping? Avoiding was easier.

Me first, this time, I thought, *or there won't be any such thing as us.*

"If you are traveling with a child and the oxygen mask drops, affix your mask first so that you may better assist the child." The words circled inside my head, their meaning finally clear.

Leaving wasn't an option at this point in time. I was too weak, too depleted of energy to visualize it.

CHAPTER 37

John returned from a three-week trip to Hong Kong. I retrieved him from Chicago's O'Hare airport and unlike most other times, he left for the office immediately. I never, as a rule, packed or unpacked his bags, but that day I decided I would unpack for him. He was tired from the long flight and he still had meetings in front of him. I was feeling sympathetic to his obvious exhaustion.

I opened his shaving kit to retrieve his electric shaver and plug it in to recharge. A prescription bottle rolled onto the counter. It was for six pills of Viagra. Only four were left.

Doris was my immediate thought. *Oh my God, he was having an affair with Doris, that woman he made me talk to.* My surety of his affair was very intuitive. John spoke of Doris for months in an admiring manner. He had touted her business acumen and spoke of possibly hiring her to assist Lu in the Pacific Rim when the business grew enough to warrant such action. My initial vague suspicions were cast aside in my belief that he wouldn't be so verbal in his admiration of a mistress. Now, I thought him clever. The best place to hide anything is in full plain view. I'm still not sure why it was important to him that I speak with Doris back in January, other than some perverse satisfaction that he had fooled me. Or maybe it was his way of letting me know that if I couldn't be there for him, he could find somebody who would. At the time, the meaning totally escaped me. It went so far over my head, it didn't warrant even the smallest upward glance.

*

I have always believed in the adage, "Don't ask a question you don't want the answer to." I had to prepare myself, not only for the answer, but the consequences of that answer. It took me three weeks to ask him the question.

I cleared the dinner dishes and loaded the dishwasher. John was sitting comfortably in his recliner watching a television program. I approached the television, turned it off, and turned to him. I was calm. I had practiced this speech a hundred times in my head.

"John, remember when I unpacked your bags a while ago when you got back from Hong Kong?"

He sat up in the recliner, face concerned. "Yeah."

"I found the Viagra in your kit, John. I read the bottle. It was a prescription for six pills and there were only four in the bottle." I crossed my arms, waiting.

I thought I saw him swallow before he began his explanation.

"I got the prescription because you asked me to a long time ago, and I wanted to surprise you one night. It's just that the opportunity hasn't presented itself yet. When I was in Hong Kong, I told Lu that I had some Viagra and he asked if he could try it. I gave him two pills."

Lu, his rep in Hong Kong was twenty-three, single, and as virile a young man as I ever met. He spent over one year training in Milwaukee, was one of my "orphans" and also spent a great deal of time with us. I knew him well. One day at Wendall Industries I caught him walking into his office with a bag filled with condoms. I teased him about it endlessly. His sexual prowess was well known and the subject of many jokes.

I was dumbfounded and had no ready response. I was not prepared for the lie John laid before me. The only thing I could muster was, "OK then, we should try the Viagra."

He never tried the Viagra with me. To this day John has not wavered from that story. The remainder of our married life, which turned out to be about four months, was celibate. Well, at least for me.

*

As unlikely as it sounds, I still saw a future with my husband. I fostered his dependence on me, and I felt responsible. I also couldn't imagine my life without John. The corporate slut was on an extended leave, not permanently resigned. I still felt invaluable to him.

And then there was always the false security that a long-term marriage brings. It would be too complicated to divorce. The fabric of our lives was inextricably tangled with family, businesses, houses, and friends. We bowed our heads together in prayer and hope. We traveled the world together holding hands. Bad as it sometimes could be, we had built a life with one another. We still shared a relationship, however changed it became. In addition to being complicated, it would be too forbidding to put fresh footprints on a path to an unknown life. Our trail may have been well worn, but we could walk it blindfolded and unaided and still find the door. There is comfort in that, however small. There is solace in routine, no fear in the familiar.

Roberta in her sassy thirties would have kicked John out without a backward glance. In the era of her fucked up forties, reticence discovered Roberta. Like a pickpocket, it snuck up on her, robbing her feistiness without a murmur—a feistiness whose, absence went unnoticed until she went looking for it. Her husband may have been an ass, but he was her ass, and if she could change his behavior once, there was hope for the future. Wasn't there always a fairytale belief that if you were happy with this person once, you could be happy again? Would it be tough to put it back together? Sure, but not impossible.

CHAPTER 38

J ohn never even murmured the word divorce to me.

It was a mild June day in Milwaukee when I opened the mail and found an invoice from the most notorious divorce attorney in town. My husband paid this attorney a retainer two weeks before, the same day I hosted a birthday party for him. That evening, he had rather conspicuously kissed and hugged me, while declaring to everyone how his love had grown stronger for me after fifteen years. I called and point blank asked him if he was divorcing me.

"Why do you want to know?" he said in a voice ice cold.

His intention was to have the papers served in a few days, when he would be in Texas and I would be home alone in Wisconsin. His attorney mistakenly mailed the invoice to the house instead of his office. Oops!

The gravity of the verbiage and my feelings regarding the conversation are etched indelibly in my brain. Yet even today, when asked "Is that all he said?" I can only respond, "I don't remember." The shock of the moment obliterated the memory of the entirety of the exchange.

Just like in the beginning, it never dawned on me that I would give up my career. My career was who I was. It defined me. Not since

"Weh...Weh...Weh...Westinghouse" had I been terminated from a position. I never saw it coming.

So when John responded to my question of, "Are you divorcing me?" with, "Why do you want to know?" my very first thought wasn't that my husband was leaving me, rather it was, *I've been fired. I can't believe I've been fired.*

As the implications of that began to register, I felt the strings of my sanity, like catgut on a violin strung too tightly, break one by one. I heard them, I felt them, and I saw them break in front of my eyes. I suddenly found my threshold, or rather, John found it for me. It would take a very long time to restring that violin.

*

Lola came that night from Chicago. In just over an hour she was on the doorstep with her suitcase. "I've brought enough clothes for three days," she said, "but I can always go home and get more if you need me to stay longer."

Dana, my good friend from Wendall Industries, came to comfort me, but ended up talking about her own marriage and how unhappy she was. The following day she called to tell me that Paul heard she was at the house to see me. She had confided to Sally, and Sally in turn told Paul. He warned her to be mindful where she swore her allegiance. She found his remarks threatening and I didn't hear from her again. Not ever.

Terror rushed toward me unabated and covered me like a shroud for the fifteen months it took to finalize the divorce. Meeting John so quickly after my arrival in Milwaukee, I had no contacts of my own and no life outside of the one that we had created together. Michael was the only attorney I knew, and I knew not to call him. The posse knew of the divorce months before I. Sally called to tell me she was sorry she knew and couldn't tell me, but John was her boss after all. It was so hard for her, she said, to keep it a secret.

It was through Sally that John obtained the name of the best divorce attorney in town. Dana once asked me to make some inquiries on her behalf; it was she who wanted to file for divorce. Not being able to reach her, I gave the name to Sally to pass along to Dana. She also passed the name to John as well.

I considered Sally and Dana two of my closest friends. Sally worked so hard for John that when I entertained her and her husband, I treated them as exalted guests. And they were frequent guests. I felt she earned the right to have someone serve her for a change. I knew firsthand he was a tough boss, so when her frustrations became overwhelming, she turned to me to vent her anger. Often, we could find a solution together to either calm him or change his point of view. I fought for her promotion to office manager when John was waffling on the idea. I fought for the raise he didn't believe she had earned because she was experiencing some health problems. She and her husband spent their honeymoon at my mother's home in Hawaii.

I was a deciding factor when Dana accepted her position as international sales manager with Wendall Industries. She was uncomfortable being away from her parents for the first time in her life and she was single in a strange town, so I adopted her. I made sure she was introduced, included, and accepted everywhere. I helped her find doctors, hairdressers, dentists, and singles' clubs. She ate dinner in my home more times than I could remember. I grew exceptionally close to her parents in Connecticut and when her mother was dying, I shared my experiences with Dana and talked her through many moments of panic as she cared for her. I flew to Connecticut for the funeral.

I called John's stepbrother, Ben the psychologist. I had been communicating with him regularly the last year about a psychological testing product he had developed to ensure accuracy when hiring. He originally approached John for help marketing the product but John didn't want to get involved. He didn't want to try the product and he didn't want to use his contacts to help Ben. I reminded him that it was Ben who had ensured his legacy at Wendall Industries and told him firmly it was payback time. He needed to do all he could to help Ben succeed. John made some introductions; he got Ben space at an industry meeting, and Ben was on his way. Yet, Ben still called me regularly because I was easier to reach.

The morning after John's blast, I called Ben for some advice and yes, even some comfort, but his verbatim response was, "I can't help you. I've been talking with John." I'll never forget it.

Bernie, the vice-president of sales for Wendall Industries, procured his job by way of my introduction to John. I knew Bernie since I was twenty-four while working as a sales rep in Ohio. I called and left word in his voice-mail at work, but never received a response.

I helped another Wendall Industries salesman secure his job there because he was a customer of mine in Dayton. When John and Bernie approached me because they were unsure if he would be a good fit, my approval sealed the deal.

These employees were like abused children and somebody had to be their voice. I stood up for them all, at one time or another. When my phone remained silent, I knew there was no one to stand up for me.

I couldn't believe this was happening. *Where is everybody?* I kept asking myself.

In the end, it wasn't just the Wendall Industries family that shunned me; it was the industry in total. I spent my entire career in this industry and formed what I believed to be lifetime relationships. I sorely underestimated John's power. Fear of incurring his wrath, losing his business, losing his line, prevented almost everyone from contacting me. There were few exceptions.

*

I received a call from a long-time buddy, a manufacturer, who tried to hire my firm to sell his product many years ago. I represented a competitive line and declined the offer, but he never stopped trying. He called me every week. I never did represent the line, but we became fast friends and sought each other's company at every show or industry meeting. He was one of my favorite people.

He called one day from Milan, Italy, and I could tell he was slightly tipsy. He was attending a trade show there and sought out John. He asked him bluntly what the hell had happened. "Is this some kind of mid-life thing?" he asked. "Are you crazy? Roberta is the best thing that ever happened to you – the whole world knows that, John."

John shrugged and said, "It's just time to move on."

My friend was taken aback by, what he termed, an insipid response. He was now calling to assure me that he considered me a good friend and solicit me to stay in touch. He gave me his new cell phone number and told me to call anytime. I was so touched.

A few weeks later, I punched in the numbers for his cell phone. I needed to talk to somebody in my world...my industry world.

It was a gruff voice that answered.

"It's me, Roberta, how are you? Did I get you at a bad time?"

"Oh Roberta...I...well...I guess I wasn't expecting to hear from you." He seemed embarrassed and didn't quite know what to say. "What's up?"

I understood immediately. When he phoned from Milan, it was a weak moment. When he arrived back in the States, reality struck. John was the power.

I quickly let him off the hook. "Oops, that's my call waiting. I'd better take it. These days I have a lot of stuff to handle, if you get my meaning." I forced a laugh for his benefit.

"That's okay. I'm just going into a meeting myself." He couldn't hide the relief in his voice. "I'll call you later. Take care, Roberta."

I never heard from him again.

I was out like the old sneakers you put in the trash because the stench is too much to bear. I was blackballed at Wendall Industries and the industry, too. The industry and its people had been my life since I was eighteen. It was all I knew professionally, and its people comprised the greater part of my friendships. I had never even remotely imagined this almost total abandonment.

The moment I opened that divorce attorney's invoice, my life was no longer my life.

CHAPTER 39

I needed an attorney. I unknowingly gave John the Hertz and I needed to find the Avis. I procured two names from a true friend from Freshwater Falls-a rare person, unconcerned with incurring John's wrath by helping me.

I couldn't locate the prenuptial agreement. I never looked at it since the day I signed it and forgot where it was filed. After a frenzied hour-long search, I found it in my files. Lola accompanied me to both appointments, document in hand.

The first lawyer looked at the agreement and said it was hopeless. Wisconsin has a long history of upholding prenuptial agreements.

The second attorney looked a little harder and after exclaiming, "I can't believe you signed this!" said she could help. I hired her.

The agreement I signed waived my rights to everything – all property, contents and future retirement benefits. I was entitled to one-half the value of the house in Milwaukee and one-half the value of the house in Freshwater Falls. John never changed the title for the condo in Ft. Lauderdale.

The prenuptial clearly stated I could keep all gifts received during the marriage, and despite the wrapped packages and declarations to all that he gave me the condo as a gift, he denied it. The legal definition of a gift of that nature meant it would have to be titled in my name. I understood why he had been stalling. The fight began.

John came home that day, after I had seen both lawyers. Lola and I were sitting in the lake room in Milwaukee. It was a beautiful spring day. My daffodils were showing the very tops of their heads, a sign of anticipation for a future summer. I saw none of that through my tears. I couldn't seem to stop crying. John walked in the lake room and Lola stood to make her exit. As she hurried up the stairs, he approached me. He chose a seat directly opposite, rather than next to me.

"Roberta, listen. I will always take care of you. The prenuptial was written in your favor and you will never ever have to work a day in your life again, I'll see to that."

My eyes narrowed and the tears stopped. After my two meetings with the attorneys, I knew it to be a flagrant lie. I maintained my silence.

He managed to look sincere as he continued. "I have no intention of putting you out in the cold. Stay in the house until the divorce is final; I'll continue to pay the bills and I'm going to raise your allowance by two thousand dollars a month so you can pay for an attorney."

How ironic. I had begged for an increase for years to no gain.

"What is it you want, Roberta? Tell me."

Finally I knew the answer to something. My attorney warned that he might ask this very question. I did as instructed and said, "I don't know yet."

"I'm going to pack a few things and I'll be at the coach house, okay?" With that, he left me sitting in the lake room and walked up the stairs.

Lola and I checked his closets after he took an excessive amount of time to pack a few things. We discovered he had packed every article of clothing he owned. I knew with certainty then that he had no intention of returning.

He took up residence at the house in Milwaukee that was our first marital home and now was used for corporate guests. It was currently being occupied by Sam, my nephew. He was spending the summer interning in the sales department at Wendall Industries, having been promised a job after his graduation from college in December. John and Sam remained roommates for the summer. Although Sam offered to come live with me, I harbored the notion that he still might work for Wendall Industries. Moving in with me could spoil his chances.

*

The forensic accountant revealed that John had put things in motion for this divorce as early as five years earlier, the same year we waged war over the title to the Freshwater Falls house. I won the battle, but he started preparing for the war.

I now understood his interference with all the design and decorating decisions. He knew that house would be his one day, and he was determined that it reflect his personality, not mine.

Wendall Industries, the bulk of his worth, was held in trust and untouchable. The Milwaukee house was free and clear, but the Freshwater Falls house had two mortgages, leaving its value at fifty thousand dollars. This was suspect. John had no mortgages on any property titled to him. Subsequent to those mortgages, which I had no memory of signing, he purchased the condo in Ft. Lauderdale for one-million-three-hundred-thousand dollars in cash and titled it in his name only. I was overwhelmed with the sense of betrayal. It plagued me. I never would have thought him capable of such deceitful acts.

I wanted cash and the condo in Florida. He wanted to give me half the value of the house in Milwaukee, half the value of the house in Freshwater Falls, less the mortgages, and no contents. The total value of his proposed settlement was abysmal considering his net worth was in the hundreds of millions. Nearing fifty, and after fifteen years of retirement, I would have to work. Because of the trust, I had no legal claim to the entity whose substantial growth I had been a party to. John's affair with Doris would have no bearing because Wisconsin is a no-fault state. I discovered she had stayed at our house in January with John, not Lu, and she was his mistress. He had purchased a house for her in Hong Kong, a tidbit that slipped accidentally from Dana, director of international sales and Lu's immediate supervisor, in our very last conversation. He took Doris to Florida a scant three months after he left me to meet my best friend Lola. But the only consequence to his action was a stern reprimand from his attorney. The court would be unconcerned with the humiliation I felt. He sought to enforce the prenuptial agreement and we sought to overturn it. The law was more in his favor than mine.

*

I was sane enough to know I was losing my mind, and sought help. At first, I convinced John to attend couples' counseling but when after two sessions he revealed he had no interest in trying, I kept the therapist, Greg, for myself. He went about the mission of helping me find my sanity. It was a grim task, restringing that violin. I needed medication to speak without crying. I couldn't focus on anything and was having trouble aiding my attorney in assembling a viable case. I was diagnosed with Major Depression. At my third session, I asked Greg bluntly if I was having a nervous breakdown.

His response was, "We don't call it that anymore." Another day, I would have laughed.

I was prescribed two anti-depressants, anti-anxiety medication, and sleeping pills. Greg explained that the theory in using two anti-depressants simultaneously was they acted on different parts of the brain. *Brain?* I thought. *What brain? If I had a brain, I wouldn't have gotten myself in this position.*

I went to bed every night praying fervently not to awaken. Although I would never take my own life, I wanted God to rescue me from the life I had now. I thought if I just wished hard enough, I could travel that tunnel of light to the next world, the next life, which would assuredly be better.

Every morning the act of opening my eyes and finding me alive elicited a bout of sobbing. My singular purpose was simply putting one foot in front of the other, so I could get through a day. "Time flies" was a lie. It dragged like a clubfoot. I left the house only when required. I was permanently attached to my recliner in front of a television that was never turned off, but I had no recollection of what I watched. I wouldn't let Harley, my cat, leave my lap. The two newspapers I received daily were put in the recycle bin still bound by rubber bands. A voracious reader all my life, I couldn't focus enough to read a book. It once took me a week to read two pages. By the time I reached the end of a page, I forgot the topic. So, I stopped trying.

I saw Greg twice a week, sometimes three. Every so often, he told me he had a cancellation after me but I suspected he kept two hours open. I no longer cared about my appearance, and I didn't wear makeup or jewelry for almost a year. I had a reputation for being extremely fashionable, but I had no idea most days what I put on my body and some days Greg would look at what I was wearing and shake his head. I became dangerously thin. I didn't know the person staring back at me from the mirror. The face that was always alive with animation and so accustomed to laughter looked dead. Because I didn't know that person opposite me, I avoided mirrors as much as possible. I had an intense intimate relationship with depression and I hated it.

The trouble with being independent is the expectation it exudes…that you'll always be independent…every second of your life. Independence is a characteristic assumed level in its disposition, solid and unwavering. I am substantiation to the fact it is not. There were moments, days, weeks, even, that I would have gladly handed my life to anyone who could manage it better than me. It's a garment, independence, like a bra. You wear it most of the time, but sometimes it feels good to go without.

CHAPTER 40

The cash amount I asked for constituted a fraction of one percent of John's worth, a pitiful decimal point that began with zero. When asked about my contributions to the growth of Wendall Industries, John told his attorney that my biggest contribution was being a good hostess. JR's never did get out of the red under my watch, so in his mind there was no contribution there. My attorney felt our best opportunity might be mediation but the process was halted when John announced he would rather lose the amount of money I was seeking in a court of law than see me have it. We were going to trial.

My attorney reminded me as often as possible that my signing the prenuptial had sealed my fate and I wasn't likely to get a fraction of what I thought I deserved. She kept repeating, "It's your own fault." I was convinced – *of course it was my fault*. It made me feel dull and dim-witted.

Depositions were scheduled for my side and the list included Michael, Raymond, Paul, Sally and several Wendall Industries employees. Our case was straightforward: to prove that I had been instrumental in the growth of the company. I would have to show I could have built an estate of my own, had I not given up my career, and that John gave me the condo as a gift. We hired a handwriting expert to prove I did not sign the mortgages attributed to the Freshwater Falls house.

The day before they were to begin, my attorney started receiving phone calls from the opposing attorney. They wanted to talk. I will never know for sure, but I suspect it was at Michael's urging that negotiations became more palatable. As an attorney and officer of the court, I was sure he would not lie under oath. I knew him to be a man of honor. I was equally certain he didn't want to admit, with his client present, that he confided in me the many things he did. Telling me I was smarter than John and might do a better job running the company, or asking me to convince John to sell JR's because he feared my lack of involvement would clinch its failure, wasn't covered by attorney/client privilege.

*

It was June 8, 2002, a typical early summer day in Milwaukee – sunny and still cold. I was a half-hour late for the proposed settlement meeting. I could see John's BMW across the parking lot and I knew that he and his attorney and my attorney were waiting for me on the twenty-second floor of the building I was pacing before, smoking my third cigarette. I was cold, not having dressed properly for the weather, and I was frightened. I don't think I have ever felt so very alone in all of my life. It was mind boggling, this continuing effort to understand my position; my particular set of circumstances in this divorce and its effect on the second half of my life. It was time to hear exactly what the offer was.

My attorney was waiting for me as I walked through the door and we silently approached the conference room. As she opened the door, I took a deep breath, trying to clear my mind.

John, slumped in a chair across the conference table, was a portrait of passive-aggression. His posture evidenced his chagrin at having to part with any of his money, yet his face held the defiance of gladiator, victory apparent as he beheld his prey bleeding on the ground before him.

John never would speak to me directly about a settlement during the fifteen months we tried to achieve one. Ready to resist my demands, he wasn't willing to endure the confrontation. When I proposed we try to work it out ourselves, he flatly declined the offer.

His attorney delivered the offer in a flat, unfeeling tone, never lifting his head from the script laid out before him. They proffered about sixty percent of what we were asking, and it was all cash. There would be no property, and contents would be at John's discretion with the exception of family antiques I brought to the marriage. I could keep the gifts, but the condo was not one of them. I would be responsible for my own legal fees, advisory fees, accountant fees and any other expense related to the divorce. In the end, the fees in total amounted to slightly more than fifty thousand dollars.

My attorney led me outside the conference room and firmly told me we could not do better in court, and risked getting less if we went to trial. She restated her familiar refrain. "After all it was *you* who signed the prenuptial agreement. You have no one to blame but yourself." As if she needed to remind me where to lay the blame.

I did not want to, but she worried me enough that I finally agreed to settle.

Now, after returning to the room and conveying our acceptance, I asked to be left alone with John for a moment. John looked uncomfortable at the suggestion, but before he could object both lawyers rose and left the room.

"John," I began, "why are you so angry with me? You're the one leaving me! I wanted to make it work. This was your decision. I still love you, John. Look at all we've been though together, all these years... you're willing to give up all these years?" I found it difficult to control my tears.

His face was stony. He had no response.

"I know you feel that I've failed you, but I just don't know where you think I failed you so irreparably that it can't be corrected. I'm not perfect, John, but neither are you. We both made mistakes. Both of us."

He looked me, his face revealing no expression at all.

I took a breath and started again. "Just try for a minute to see my side. What you are offering here can't support me until the end of my life and you know that. I worked hard for you, John. I gave up a lot for you, for us, for the business. It would be unfair for you not take care of me now. What I am asking would make no difference to your bottom line, but my lifestyle would be forever changed. If you gave me what I was asking, you wouldn't be sacrificing anything – you wouldn't have to sell a house or a car or a boat, or anything. It's not that much to you, but it's all I'll ever have."

The look on his face remains a vivid memory. His once soft brown eyes turned black with silent rage. The wrath was palpable – I could feel it in my chest. He was having trouble controlling his anger.

"What makes you think you're *entitled* to a lifestyle, Roberta?" he said, his face slightly twisted. Only our location with both attorneys just outside the conference room doors prevented his shouting. "When I found you, you were a nothing, an absolute nobody. I *made* you and it cost me a fortune with your clothes, your two hundred pair of shoes, your houses, and your insistence on first class accommodations wherever we went. You're a great hostess, Roberta, but big fucking deal. I can hire a hostess, hire a chef, and hire a manager for far less than you've cost me already. It was *me* that elevated *you* to first class status.

And don't even think of mentioning JR's, Roberta. What the hell good did you do me there? Jesus, you couldn't even pull it out of the dumpster before you made me sell it. So don't bring *that* up. You haven't earned a lifestyle Roberta, you haven't earned shit. Whatever money you think you deserve now, you already spent. Too fucking bad, Roberta, it's just too fucking bad."

It felt like all the air had been sucked out of the room. I had barely been able to stop crying through the entire divorce process, but this litany stunned me so totally that it stunted my tears. It was the most classic case of projection I have ever seen.

I transitioned, without thinking, to classic corporate slut mode. *End result, end result, end result....Think quickly, Roberta, what does he need to hear to net the result you want? Keep your eye on the ball, Roberta. Keep it together.* I wanted to know if I could still do it – if I could still bend him. Spontaneously, the corporate slut was reborn. I felt my chin rise, my shoulders square, and for the first time in months, my head was clear.

"OK John," I started. "I don't think you mean that...not really, but for argument's sake, let's assume that you're probably right. I certainly have an expanded wardrobe since marrying you and of course the jewelry is spectacular and you know I love all of it. But you also know that I was more than just a hostess for you, John. Give me some of my due...it's only fair. It's just that I need some additional seed money on top of what you've offered. I need startup costs to cover moving, attorney fees and all those things we never think about that somehow manifest at the last minute."

"You're getting plenty, Roberta! I'm making you rich by most people's standards. Don't you get that? You're above working now, Roberta? It's really more than you deserve, and far more than I have to give you according to the agreement. I cannot believe the audacity.

I supported your mother, loaned your sister money and let you buy whatever the hell you wanted...and you can stand there and ask me for *more!*" His hands clenched into tight fists on top of the conference table, and his face was pink in an effort to control his anger and the volume of his voice.

His tone, so full of hatred, startled me anew. I looked at him and saw the coldest eyes I ever beheld. I realized then that John left me a long time ago. I wasn't exactly sure when, or why I hadn't noticed.

I felt the tears, bitter, sting my cheeks. "I'm almost fifty years old and I have to start a new life without you, when you know I don't want to, John." I attempted a laugh, but it came out a squeak. "Why didn't you leave me when I was forty and still cute? I might have stood a chance."

He actually managed a small smile. Did he appreciate my attempt at humor, or was he enjoying my distress? It likely was the latter.

"The day you told me you wanted the divorce you promised me I wouldn't have to work. This settlement won't assure that promise. I need a leg up now, John, and you're the only one who can do that for me. I'm afraid, John, afraid I can't do it. I'm asking you, please. More money would give me some breathing space and a chance to beat this depression."

He held up his hand and said, "Enough Roberta...I've heard enough."

I wiped my cheeks quickly as he summoned both attorneys back to the room. I wasn't sure what was happening. My stomach was tied into a sickening knot. I could feel my lower lip start to tremble.

As the lawyers entered, he reached over and took my right hand in both of his. I was taken aback because it was a protective and loving gesture. His face softened instantly and his black eyes reverted to a soft brown once more.

"I've decided to give Roberta another hundred thousand. Amend the agreement and let's get this over with." His actions, his gestures, were intentionally designed to demonstrate abnegation, his generosity through sacrifice.

It was exactly what I'd counted on. It was sweeter than honey freshly harvested from the honeycomb. So very rich with irony, it was the greatest victory of my career. The amount of money obtained mattered less than my ability to procure it. I guess being a corporate slut is like riding a bike.

Both lawyers were stunned. My attorney in particular looked embarrassed. I had accomplished more than she did. A few moments later I found myself at the water cooler, sipping cool water and trying to calm myself, when John's attorney approached me. Making sure no one was nearby; he leaned into me and whispered, "I wish you had been my client."

Before I could ask the question, he turned and scurried down the corridor, the back of his grey pinstripe suit waning quickly. I never did ascertain if he meant because I was a nicer person, or he could have done a better job on my behalf.

CHAPTER 41

The house in Milwaukee sold within a week at asking price. The buyers wanted to close in ninety days, and I had yet to purchase a place in Ft. Lauderdale. It was a quick trip but one week later, I placed a deposit on a condo there.

Dividing the contents was dreadful. I was humiliated by the act of having to ask for items I had purchased on my own, or things we purchased together that once held sentimental value. Each carried memories of places we visited. To get what I wanted I feigned indifference or made sure John believed it had no monetary value. His intent was to make sure I left with as little as possible, and what I did get had little value.

I requested the Waterford chandelier I had purchased in London so many years ago. He denied the request. Later I discovered he did not keep it for himself, but gave it away. He didn't want it; he just didn't want me to have it.

Going from room to room in the three houses where contents were divided, he reigned like a malevolent and spiteful king. My every request was subject to his fancy.

Friends were no different. In public he urged people to remain friendly with me, but endlessly harassed the few who did. One caller said, "I'd like to stay in touch, Roberta, and John *says* its okay, but you know how John is. He really would be pissed. I just called to wish you luck."

*

In leaving me, John pursued his own happiness. In that regard, he was braver than I and in the end I could never blame him for that. We all owe it to ourselves and the world to find happiness. Ultimately, it wasn't his leaving me that hurt the most. It was his unwillingness to take care of me after I took care of him for so many years, particularly at no cost to his lifestyle. He pursued hurting me with unmitigated enthusiasm. It was his delight at my obvious terror that caused me the most torment.

What support I did have was steadfast. Lola called every day and drove to Milwaukee with lightning speed if she heard that little glitch in my voice alerting her that I was desperate for a hug. My lifelong friends from Cincinnati, Grant and Marie, visited to assure me I would always have their support and more importantly, their love. Depression still in control, I slept through most of their three-day visit.

When I shredded a ligament in my right index finger that required surgery, Marie came to care for me, and returned yet again to help pack, because I was still in a cast. They called frequently.

John's stepsister, her two daughters, and their children were and are still among my closest friends. They called, they visited, they encouraged and comforted. Their assurance that I would always be family soothed any fear I had of losing them—this family I always dreamed of and fell madly in love with. Sam, in spite of living with John all summer, called daily and I saw him at least once weekly for dinner. He endured a lot that summer, with John constantly trying to sway his opinion against me, his aunt, and the one he called his second mom.

Marie and Grant's oldest son, Blake, together with Sam, devoted four full days to packing my house. They packed the furniture I was moving to Florida and loaded what I had given them into a van for transport back to Cincinnati. They stayed a day longer to assure my workload would be considerably smaller. We hauled over six hundred books to a resale shop and that night, at the restaurant, they paid the bill before I could reach for the check. I looked at them and thought, *my God, they're grown up. Where was I?*

Harley, my remaining cat "child" and constant companion, fell victim to the same mysterious illness as Porsche and just before moving to Florida had to be euthanized. I was overwhelmed and positively desolate with the loss. It wasn't so long ago that I lost Porsche first and my mother shortly thereafter. I was convinced I was being given some sort of karmic payback and must have been Genghis Kahn in a former life.

I wasn't sure, some days, if I could endure one more dreadful event. Greg wasn't piecing together a puzzle; it was more like a Rubik's Cube. I felt I was barely clinging to what was left of my reason.

When I was a child, I dreamed, like all other little girls, of the way my life would play out. I used to run around with a slip pulled backwards over my head, like all little girls, and pretend it was my wedding veil. I saw myself walking down the aisle on the arm of my father toward the man of my dreams, certain to spend the rest of my life in utter bliss with the most handsome man, the most thoughtful man, and the man who believed *I* was the most beautiful and most brilliant woman of his life.

Together we would sire gorgeous babies who would grow to be loving, thoughtful, and uncommonly bright adults. My husband, my only husband, would be a man much like my father, a man on whose lap I could curl and who asked nothing more of me than to be the best I could be, for me. He would be a man who encouraged imagination, independence, and excellence so that I might be fulfilled rather than be those things to benefit his needs. He would be a man that found me beautiful in every way and made me believe that I was.

I am not unique in that my life does not even remotely resemble the dreams of my childhood. It's puzzling to me how far from the mark I landed. I assume all responsibility for the choices I made that made it not so.

The dreams of my childhood were swamped by the reality of my life with John Wendall, like small sailboats in a North Atlantic storm. I believed them lost, but on the contrary, they've resurfaced, and now dictate my active pursuit of bliss in the second half of my life. "Never give up Roberta, believe in yourself." my grandmother whispers to me every night. Her words are a mandate I have every intention of heeding.

I am no stranger to hard work; it's what I do without question no matter what the goal. My newest objective is happiness. I've learned that hard work will provide the key that unlocks the treasure chest of contentment and keeps it open forever.

EPILOGUE

It was moving day. Mark, my Wendall Industries IS mentor and friend, brought his daughter to say goodbye. I was touched by his courage. He was the only person of the Wendall Industries family who demonstrated the bravery to stay in touch with me, both by phone and in person, when he could pry me from the safety of my recliner. We went to lunch. He never tried to hide our continued friendship and because of that he was subjected to unspeakable insults by John and his loyalists. We hugged goodbye and promised to stay in touch, but we both knew I wouldn't be back. There was nothing left for me there.

Mark and the moving truck pulled out of the drive almost simultaneously. I lived in Milwaukee for eighteen years and this house for fifteen of those. It was the longest period of time I have ever lived anywhere.

I stood in front of the home that bore witness to my marriage, good times, and bad. I looked at the English Tudor that I decorated so meticulously in the period style and the clump of birch trees we planted so long ago that now was as tall as the house. I smiled at the stately stone lion that I used to dress for every holiday and Green Bay Packer game days. My costumed stone lion was always the talk of Lake Drive. I wondered if the new owners would keep the tradition.

I pulled out of the drive slowly and made my way down the street. I passed the grocery store where every butcher, every checkout person and store manager, and I exchanged jokes and a few laughs almost every week for the last fifteen years. The girl in the deli started my order when she saw me walk through the door.

On the corner was the variety store where the owner helped me outfit my stone lion for as long as I had dressed it. They were fun afternoons, with he and I laughing at what we conjured.

Next door was the small private pharmacy that brought me prescriptions when I was too sick to fetch them, and treated me with such kindness when the only prescriptions being filled were anti-depressants, anti-anxiety medication or sleeping pills. They snubbed my husband, hoping it would make me laugh or at least give me some satisfaction knowing they liked me better.

These are what were left of my friends in Milwaukee and I knew I wouldn't see them again. It was a short drive to the highway but those eighteen years, like the familiar landscape, flew by my car window with implausible speed. It felt like closing a photograph album for the very last time.

I was on my way to the sunshine state to start a new chapter and wondered what career would find me next, or, given my age, if I'd have to seek one for the first time. It couldn't be in foodservice and I was absolutely certain I would never again be a corporate slut. I'd been there, done that. The tight ball of anxiety alive in my gut so long, suddenly gave way to butterflies of excitement in starting something brand new.

It was an astonishing journey. Greg kept urging me to consider that this journey had made me a remarkable woman, I was beginning to believe him. Together we had restored at least one string of my sanity. The others were curving in the general direction of well being, too. There were still a few days when I felt totally lost and void of any reason, but restringing a violin happens over time. The laugh resounding from the interior of my car no longer sounded maniacal. It was pure Roberta, finding humor in every part of being. I used to think new adventures, new challenges, were suited mostly for the young, and then I realized…I *am* young, and no matter my age, I would be young forever.

My spirit has always been and remains indomitable. Nobody can take my laughter for long. I have a ton of character, I know. The scar tissue, not visible, is testament to my strength. It's been hard gained, but worth it. Free at last from the burdens of satisfying John's overwhelming needs I could discern Roberta resurfacing. I was pleased to become acquainted with her once again. I may have bounced over my forties on a trampoline of tragedy and circumstance but in this new day, this new era, I was determined to pursue and capture fabulous at fifty. I knew it was mine for the taking. I settled in the driver's seat, ready for the long drive ahead. The destination of my own choosing was getting clearer with every mile.

ACKNOWLEDGMENTS

I would like to acknowledge all of my many readers and the people who gave me hope from the very beginning. Shelly Rosenberg, my first professional line editor who wrote to me after the first chapter, telling me I had written something wonderful. Thanks to William Greenleaf for his valuable critique. To Geoff Kemp and Mike Roumell, who not only read many versions, but gave me valuable suggestions that changed the tenor of the work. Jane Burgess, Candace Andreozzi, Cathy Liebowitz, Kay Hahn, Carin Puglisi, Ronnie Dennis, Dana Isbitts, Todd Metcalf, Kayla Metcalf, Erin Sheley, Annie Kessler, Mary Kay Meyer, Nancy Miller, Linda and Terry Conley, Charlie and Allyssa Gum, Leslie and Craig Werner, Darlene Orlov, Mark Hopkins, Talmadge Cesco, and Judy Rickard, whose belief in the work sustained me when I was so doubtful. Thank you to Jonlee Peterson for your very special efforts with your many contacts and your wildly contagious enthusiasm.

Much gratitude goes to Julie, Jennie, and Nancy for reading and reminding me always that I'm still family. And to Charlie for allowing me to share his life and pretend that he's my very own child when I need one, and sometimes when I don't.

Thanks to all of the Wrights – Chris, Gary, Brad, Bridget, Mike and Robyn for not only reading but for their unwavering support all of these years, and for making me feel loved even in my worst moments.

For Ross Brown, of The Editorial Department; thanks to you for leading me to Catherine Knepper my editor and Catherine for helping me make this a real book. This would never have happened without your encouragement and valuable work.

Most importantly to DW who still inspires me to write every day; you will forever be my muse.

Printed in the United States
119201LV00001B/133/A

9 781434 344915